DEAD
BOMB
BINGO
RAY

DEAD BOMB BINGO RAY

JEFF JOHNSON

TURNER

Turner Publishing Company
Nashville, Tennessee
New York, New York

www.turnerpublishing.com

Deadbomb Bingo Ray

Cover design: Maddie Cothren
Book design: Tim Holtz

Library of Congress Cataloging-in-Publication Data

Names: Johnson, Jeff, 1969- author.
Title: Deadbomb Bingo Ray / Jeff Johnson.
Description: Nashville, Tennessee : Turner Publishing Company, [2017]
Identifiers: LCCN 2017021936 (print) | LCCN 2017026461 (ebook) | ISBN
  9781683367260 (e-book) | ISBN 9781683367246 (paperback : alk. paper)
Subjects: | GSAFD: Noir fiction. | Suspense fiction.
Classification: LCC PS3610.O3554 (ebook) | LCC PS3610.O3554 D43 2017
(print)
  | DDC 813/.6--dc23
LC record available at https://lccn.loc.gov/20170219369781683367246

Printed in the United States of America
16 17 18 19 20 9 8 7 6 5 4 3 2 1

Measure twice. Shoot three times.

DEAD
BOMB
BINGO
RAY

CHAPTER ONE

▶ LES FEUILLES MORTES. THE ROSENBERG TRIO

Ray was eavesdropping when the breakdown on the setup came through. Three kids at the table across from him in the anarchist café were talking about video games and scotch, and how children younger than cigarettes don't care for jazz. One of them was named Paul. Ray watched their lips from behind his shades while listening to a conversation in the office down the street through a wireless earbud. Deadbomb Bingo Ray was going to burn, they were saying, torched for a crime he'd committed (last year—get over it) and the wrong kind of roachlife would bounce out of federal, all in the same astonishing move. They were talking advanced chess. A single taco with every known ingredient. A brilliant plan, except he knew they were planning something, which was why he was spying on them and pretending to eavesdrop on these kids in the first place.

"When it's all over, Anton Brown will return to the fold," Tim whispered in his ear. "And with that one man . . ." he paused dramatically, a familiar self-awe in his voice. Ray could almost see him, holding his thumb out in that Clinton gesture, "I will change *everything*." His fist hammered the desk, not especially hard. "This isn't like winning a race I was disqualified from, people. This isn't even competing. This is blowing craters in the racetrack and kidnapping the judges before the event."

1

Tim Cantwell was the mouthpiece in the spendy suit at the big desk in the new office. His endgame circled back to hedge funds, which was where everything went to shit the first time. Absolute return as a lifestyle had been behind Anton Brown's destabilization. The constant lies regarding net asset value had broken his underpowered soul, and at a pivotal moment too. When Tim's house of cards was hit with a regulatory colonoscopy, Anton had flipped his wig. He didn't give up anything to the Feds, but he didn't help Tim either. As a result, four hand-wringing peons with bad lying skills took a four-year mandatory fall. Tim escaped with an unscheduled bankruptcy, which of course didn't mean anything, and a fine he paid with other people's money. The resulting downtime was a working vacation, which he used to plan 'n' tan poolside in Costa Rica, where he turned a sunny, tropical walnut and devised the masterpiece he'd just outlined.

Ray got up and buttoned his coat. It was warm for November in Philadelphia, but it was still November. He adjusted his shades and took one last sip of coffee as the Paul kid paused mid-nonsense and gave Ray a brave but boyish once-over. A guy in a suit had no business being in that café, Paul's squint said, especially not one who knew how to tie a tie and comb his hair. In his ear, Tim launched into a lurid side-pocket smokescreen set up to "value" his new crappy assets, and the confidence in his voice put a spring in Ray's step as he took to the sidewalk and headed for his car.

Tim knew that Ray had been paid to give Anton Brown a push in the wrong direction, along with everything else, by a small pool of wealthy investors looking for revenge. No one in Tim's world knew that Ray had kept pushing Anton afterward. A month after Anton snapped and left Tim and his team at the mercy of the Feds, Ray had arranged for him to snap again. And again. And again. It had been easy to turn Anton Brown into a bank robber, to make him so crazy that he turned on the industry he mistakenly believed had made him crazy in the first place. Ray had begun to suspect that all that crazy had contaminated him about a week ago, just before he learned that Tim Cantwell was back from vacation. A solid year of redirecting Anton's stale, colorless little mind had made him feel curiously bloodthirsty in a brand-new way. Now here he was, on his way to have lunch with Abigail—Anton's new boss, the object of Anton's desire—to make Anton Brown freak out yet again.

Abigail seemed a little crazy too.

II

CHAPTER TWO

▶ 400 BUCKS, REVEREND HORTON HEAT

R ay had four cars at the moment: a 1971 Chevy Nova, gold with black leather interior; a 1977 Coupe de Ville, chopped and fleck-toned throughout; a black 2016 Mercedes something-or-other (who cares); and the white Camry parked down the street in front of the overpriced food co-op. It had a little silver Jesus fish and a Dave Matthews bumper sticker, empty kid seat in the back, and a cop would have to be Batman to look at it twice. He could glue a severed gorilla head to the hood and possibly get away with it. His invisible car, the opposite of a red boner trumpet in every way. His favorite.

Its offensive capabilities were subtle. The radio turned on the instant the door opened, and that was it. He listened to the Reverend as he made his way to Fishtown, cruising in polite autopilot mode. Lunch with Dr. Abigail Abelard. Lunch date number three. Dinner and pussy was right around the corner, even a little late at this point. He glanced over at the book on the passenger seat. *The Physics of Star Trek*. Abigail was a physics geek, nerdy, and hot in a nerd chick way, but not a bombshell like Ray's assorted weekly runway trash. But she had a laugh and a light in her, and after their first encounter and the ensuing coffee that led to lunch, he found himself thinking about her more than he should have.

Anton had gone to work for Abigail as a part-time accountant. In the beginning, Ray was sure that Anton was setting her up for something—a small-time solo investment sting maybe, or even a straight-up numbers shuffle once he had her account information. As impossible as it seemed, by the end of date number two Ray had surmised that Anton might have finally lost his shit all the way and gone straight, that he actually was a part-time accountant, with a real cubicle, a computer, and a ten-dollar tie, even his own parking space.

Confusing.

He broke into Anton's apartment again to investigate and discovered that Anton had bought a dining-room set. For a year he'd had a couch, a coffee table, a bed, and nothing else. Two of the doors in the apartment were always closed, like he was scared of what wasn't there, as though the empty rooms were a reminder of his empty life. But Anton had finally moved in. It gave Ray chills to look at the table and chairs, because it could mean only one thing: Anton had become a ticking time bomb, the timer had dinged, and he had bought . . . furniture. He had a job. There was no reading someone when they were that far gone.

Deadbomb Bingo Ray got his name reading people while earning his bones on the pitiful side of Detroit, just across the imaginary derelict tracks from the crappy side. Name night came about during a lucrative conflict with a cardsharp named Max Ripple. It was more than twenty years ago, and Ray was working as a croupier at a private game, which was half of a hustle all by itself. The Ramirez brothers were running the show, and they knew who this Max character was but thought they could take him; that's why Ray was there—the young Vegas dealer who could spot bullshit no matter how cleverly gift-wrapped it was.

But he couldn't. Max Ripple kept winning and winning far into the night. By four in the morning, the Ramirez bank was down two million and Ripple was wasted and gloating and far from done.

At the piss break, Ray had been informed that he would not be returning to Vegas with any of his fingers if the fortunes of all didn't reverse in a big way, and fast.

Ray didn't have a gun with him. If he had, he would have killed everyone on both sides and hit the card circuit in Rotterdam or Singapore, places he'd never been but had heard good things about. But as luck would have it (his luck), one of the Ramirez brothers was using a grenade for a paperweight in the office. They kept it there to scare pussies like the bartender or the UPS guy. Ray stole it. He was improvising, but he was hopeful too. The last player at the table with Max Ripple was Jose, a hustler on a losing streak backed by the brothers and slated to make the transition from hands to flippers also. Ray had to warn him somehow. What happened next was the stuff of legend.

When the game resumed, Ray began a complex communication with Jose, incredibly dangerous, right in front of everyone. The Ramirez brothers watched the game from the bar, two fat, extremely pissed-off Mexicans with murder in their eyes. Their controller, a mute named Rob or Bobby (depending on whom you asked), hovered behind Ray. Max Ripple studied his cards for a microsecond and then x-rayed everyone, unblinking and supernaturally confident. Jose looked at his fingers, counting them toast.

Using the tools at hand—a blank Palmer Practicality ABC bingo card from a box of them in the office and red lipstick from the back of the toilet—Ray had composed a message for Jose and slipped it into the doomed hustler's suit coat. "Dead" and "Bomb." "Grenade" didn't fit. It had to be four letters, and that was pretty much all Ray could spell out.

When he finally met Jose's eye, right after they both lost again, Ray glanced down at his own breast pocket and then at Jose's. It was all eyes, that game, and Jose knew what to do. He excused himself and went to the bar, read the message, and whispered something to the Ramirez brothers. Then all three of them looked at the table.

"Deal," Ripple intoned. He tossed out a chip, stone cold.

Ray stepped back from the table and raised his hands, signaling a table check. Rob/Bobby stepped up and took out the idiot wand to sweep the table. Ray didn't approve of that wand in the least. But it did pick up the quarter Ray had slipped into the cardholder. When both men leaned in, Ray dropped the grenade in between them and hit the deck behind Rob/Bobby.

The explosion was much bigger than expected. The table was simply erased, on a molecular level. The mushroom cloud of fire blew the roof off, and the donut shock wave blew Ray back into the bathroom and broke his leg when it did. Poor Jose died, as did one of the Ramirez brothers. The surviving one came to holding a bingo card with "Dead Bomb" in red. Afterward he approved of the action, even took credit for it. He'd almost been swindled out of two million by his piece of shit brother and two of his lackeys, but the final card had been up his sleeve—the infamous Vegas fixer known only in the highest circles, the man called Deadbomb Bingo Ray.

Ray made a new career out of it. That was the kind of bomb he was.

He didn't understand Anton Brown at all at this point.

▶ SOUS LE CIEL DE PARIS, TOOTS THIELEMANS

Ray parked far enough away from ENOS restaurant to hide his invisible car, which didn't seem out of place in the least, and walked the three blocks. Fishtown had undergone a sticky spurt of gentrification over the last few years, and the flavor of the ubiquitous Philadelphia litter had changed to something jarringly pleasant, like upbeat disco and Crayola rainbows in a discount graveyard or a toothless, hollow-eyed mental patient smiling at a clean new teddy bear. A Little Mermaid Band-Aid over a spider bite. Wrong, essentially, but lively about it.

ENOS had gotten rave reviews, and Ray was a little excited in spite of himself. The wash of warm air when he entered smelled like bread and rosemary and roasted meats. It was mostly full, and the vibe was semiloud and tipsy-happy. He scanned the room while the peppy greeter woman gave him a crotch shot with her eyes. Ray was handsome, a hard and even six-footer, with dark hair, almond-shaped brown eyes, and spare, bony features. There was a scar under his left eye from his nine-minute career as a bouncer at Flodette's in Baton Rouge that gave him character, and his suits were tailored Italian.

"Two?" the greeter asked. Ray smiled at her with his whole face.

"Yep. I'm meeting someone, but she's not here yet."

"This way." She took two menus and struck out through the door cluster. Ray followed, looking for Abigail, but he didn't expect her just yet. He was five minutes early, and Abigail was one of those incredibly rare people who was always exactly on time.

"Drink while you wait?" The greeter gestured at a little two-top. Ray shucked his coat and draped it over the back of the chair.

"You know, I just might. I'll have . . . let's see . . . vodka rocks. Might have to do some kissing." He sat and she smiled, then spun away.

Ray thought about his Star Trek book. Abigail was deep in her second start-up, and carbon was her game. The Wikipedia entry on carbon was lengthy and unenlightening, especially considering that Abigail seemed to be dealing with carbon in the singular, as in one carbon atom. By date number two, she had politely refrained from rambling on about things that he clearly didn't understand. They settled into a topic list that didn't include work, which was convenient as Ray didn't have a patter about his media-company front that could stand up to bright scrutiny and he didn't particularly want to beef it up.

His drink arrived, dropped off by a busy guy on mute. Ray sipped and looked out the window. It would snow sometime soon, and he wondered how much carbon was in snow, how much of the weight of snow was hydrogen, and what hypothetical media value snow carbon might have. He was going to need to get a new watch soon, and the options therein stole into the forefront of his mind.

"Raymond!"

He looked up as Abigail leaned in for an all-lip, no-spit kiss, smiling as she did. Her breath smelled a little like cat food. Ray felt a warm thrill as her fresh, clean face pulled away. She was wearing tight black jeans and a big gray sweater that reminded him of Maine or Connecticut. He licked the aftermath of the kiss away and rose a little in his chair.

"Abby, you look just like this woman I dreamed about last night."

"Cold snap," she said, settling. Abigail was generally oblivious to the mood of a room, unlike Ray who morphed along vibe lines effortlessly. She sniffed loudly. Her motions ranged some 20 percent faster than those of others around her, her body language still out-side, causing an unconscious volume drop in a twenty-foot radius. Ray politely sipped his drink, soothingly slow and calm.

"Feels a little like snow," he offered. She looked at his drink and then cast around for a waiter.

"I should go coat shopping," she said, quieting a little. Ray had more than fifty coats, but he wanted a new one too. She caught the eye of someone behind him and waved frantically. Ray leaned back and waited.

"Can I get some tea? Any kind is fine." She said it as the guy with the beard was still approaching. While he reeled off fifteen dif-ferent kinds of tea and their country of origin and tossed in trivia about workers' rights and free trade, Ray surveyed the room again. The trend in trendy among the staff at ENOS was hair-intensive, he noted. The men, their waiter included, were of the beardo variety: short hair with big, full beards that they no doubt perfumed with artisan bacons and brewer's yeast. The women boasted wire-bristled teen boy legs and dark, Parisian armpit forestry. An imaginary pubic hair caught in Ray's throat, and he turned back just as the waiter wafted away.

"How's your day so far?" he asked. He passed her one of the menus.

"Very good," she replied. She skipped straight to the back and scanned it, obviously hungry. "Had an engineer from Penn out this morning to help me with the new computer." She looked up and grinned. "What do you think's better than good? I mean super-duper."

Ray turned his menu over. "Grilled twentieth-century pear with white beans, lacinato kale, and candied pumpkin seeds."

"Penn Cove mussels with a coconut date and ricotta salata," she said, rolling it off her tongue. She looked up, and they smiled at each other and kept smiling. She was horny, he realized, maybe all of a sudden. And suddenly he was too.

"We can share," he said.

Her eyes twinkled. "I'm a fan of pears. Forever and always."

The moment stretched into two, and then the tea came. They each placed an order. When the beardo left, Abigail smelled her steaming cup with her eyes closed while he watched.

"Moroccan mint, dried by Berbers." She put the cup down to let it cool. Ray tapped his tumbler.

"The house vodka. Brewed in steel vats by English majors and decanted by minorities." He smiled. She smiled, too, but not hugely this time.

"Vodka at lunch? Is it that kind of day, Ray?" It rolled out just like the ricotta salata.

"Yeah, well." He shrugged easily. "Media . . ."

"Lucky you. Know what I did last night?" Mischievous.

"Ate pizza in your pajamas and watched *Real Housewives of Orange County*."

"Nope."

"Drank most of a bottle of cucumber juice in the bath and then fell asleep on the couch with something in the oven. The fire department woke you up, and one of them gave you his number."

"Very specific, but no." She lowered her eyes at him.

"Well, then . . ."

"Chemistry!" she chirped. "I made you a present."

Ray expertly hid his immediate discomfort.

"You might be thinking of synthesized ambergris or casto-reum—seamless travel from the top notes through the heart and down into that dark base—but as cosmopolitan as that might be, I hunted after what I considered your personal essence."

"Which is?"

"Animalic, with an aldehydic woody resin."

"Ah." That was definitely horny. No doubt about it. She was talking about cologne. She'd manufactured him a perfume.

"Yes. Site I found online. My headspace effort was entirely a projection. I dreamed your distillation into my laptop. It will be here next week."

"I see." He looked deep into her eyes, searching for some clue as to how far he'd sailed into those waters. She tittered.

"Don't let that go to your head, now," she chided. "I like this kind of thing. It's been a long time since I monkeyed with big, fat molecules."

"Weeks?" he guessed.

"Years," she purred back.

"Hmm." He was enjoying himself; he didn't care why. "I won't let it go to my head then. But what should I get you? I can't design a fragrance, but I tell you what—how about dinner this Friday? My place. I'll cook for you, and you can pick the records before, during, and after. And I won't even complain if you have DJ emotional monotone or dig my operas out of the back and play the screechy parts back to back."

"Deal," she said. She finally sipped her tea. After savoring it for a moment, she slyly looked around. "What's your impression of ENOS? I like the mixture of rustic wooden farmhouse and pharma-ceutical laboratory."

"Nice," he said, joining her appraisal. He shelved his hair observation. "I read that most of the kitchen staff came from Borto. Too bad they didn't bring the pickled beet salad."

"Mmm. Last winter I went to a conference in Chicago, and there was this cute little place down the street from my hotel that kinda reminds me of this. It was even colder, more lab metal, but they had a big wooden barrel of hot cider right by the door."

Ray glanced at her as she people-watched. Abigail had one setting, a blend of happy and interested. She saw something that captured her attention at that instant, and she made a little *O* with her mouth and took an unselfconscious breath of delight, like a kid looking at a birthday cake. Turning to him, she raised her flat hand and pointed through it.

"Hands under table," she murmured like a ventriloquist. "Hands under table, two o'clock . . ." More pointing.

Ray looked with just his eyes, miming a doll. Abigail snorted at him. Two tables over, a man and woman had their hands high up each other's thighs, shielded by the tablecloth, but visible from where they were sitting. There was something so aching about it, so secretive and moist, that Ray felt an impulse to buy them a fruity dessert. He looked back at Abigail. She was blushing.

"I think they overheard you talking about cologne," he said. She tsk'ed and looked out the window, grinning again. Ray finished his vodka. When the waiter hurried past, Ray caught his eye and motioned at his empty and got the nod. A quiet moment later their lunch came, his drink with it.

"Trade some?" Abigail eyed his twentieth-century pear halves, pan-seared in olive oil and stuffed—the bed of creamy white beans, the crispy fronds of glistening lacinato kale, the glossy candied pumpkin seeds. He eyed her plump, steaming mussels, open and juicy, and his eyebrow went up.

"Perfect."

They ate in silence, passing their plates back and forth, and eventually they were passing their forks back and forth as well. At that point Ray knew, and he knew she knew too, that Friday was going to be a slumber party. As he ate the last mussel, chewing and nodding to her and making a low rumble of contentment, and she nibbled slower and slower on the final candied pumpkin seed, he realized that without thinking they'd turned lunch into something else.

"I like this place," Abigail announced.

"Me too. I like everything about it."

She sighed. "Back to work then." She wiped her lips.

"My secretary has all kinds of action lined up." Ray finished his drink and signaled the waiter, who was eager to turn the table after their slow courtship ritual. He appeared instantly, the check already prepared.

"My accountant has the same kind of thing going," Abigail said.

"He's working out? Anton?"

"Mmm-hmm. Makes a little extra work for himself, but there's so much to be done."

Ray slipped a few bills into the waiting folder, and the waiter seized it. A busboy swept in behind him and started clearing. Both Ray and Abigail noticed for the first time how full the place was now and how many people were waiting in the doorway out of the cold. They rose hastily and moved through the tables and out the door, walking so close that they were almost touching.

Once outside, Ray put on his coat. Abigail checked the messages on her phone, her soft blondish hair rippling in the mild breeze. She looked up.

"Better run," she said sweetly.

"Walk you to your car?" He held his elbow out.

"Nah. Gotta make a stop or two. I'll call you." She looked back down at her phone and started walking, and that was that. Ray watched her go. An abrupt, slightly confusing ending, but it didn't faze him. He already knew she was a socially awkward woman, and he found it charming, even refreshing, after years of dealing with women who could easily have been diplomats or hypnotists. He lit a cigarette and headed in the opposite direction. There was always something to do, but at the moment none of it was pressing, so he strolled and considered breaking into Anton Brown's house again, just to see if there was anything new. He thought about buying a crate of grenades from a guy he knew in Chinatown and fobbing them off on the hard Russian dummies in Jersey City for an easy payday. But mostly he thought about Abigail's expression when she had eaten that last pumpkin seed.

II

CHAPTER THREE

▶ THE CRAVE, JELLY ROLL MORTON

Gruben Media was on the fifteenth floor of the Craft Building downtown, a two-room office with a view, lost in accounting firms, PR fronts, advertising think tanks, and nonsuggestive acronyms with unrevealing logos. Ray's last name wasn't Gruben, media was a blanket term that still didn't cover him, and his only employee, Cody B. Hooper, was in his third year of college so his mother was filling in. Agnes Hooper was a heavy-duty burnout from the transition period between the beatniks and the hippies, but you couldn't tell from looking at her. She dressed sweet old librarian, down to the bifocals she peered over the top of, and she brought her own lunch every day in a little paper bag. At some point, she'd legally changed her last name to Capsule and never got around to changing it back. Drugs, she claimed. Agnes Capsule had a few other mushrooms in her belfry. She was bad at most of the clerical stuff and had no idea how to use a computer, but excelled at tricking other people into doing that part of her job, and she refused to carry a gun. She also had what Ray considered an unhealthy interest in killing Woody Allen, he assumed with poison, though maybe not. The important thing was that she loved Cody, whom Ray had an older-brother thing going with, and that translated into a half-love toward Ray. Plus she had unbeatable old-lady charm, which was endlessly useful.

"Hello, dear," she said when Ray came in. She was doing something complicated with Rolodex cards. They were arrayed over the receptionist's desk in a modified solitaire, with some of them turned sideways and some of them stacked in spiral fans.

"Hey." Ray took his coat off and draped it over his arm and then crossed around to her side of the reception desk. "Any calls?"

"Hmm, no. Not really." She looked up at him and smiled. "Cody is going out with his new girlfriend again. Quite a steady item now, eh?"

"He say anything about bringing her home for Christmas?"

"Not yet. I didn't ask." She looked back down at her cards. "Maybe I should." She sighed. "Don't want to pry."

"I can ask if you want." Ray carried his coat into his office and left the door open so they could talk. His desk was modern and uncluttered, with their only computer and a blotter with a single pen. There was a small bar, a black leather couch, a glass coffee table with a few travel magazines he subscribed to, and a bookcase with a rotating stock. The wall behind the desk was floor-to-ceiling windows, responsible for more than half the rent. He tossed his coat on the sofa and went to the bar.

"Did you have lunch with Abigail?" Agnes sounded distracted, but he knew she wasn't. "I thought that was today."

"Yep." Ray poured himself two fingers of bourbon and carried it to the windows. From fifteen floors up, the Philly litter problem looked far different, more like patches of discolored snow. Clouds were rolling in.

"Did she have anything more to say about that boy? The one you're driving crazy?"

"Not much. He's nuts as shit, though. Primed to explode, which is handy." Ray turned away from the windows and walked over to the doorway. "The bug you planted in Tim's new office worked like a charm. I almost feel bad about fucking those guys over again, but it looks like we have to."

"That Tim is a horrible little bastard, Raymond. You should be happy for round two."

"Yeah." Ray swirled his booze. "He wants Anton back."

"Your pet crazy boy?" Agnes turned. "So he doesn't know what you've been doing?"

"No idea. I guess they think Anton is just cooling his jets, holed up in his little apartment watching Netflix."

They stared at each other. Eventually Agnes shrugged. Ray walked over to the visitors' chair across from her and sat.

"When Tim's hedge fund burned those clients of mine, I dunno. After I cracked that pack of shitheads apart, I kept after Anton because he wasn't supposed to escape. He was supposed to go down with the ship."

"That only made it so much worse for him, dear."

Agnes was trying to make him feel better. Ray leaned back and relaxed. He liked the chairs in the reception area. Agnes looked up and fixed him with her curious look, the one that meant she didn't mean to pry but might like a story to pass the time.

"You never did tell me the whole of why you've been after that boy. Tim Cantwell and his little band of toads, well, that was more than a year ago, and it wasn't even one of our more complicated cases." She liked to call what they did "cases." They clearly weren't, but there was no stopping her.

"Anton is my most treasured variety of mark," Ray began. "He likes to rob banks now rather than work at them—I think I told you that—but the douche hides the money in a black trash bag under his bed. Maybe that's some kind of kink left over from his banking days, I dunno. Anyway, I just liked watching him there for a while."

"Hmm." Agnes held a card up and inspected it.

"When I watched him go on that first grand spree of his, no doubt motivated by something easy to understand, I broke into his apartment and stole the money. You remember . . . little over two hundred and sixty thousand dollars, so not bad. He also had this collection of nautical charts. I guess that's where the game really started for me. I took those too." Ray sipped and remembered, smiling. "And his dog was a docile little Pomeranian."

Agnes smiled. "Pepper."

"Yep. And we all love that dog too. She begs when I eat, which is annoying, because I get her the best dog food there is, you know. I let her steal little bites off the edge of my plate when she thinks I'm not looking."

"Raymond!" she scolded.

"We make our humor where we can, Agnes. Anyway, we had other things to do for a while. That tasteful little hijacking. . . ."

"Our foray into real estate," she added.

"Who could forget? Jesus. And there was that midlevel drug dealer what's his name. The weirdo who hired us to steal that boat. But I kept going back to Anton again and again. I think walking Pepper reminds me of him all the time."

"I should take Pepper to the groomers," she said. "She loves a good nail trimming and a bubble bath, the little tooter. But go on . . . about Anton."

"So then he robs the Interstate Savings and Loan, almost right after I picked him up again full-time. 'Bout a month and a half ago, I guess. He pulled that job off with a measure of style that marked a graduation for him. In and out in less than three minutes. But rather than hit the freeway, which is sort of customary for Anton and the stick-'em-up guys, he used a series of cars he'd stolen that very morning in a shuffle. That was the part I enjoyed the most. He left the bank dressed as a clerk from an office-supply store, but by the time he got out of car number three and into his own, he was dressed as an accountant in an off-the-rack Sears suit. All the way back to the disguise he wore with Tim and the pit bulls. The police swarmed the freeway and the fast getaway routes while that fuckin' greasebag sat in a Burger King reading a fly-fishing magazine and chewing his way through a double with cheese and fries."

"Signs of development," Agnes offered.

Ray nodded and looked into his glass. "Totally. I popped the trunk of his Town Car while he was eating and transferred the money to my Impreza, and then, as I stood there in the parking lot, I felt strangely empty, Agnes."

"You weren't hungry for that plastic food, were you?"

"Nah. It was this feeling I've been experiencing on and off since I was a kid—kind of thing everyone feels every once in a while, I guess—but right then an unusually powerful wave of it made me go numb. I drifted up to the window and stared at him." Ray sat up, a faraway look in his eyes. Agnes narrowed her eyes at the sound of his voice, which had grown distant. "Anton was less than three feet away. I . . . I raised my hand, and the shadow of it fell right over his face. He didn't even look up. Then I walked away."

They sat for a moment in silence. Ray looked back down at his drink and sipped, and then he sat back again and took a deep breath.

"That moment, Agnes, that defining instant—the passing shadow of a hand on the face of a bank robber—eventually led me to the greatest theft of all, and I didn't even know it until lunch today."

"What is it?" She gave him her best old-lady smile, the wise and patient one.

"The immortal soul of Abigail."

Agnes considered. After a moment, she paused in her game of Rolodex solitaire and snuggled down into her little-old-lady sweater, the baby-blue button-up.

"It used to be that a man didn't say that out loud." She thought, her lips pursed. "Clancy! I haven't thought about him in years. It was the spring of 1968, I think. We took mescaline at a music festival in Shasta. Scored it off a Korean trumpet player, my word. Anyway, that night while we were watching the sky, Clancy told me the very same thing. He wanted my immortal soul." She gave the memory a pleasant smile.

21

"What'd he want with it?"

"Oh, I don't know. I think he wanted to eat it."

Ray got up and went back into his office. Agnes began humming, a soft, lilting tangle of Holiday's "Pennies from Heaven" and something else. She never hummed one song at a time, instead playing back random samples of everything.

"So what was the story out of the bug?" She'd been putting off asking. Agnes had been delighted to pose as a potential target for Tim, a widow with money to lose. She said planting the bug had made her feel like James Bond's stepmother. Ray drifted back into the doorway.

"They have a pretty solid plan. Eerily, almost exactly what you'd expect from a hedge-fund manager. Some woman is going to approach me with a job in the next few days. She'll have a problem that's right up my alley."

"Let me guess—a small gamble with a huge payout, but it's just a trap with pretty legs. What's the story on how she's supposed to know anything about the infamous Deadbomb Bingo Ray?" The Rolodex cards were in discrete piles by then. She took four little plastic Dollar Store boxes out of her desk. A fortune in contact data. The rebels of Agnes Capsule's generation had rabies for the Tims of the modern world.

"Racetrack. Freddy Hobbs got a cool fifty large to vouch for her."

"What a shame. I always liked Mr. Hobbs." She turned in her chair and looked at Ray over her glasses. "I assume he goes down after the fact?"

"Fifty plus the vig. I always liked Freddy, too."

"Then?" She turned back.

"The bait gives up some poon, that kind of thing. She'll tell me she's being blackmailed by someone, blah blah blah, and she wants to pay me twenty Gs in cash to break into someplace and steal the evidence."

"I bet the cash she pays with is on the federal watch list."

"You got it. Tim bought it for twice the corner value from a laundry he has ties with. Comes from a bank job with a huge body count."

"It has to get more complicated than that," Agnes said, disappointed.

"It does. The blackmail documents are real, just not in play. The holder of them would be in an ideal position to make Tim do anything."

"So you get picked up by the Feds and Tim squeals, shifts the whole mess on to you."

"Yep. Says I made him do it all, that he had no idea that what I was doing was that bad, and that on top of it all I'm a crazy-ass killing machine. Feds toss my place and find the cash. *Bam.* Tim and his banking posse get a pass, I take the fall for every crime they've ever committed, plus I get slapped with life on top of it for the bank slaughter."

"Sweet. What are we gonna do?"

"Dunno yet. Something good."

"I just don't get it. If they want you dead, why not just hire a gun? This is Philly, for goodness' sake. Every other monster on Market Street would pull a pistol for twenty bucks. Kensington even less. Those people will gun someone down for a few extra bullets so they can kill their friends."

"Tim's eternal motivation is greed, straight up. He can't play at anything without making a run at the whole pie. Dude could care less about making me dead, as sick as it sounds. He wants his whole team sprung and cleared and reinstated. He wants a second shot at the back seat of the limo and a night with every name in my call-girl catalog. Shuffling me into prison for life in the same move so I don't fuck with him again . . . totally gives him wood."

"This is the kind of grandiose thinking that got him into trouble in the first place," Agnes grumbled. Ray detached from the doorframe and wandered back into his office to the bar, talking over his shoulder.

"It's an example of something so common anymore, I just can't believe it." He poured himself a second bourbon, very small. "Big screwball mess like this. . . . Tim thinks he's learning, that this is some kind of test, like a Rutgers dissertation on cannibalism or the entrance exam to the Illuminati. In the world of high finance, the own-your-own-skyscraper set take people like me apart all the time. They have to. Moving money is a hard-core scumbag racket, even when it's legal. You burn people all the way down all the time for a living, and most people take it lying down with their mouth open and their eyes closed. But every once in a while someone is bound to freak out. It's just the law of averages. And when they do, rare as it is, they find a fixer to fix it."

"So Tim thinks he's—"

"He thinks he's getting better at the game, Agnes, simple as that. Now he's buying into the big-boy tournament, the no-limit table."

"Gracious me."

"Yeah. I'm the house again. I dunno, I guess I screwed up last time around. He was supposed to learn not to play in the first place."

"My word." Agnes put her boxes away and opened the drawer where she kept her lunch. She took her tea thermos out and poured herself a cup, all very tidy, and then turned around in her chair. "You're going to have to hit the incoming pussy hard, Raymond. I hope it doesn't throw a monkey wrench in things with Abigail. I like the thought of adding a science lady to our little mix. She could help Cody with his calculus."

‖

CHAPTER FOUR

Ray tossed his keys on the stand by the door. Normally he was glad to be home. His brownstone had three bedrooms with a converted home office and a library on the second floor. The ground floor in front of him was a huge living room that opened onto a big dining room that in turn opened onto a big kitchen with wooden counters and a six-burner stove, in a sweeping, airy flow. Japanese art, cherry-picked oils out of Rotterdam and Buenos Aires, an unbeatable sound system, and no TV. Paradise. But he frowned. The Friday-night dinner for two was the day after tomorrow, almost exactly forty-eight hours away if Abigail stayed true to her word, and the place was full of weapons.

▶ LIFEBOAT. NATHANIEL MERRIWEATHER

Pepper was sleeping on the couch again. She ignored him, but her tail gave her away with a single thump when he didn't move. The little fox dog looked up apologetically.

"Hey, Pep," Ray said. That rewarded him with active wagging and the lowered head of faux guilt. "You get off that couch, and I swear I'll give you the good food. The special treats."

Pepper grunted and stretched and then closed her eyes. She already knew she was getting the good stuff. In the beginning, they'd had an arrangement when it came to the furniture. She stayed off it. Then, gradually, they both stayed off it. Now they were in yet another protracted negotiation phase, where she staked out certain spots. The right side of the couch was one of them. She wouldn't budge until she heard food sounds or he opened the back door. It was as simple as that.

Ray took off his coat and hung it in the closet, kicked off his shoes, and loosened his tie as he made his way through the place to the kitchen, turning lights on as he went. There was half a bottle of a decent red on the counter. He grabbed a glass, pulled the cork, and poured some and then looked out into the back yard. The fountain was dry and silent, and the security lights were all off. He turned off the motion sensors.

"Dinner, or your nature walk?" he called.

Pepper padded in and glanced at her bowl and then walked to the back door and glanced at him. Ray put his hand on the gun strapped across his chest and dutifully opened the door for her. She sniffed the cold air and then bounded out, tearing off into the darkness. Maybe she could sense the coming snow. He waited, watching the night and listening, until she returned. While she watched patiently, he took down some of the Japanese kipper-flavored superfood and put it into her bowl. Pepper ate in a regal, patient way, unlike any of the other dogs he had ever been aware of. It was true that almost all of those dogs were from dog-food commercials—and he watched TV only when he had to, which was almost never—so he didn't have any real point of comparison. He thought Pepper ate like a cat might, and he liked that. It made him feel like he was doing a good job caring for her.

He carried his glass into the living room and took stock. There was at least one handgun in every room, all of them the same model: Beretta M9, with handy interchangeable clips. Fourteen guns if he included the pantry. He sighed. The two shotguns upstairs, the rifle under the kitchen sink, the armory under the dining room table—almost all of it would have to be moved out to the garage. But that wasn't all.

He got up and walked over to the nearest painting, sunflowers in a Turkish landscape. Resting on the top of the frame was a sharpened bicycle spoke. He took it down and inspected it. A vicious, terrible weapon, favored by South African street gangs, and there was one on the top of every painting. If she found even one of them, she'd think he was crazy or paranoid or both. He'd have to take those out to the garage too. He carried the spoke back to the couch and set it on the coffee table and then finished his wine and made a mental list. Razors taped here and there, a dive knife in the vase on the lintel above the fireplace, four feet of heavy chain in the fireplace itself. . . . Two hours. It would take two hours to box it all up and lock it in the trunk of the Cadillac. He'd leave two guns on each floor, hidden really well, and he'd put the sharpened spokes in the kitchen in a decorative glass jar. If she got curious, he could claim they were skewers, which was totally believable.

Tomorrow, or maybe Friday before his date, Tim's actress would take the stage and start the setup. They knew where the Gruben Media office was. Hobbs from the racetrack knew too. But he doubted anyone would show up or call. Ray's night spot was always the same, the bar attached to the Kimpton Hotel over by Liberty, an easy ten-block walk from his house. On Friday and Saturday nights in winter, they opened the club on the roof. He knew every floor, every room, every employee. That's where it would start, when he was drinking and already waiting for bad news.

He'd drink there tomorrow night, and from there he'd wing it and wait for the situation to loosen up enough for him to squeeze a bomb into the cracks. But tonight he needed to focus on moving weapons and dealing with the menu for Friday.

Ray went upstairs and changed into jeans and a T-shirt and then came back down, took his empty glass back into the kitchen, poured one more, and checked the refrigerator. He took out cheese and smoked ham from Di Bruno's and made a sandwich, ate it, and then rinsed and dried the plate, during which time a reasonably impressive menu gradually formed. He carried the wine upstairs and went into the master bathroom and turned on the shower. While it heated, he stripped and then studied himself in the mirror.

The naked part would be difficult. He worked out for a few minutes every day and had for years, so he had a hard frame the fat had been torn out of a long time ago. The scars weren't bad, considering what he did for a living. He'd been shot in the hip, but it was a grazing that hadn't even cracked the bone, and the scar looked oddly like a fashion-related accident in the right light. He turned sideways and checked out the edge of his back on the left-hand side. Three small puckers of white where some worthless shithead named Leon had stabbed him with a broken beer bottle. Again, not too bad. He looked down at his feet. All the toes were there, but there was a skin graft and surgical scars on the top of the right one. That had been a bad night.

He nodded in the mirror. A patch of frostbite where a belt buckle would be, pink years later, and a bald patch in his chest hair from an electrode—same night. In total, it was not much of a collection as far as scars go, a testament to his caution and effectiveness, but that was a hard thing to brag about in the wrong company. He showered, toweled off, and then got back into his jeans. In the end, he decided to transfer his weapons around at the last possible moment. Instead, he went into his little library room and sat down in his recliner. Ray never carried a cell phone, but there were always four or five disposables from Colorado kicking around, and there was one on top of the library Beretta, in the drawer of the lampstand next to him. He took it out and dialed a number from memory. The answering voice was low and Barry White–smooth.

"Raymond." Clink of ice in a glass.

"Talk to me about Freddy Hobbs."

"Racetrack Freddy Hobbs?" Barry White was already bored.

"The one."

Pause. "Freddy's okay. Bookie with a rosary of midrange Democrats. Big spender when it comes to pills, buys off Tito at the Grace Church. Viagra mostly, 'cause he likes the happy endings at the Wellness Center on Baltimore, Mondays and Thursdays. Little Thai bimbo calls herself Caroline, wears cowboy boots. He drinks like a Russian, but he has a handle on it. Total lifer. Wife's name is Claudia, real disgusting old bath slipper of a broad. Treats the kids at the corner grocery like trash, takes her toy poodle to the post office." Deep breath. "That kind of thing."

"Huh. You ever hear of anything that could be used to corner him? Not with the Feds. I mean real heat, like the Syndicate or whatever."

"Hmm. Not really. Why?"

"Speculate for me. What kind of shit could he get into that would make him introduce the wrong kind of person to me?"

"No kind of shit at all. The only way in the world Freddy Hobbs would intro you to bad news is if he had no idea it was bad news."

"That's what I thought. Word is he's getting a little cash out of setting me up for something, but——"

"He likely got played. Give Freddy good news, and then ask him to do a little somethin' in return. Freddy isn't rat material. Old school, plus he fears the bingo card more than he fears waking up in a blood-filled bathtub with Santa Claus and a dick in his ass."

"I guessed as much."

"Then why ask?" Tinkle of ice cubes in a glass again.

Pepper came in and hopped up into the other chair. Her chair. She gave him one look and then curled into a ball.

"Thinking out loud. Guess I'll hit the tracks next week and talk to him, hear what I hear. Your mom wants to know if you're coming home for Christmas. And if you're bringing the new girl."

"Jesus. Her name is Kate, for the tenth fucking time, Ray. I don't want to bring her home if Mom's gonna go off on her Woody Allen shit. It's fuckin' embarrassing, man." Cody's Barry White had gone James Brown, just that fast.

"Whatever, little dude. You comin' or not?"

"We stay at your place?"

Ray rolled his eyes. "So it's we?"

"Not sure yet, but if Kate tags along it's your place or the Kimpton. I like this chick, Ray. It's too early on for anything too . . . you know."

"What's her major?"

"Art history."

Ray laughed. "So if she can get past your mom and the whole 'assassinate Woody Allen' stuff, your job history, and your likely employment future, plus all the secrets you'll never be able to keep, you'll find yourself saddled with a pretty ambitious gal. Four years of college studying something other than what you're going to be doing for a living is wicked brave. Art history is incrementally more worthless than an English degree, Code. Kinda makes you wonder what her real plan is."

"Fuck you."

"They teach you how to think that fast in school?"

"If I do bring her home, you keep your fucking mouth shut too." Ray could hear Cody pouring himself another drink. "So what's this thing with Hobbs? You gonna tell me?"

"It's nothing. Some boomerang bullshit with that dipshit Tim, the banker."

"Huh. I guess I didn't see that coming; but now that you tell me, I can't say I'm surprised either. That guy's special."

"So Carol, art history. What else?"

"Kate. Shit. Nothing else, Ray. You want, you can always come visit." Cody was at UCLA.

"Night, Code. I'll tell your mom you said maybe."

"Tell her probably. And tell her if Kate comes, we aren't staying at her place 'cause Kate's loud in the sack."

"Kate, art history, opera babe. Check."

Cody sighed and hung up. Ray put the phone back and went down to the kitchen, made tea, and then carried it into the dining room and crawled under the table. It was comfortable under there on the strip of carpet. He slept there often, especially on nights when he'd just learned that a setup was going down. Duct-taped to the bottom of the table above him was a Beretta M9 and an extra clip, a Benelli tactical shotgun with a round loader, and a suppressed SCAR assault rifle with an EOTech holographic sight with night vision, plus a good old-fashioned tomahawk.

"Pep," he called. Pepper zipped down the stairs, checked out the kitchen, and then silently came to him and lay down at the edge of the pillow. He patted her little head. "Keep your guard up, kid. We're on yellow alert until this time next week."

Pepper sighed and made herself comfortable, but she kept her eyes open. The book Ray was reading was still on one of the chairs. He took it and leaned back on his elbow and spent a few minutes reading before lights-out.

II

CHAPTER FIVE

▶ THROUGH THE DARKNESS, TIGER ARMY

R ay spent the morning in what appeared to be an aimless, random fugue generated by boredom and lonesome shittiness, but that was far from the case. He was, in fact, engaged in the kind of highly calculated activity that gave people names like Deadbomb Bingo Ray.

The first step was to circle the tail he knew was waiting, get the make and model and maybe a face or two. That turned out to be neither hard nor easy, so suspicious. There was only one car, a dark-blue Taurus, and it shadowed him between two and five cars back for about half an hour, disappeared for a few minutes here and there, and then fell back in with a randomness that was too perfectly random.

There were a thousand ways to spot a tail, or so it went, and an equal number of ways to lose one. But the layman's gossip and the spy-buster bestseller tricks, the coo-coo bird dipshittery in Tom Cruise movies, the loopy hair-and-mirror gimmicks out of comic books, none of it worked quite like parking and getting out of the car.

Ray left the Camry at the edge of Chinatown and headed in on foot. It had rained during the night, and the gutters were so clogged with trash that big puddles of sludge had formed on almost every corner. He stayed out of the spray zones and at the same time avoided looking at anything reflective. One glance in a window would give him away. Losing someone in Chinatown was easy enough, especially when you were banking on it, literally.

Emerald Alley—a generalized crap store with tourist junk, phony antiques, and expensive bottled water—was one of the dozen or so places on Ray's payroll. The Chinatown payroll was coin-operated, almost impervious to penetration, and accessible at any hour. He'd set it up with Cody almost four years ago, and they'd used it only three times: once to test it, once to escape a net cast by a dead man named Roger Fish, and the third time to evade a woman who needed to be evaded (Bianca Dellafortuna, who had thankfully returned to Portugal and married a truly unfortunate man).

Cody had paid a kid named Bronco to drop off two hundred dollars a week at four restaurants, a twenty-four-hour convenience store, a grocery store, two dry-cleaners, a dress shop, and an antique store. It was expensive, and after four weeks all of them were freaking out pretty bad. Then Bronco went around and gave each of them a final payment plus a 1978 quarter, and this time he gave them a message: if a man named Coug Rollins came around and slapped a 1979 quarter on the counter, it meant he needed a hand with something easy and legal, no big deal. A 1980 quarter, on the other hand, meant he needed help with something hard, and he would pony up big-time.

None of them tried to give the money back, and the Chinatown network was born.

Ray went into Emerald Alley and put a quarter on the counter, 1979. The ancient Chinese man behind the register glanced at it, squinted, and then squinted at Ray, his expression unchanged.

"Coug Rollins," Ray said. "You got a way out of this building that isn't back through that door?"

"Back door, basement maybe. . . . Maybe roof, you like?"

"What's in the basement?"

"Rats. Water. More rats. Big hole." He said it like it was nothing, like looking for a big hole while wading through black water with rats in it happened to him all the time.

"Back door leads to? Fuck it. Which way to the roof?"

The man pointed over his shoulder with his thumb. Ray looked around him at the curtain doorway and then walked around the counter and went through it. On the other side were stacks of boxes and a narrow staircase leading up. The old man peeked through.

"Go up, up, more up. Close roof door, please." Up three floors. Ray nodded.

"Someone's coming in looking for me. That camera out front actually work?"

The man nodded.

"I'll be back in an hour to look at the tape. After that, we're good."

The man disappeared. Ray made his way up the three flights of stairs, paused at the top landing to listen, and eventually climbed out through a square metal hatch onto the roof. It was sprinkling again, but there was plenty of crap on the roof for shelter. He dutifully closed the door and scuttled under the overhang of a dead chunk of heater.

It was quiet. Muted traffic sounds rose from below. Wind whispered through metal housings and around pipes. It was cold, and the sky was one flat, low cloud. He carefully settled into place and scanned the adjacent rooftops, taking his time and being careful about it, going foot by foot and memorizing details—Philadelphia colors, the various shades of pencil lead and rust, the city's uniform—in case he had to run. Once he had several routes mapped out, he relaxed. A few minutes after that, he thought about cell phones.

Ray was happier than he could easily convey that he didn't regularly carry a cell phone. When they'd first become popular, he was sure it was a fad that would collapse in on itself, that no one in their right mind would want one after owning one for a few months. But they got smaller and cheaper fast, and he admitted that he'd been wrong. Then he gradually became happy that everyone had one, and happier still that he didn't. He would never have been able to enjoy hiding on a roof in Chinatown in the rain with a cell phone. All the little moments of peace would have been lost.

He closed his eyes. He was pretty sure it had been a woman driving the Taurus, but it could have been a slender man with longish hair. Brown hair, not black. That was all he had so far. He drifted through his options in confronting Hobbs, playing scenarios out from start to finish, and then his thoughts turned to Abigail and Anton Brown.

Abigail gravitated toward seafood. She also liked greens of the dark variety, she used honey instead of sugar, and she had terrible taste in men. All of it was true. She'd ordered the salmon, then the halibut, then mussels, in that order; with kale, kale, and kale respectively; tea with honey all three times; and she'd hired a former hedge-fund con man turned bank robber turned nutjob as her accountant, and she was dating with the intention of getting down in disco town a guy named Deadbomb Bingo Ray. He shook his head.

What had started simply enough had gotten complicated. It was like he'd knelt in a field to inspect a round gray dot and discovered it was the tip of a dinosaur skeleton. Totally random and not necessarily good or bad, just big and weird. He had dreamed of her last night while under the dining-room table. In the dream, he'd been drinking orange juice and she was laughing, wearing a bathrobe. It seemed like morning. Then he'd tied her hands to the bed with her panties. Then they were someplace far away, like Spain, and it was winter and they were wearing big hats and he'd just killed someone. Then he was eating off of her naked ass while she flipped through the channels on a TV.

He didn't try to take the dreams apart; that was one of the many roads to madness, in his opinion. But it was all unusually vivid. He thought about the kiss in ENOS again, the firmness of her lips. Call girls in the thousand-dollar range had full lips, half of it collagen, every last one of them. He didn't mind, but he'd forgotten how firm a woman's lips could be and what it was like to have a mouth close to his that didn't smell like mint and makeup, which is what he now imagined his dick and all other dicks smelled like.

Her fingernails, too, were different. Blank, like a monkey's. Small and colorless. She never wore jewelry. She wore sensible shoes. Her eyes were the greenish blue some natural blond women had, made hypnotically bright by their clean presentation and the enormous mind behind them. He shook his head and looked at his watch. Forty minutes had passed, and it almost scared him. He got up and stretched and then walked to the edge of the roof and looked down. No blue Taurus, no one loitering in front of Emerald Alley. He gave it a few more minutes and then quietly went back down.

The ancient Chinese man greeted him at the bottom of the stairs and motioned for Ray to join him at the register. The store was empty. He knelt and opened a cabinet. Inside was a discount video setup.

"Two people come in. My neighbor Wong and later a woman. She look at stuff and buy water, leave. Stand out front and drink it, walk away. I look, she gone."

"Show me the woman," Ray said. It was already cued up. Ray paused it when the camera had a clear view of her face. Tim's actress was a beauty. Shoulder-length brown hair, full lips, wide cheekbones, huge eyes, slender shoulders, and a heavy chest pushed high. Her expression was oddly perfect in that frozen instant—confused, searching, a tiny bit depressed, like a waitress in an Alain Delon flick. Ray clapped the Chinese man on the back.

"Good job."

"We even?" The Chinese man had the eyes of an experienced assassin. Ray nodded. The man nodded back.

"Coug. Like your money, Coug. I Cixin. Maybe like your money again, see? Anytime. Anytime."

▶ THE NOTORIOUS & LEGENDARY DOG & PONY SHOW. FIREWATER

The rest of the day was easy. Agnes would tell anyone who called the office that he wasn't in and that she had no idea when he would be, which had the merit of being true. He disappeared all the time, and her attention wandered anyway. She might have even taken the day off. He left his car where he'd parked it and caught a cab to Thirtieth Street Station to wait until six, when it was common knowledge that he'd be at Casey's, the bar in the Kimpton. In that way, he scheduled the meeting.

The train station was centrally located, and Ray liked the place. He'd spent all of a particularly shitty winter there unraveling a knot with ten strings—day after day of tracking commuters, narrowing down who was going where and when, looking for weak spots in the Skidmore Fountain Collective.

They were an upscale hunting pod of fraternity coke dealers out of Rutgers who brazenly tried to apply economic rape theory to the volatile Philly drug world. They assembled an expansion team with "associates" and held production meetings with spreadsheets and PowerPoint presentations, had a nine-to-five office getup, business cards and expense accounts, the whole nine yards. Ray had been hired to identify all the players, great and small, and in four months he'd done just that. Then in one night, in the span of seven minutes, they'd all vanished completely. New York ruled the landfill called Philadelphia, and the Rutgers kids didn't survive to learn the hard lesson that you were supposed to move after graduation. As an institution, Rutgers produced the most bloodthirsty criminals in the world. Generation after generation of shadowy human shells trained in no-mercy people-harvesting, and Philadelphia was their playground for the time it took for their souls to burn away. But they were supposed to leave and bring hell to the rest of humanity once the process was complete. Ray had been hired by Rutgers graduates ten years senior to Skidmore Fountain. Once the competition was gone, his clients decided to kill Deadbomb Bingo Ray to tidy up the loose ends. The explosion that killed them in turn wiped out half a block in Queens and left Ray with his biggest scar, the one on his foot. It was snowing on the drive home, and he wrecked his BMW, tore up his foot, and got frostbite from his belt buckle while he was waiting for the ambulance.

So he knew the train station well. He knew its patterns, the timing in the flow of passengers, where it was loud and where it was quiet and why, how to get lost, and how to find anything. There was no way to sneak up on him in Thirtieth Street Station, and a public place dialed in that tight was sacred ground, real estate with numinous value.

He went to the bakery and bought a bottled water and then drifted down to the pretzel place and got one, skipping the mustard. There was an area with tables ahead, but he went back to the main theater with the old wooden pews and sat in the center, facing the towering black angel statue. Twelve pews in and two up was the optimal position. No one ever sat there, possibly because it was visually loud in a peripheral way, but you could see and hear everything. He ate his pretzel and watched the people, letting his mind wander and listening to where it went. He didn't move for more than an hour. When he finally did, he headed up to the pay phones by the commuter train terminal.

He was alone among all those strangers, as alone as he would be on the surface of the moon. No one was watching as he dialed a number from memory and waited for it to pick up.

"Jay's Garage." Quick, clipped, Jersey accent.

"Jay around?"

"Nah."

"What about Jimmy?"

"Big Jimmy or Little Jimmy?"

"Little."

"Hang on." A minute later, the phone jostled around.

"Little Jimmy."

"Hey, man, it's Ray. I need a small favor. You gonna be around tonight?"

"What time, bro? I mean yeah, anytime you need, but what time?"

"Hard to say . . . like between eleven and maybe as late as three in the morning."

"I'll leave the back light on. Be here with one other guy."

Ray hung up and walked back down to the horse fresco and looked at the giant clock across from it. Thursday drinking hours were six to nine, and it was time. Time to go get half drunk and walk into a trap.

II

CHAPTER SIX

▶ SCREAMS IN THE EARS. BILL FAY

It was crazy, but the universe seemed to be governed by irregular magnetism. Cheerful people attracted cheerful people, bored people the boring, the horny the opportunistic (another form of lust), and of course sadness had trouble being alone. The exception was depression, which drew out the monsters of the world. That's what Ray thought about in Casey's at the Kimpton Hotel, while he watched and waited and drank and listened. When his tail finally showed a little after eight, she was indeed exceptionally attractive in life; but as she scanned the room for him, he once again caught the ghost of a bummer around her eyes. A depressed woman in a bar, paging one Deadbomb Bingo Ray. Sometimes being right was bad for his self-esteem, a forever-private paradox.

"Gary," Ray grumbled, flagging the bartender. "Switching to bourbon. Make it an emergency double." He leaned his face in a little closer to the bar and leered sideways at the woman, who was still in the doorway playing those haunted eyes over the room.

"That kinda night, eh, Ray?" Gary started pouring.

"Slouching toward Bethlehem. Ah, fuck it." She'd seen him. He turned to his drink and sat up a little, picked up the tumbler and drained it, motioned for another. Gary raised an eyebrow.

"Two glasses this time, Gary. Christ."

The woman settled on the stool next to him and smiled politely at Gary, who smiled back and set a tumbler of bourbon in front of her. She looked confused for an instant, until Gary set another in front of Ray. Then she looked sideways at him, and he picked up his drink, clinked the edge of hers, and looked her in the eye.

"What?" he asked.

"I . . . I . . ." She raised a hand to her throat and tried not to blush. Gary drifted away with perfect timing. Ray frowned and waited.

"I . . ." she started again. Then she looked at her drink.

"You're made, lady. Followed me all morning. So you want to hire me for something. It happens this way all the time. So all fucking morning you try to get up the nerve to open your mouth. Instead, you wander around Chinatown like a tourist, then go to my office and sit around listening to shit about Woody Allen, and now you're here, all loked up on a whole day's worth of the courage you collected like spit in your mouth. You'll need that drink for the next part, because you're going to try to use that ass of yours as a weapon, to fuck me into a state of emotional investment. Drink up, baby."

She did. Once the burn in her throat faded, she turned to him fully and the bummer in her eyes went stale.

"You're as horrible as they said you were." It came out religious, all conviction with no wiggle room. Ray snorted.

"Bingo. Go fuck yourself." He turned forward and watched in the mirrored backsplash as she stared at the side of his head. After a minute, she left. Ray summoned Gary for one last round and the check.

"Friend of yours?" As in an escort. She was pretty enough. Ray shook his head.

"Colleague."

Gary set the fresh tumbler out and made change for the bills Ray slid across. Ray sipped while he waited, then he leaned back and glanced into the hotel lobby. No sign of her. He nodded to Gary and then slid off the stool, got his coat, and walked into the lobby. There was a short line at the check-in desk, so he picked up the paper and read the cover until it was his turn. He was a regular and the lady knew him, but not by name. She smiled, though, and Ray smiled back.

"Philadelphia again?" she asked brightly. She seemed to be under the impression that he lived in New York but occasionally had business reasons to stay overnight.

"Super-early meeting in the morning," he replied, taking out a credit card. "Sleeping over so I can show up with a proper hangover."

They went through the check-in process, and he got his room card, put the paper back in the stand, and walked slowly out front. The night had grown bitter, the coldest of the year so far, and the wind had picked up. Ray lit the cigarette he'd bummed off Gary and nodded to the doorman and then took a left. Random drops of small freezing rain blew out of the black sky and haloed the streetlights. A slow half block down, the woman fell in beside him.

"I only got the one cigarette," Ray said without looking at her.

"I need to talk to you, Mr. Ray." Her voice was firm, in no way imploring. He was irritated at what a crappy job she was doing. If she hadn't been the tip of the spear in a setup, he would have kicked her in the stomach. Instead, he sighed smoke.

"Talk. And it's Ray. Just Ray." He shook his head in disgust and kept walking. At the corner, he led them left again.

"I have a problem, and a friend of a friend said you're a problem-solver."

"Fixer." He picked up the pace a little as the cold started biting. "The term is fixer."

"Okay." She drew it out, in the snotty, patronizing way college kids did these days, a long, upturned mouthful of disdain. He stopped and turned.

"Listen, you idiot. Spit it out, or I put this cigarette out on your fuckin' forehead. I barely, barely give a shit what people like you want *after* they've paid me, so right now you're on the wrong side of a minus at night in the dark with no witnesses. Be compelling."

"I'm being blackmailed by a man who makes you look like a saint. Five thousand a week for seven months now, and it's graduated to sexual favors scheduled for next weekend—two days in Atlantic City crawling around on a motel floor with a horse bit and a feather duster sticking out of my ass. I want him buried alive. Good enough?"

Ray thought. "No," he said eventually.

Her eyes watered. "Please," she hissed, and there it was. The desperation he'd been waiting for.

"What kind of blackmail? Don't bother lying to me." He flicked the cigarette away and rubbed his hands together.

"My late husband ran an art gallery in Chicago. Packhouse Water. After he died, several of the investors . . . courted me. I had the insurance money, there was the sale of the house. Essentially, I needed investment advice, and these were investors."

"So you're on the line for insider trading, and you don't want to do a Martha Stewart and make cupcakes in the big house."

"Right." She looked down and then back up into his eyes. A shiver ran through her. "Can we go back to the bar? I'm freezing."

"Too loud, plus we have to talk money and details." He turned around and led her back to the Kimpton. "I have a room. We'll raid the minibar and warm up while I take notes."

▶ LOOK FOR ME (I'LL BE AROUND), NEKO CASE

They didn't say anything on their way through the lobby, and the ride up in the elevator was the same. On the fifth floor, Ray led them down the hall. They walked abreast, bonding in the way that strangers headed for a hotel room unconsciously do. Hardwired into the base code of the human behavioral program was a mutual awareness of their genitalia. Ray found that the woman's depression had infected him on some level, so in front of the door he stopped and got back into character. He turned to her with the room card in his hand.

"Your name, before I open this door?"

"Mary. Mary Chapman."

Ray nodded and led them in. The room was high-end hotel standard, with high ceilings and a beige-and-gold motif. He took off his coat and went straight to the bar to avoid looking at the shower with her, tossed his coat on the bed to turn it into something other than a bed. None of it worked. He opened the mini-fridge, and his heart sank as he caught her surreptitiously inspecting her hair in one of the many mirrors. He didn't normally drink with the express purpose of going past drunk to blasted, but there wasn't much of a choice, so he pulled out all the little bottles with anything brown in them and rose, looking at her. She smiled.

"Make yourself comfortable, Miss Chapman." He gestured at a chair with his handful of bottles. She took off her coat. "So, what brought you from Chicago to Philly? Drugs? Flaming street mattresses? Burned-out cars? Or are you just some kind of pervert, into riding with low-rent junky villains in vans with no wheels?"

"Ray," she said slowly. "Can you be nice?" She sniffed, and Ray froze. The first little inarticulate beep came out of her, and he took an instinctive step back. And then she was sobbing wretchedly. Abruptly, she threw herself on the bed.

"Oh God, no," he mouthed silently. He put the bottles down and then tore the lid off one, drank it without even reading the label, repeated the process, his eyes glued to her heaving back. She was wearing a red dress, the fabric slightly shimmery, and she smelled like Chanel N°5 and hair spray. He loosened his tie and sat down next to her and patted her on the back, resigned to his fate.

"I'll fuck him up," he said soothingly, rolling his eyes. "Twenty-five large and he'll spend his final days in the trunk of a car on Market Street with a hundred live sewer rats and a can of gas and some matches. Let him pick his own entrance to the afterlife. That good enough?"

She turned her smeared face to him and shuddered all the way down into still. "You'd do that for me?" It came out quiet. Her eyes were wide and fixed on his face as she wiped her nose with the back of her hand.

He nodded. "Twenty-five and—"

"I have seventeen five," she interrupted. He frowned.

"Twenty-two five is as low as I can go. Even in this godforsaken broken mouth of a city, a running car and a hundred live rats will—"

"Nineteen," she countered. Ray considered.

"Twenty-one," he said. "My final offer. And you're down to fifty rats or a big, blind possum. Maybe just cats, but—"

"Twenty even," she said, propping herself up on one elbow. Her hair fell across one eye, and she gave him a damaged, lopsided smile. "Twenty and . . ."

Ray got up and went slowly to the closet, opening the door while she watched. Then he closed it and went to the dresser and opened the top drawer.

"What are you doing?" she asked, putting cute into it. He looked at her, and she bit her lower lip.

He winked. "Looking for the feather duster."

She fell back and stretched like a cat. "Closet by the door, above the ironing board."

▶ I'M YOUR MAN, NICK CAVE

When the whole sordid thing was over, Mary staggered into the bathroom. Ray just lay there on the bed, staring at the ceiling with no expression at all. He heard the shower turn on. Instantly, he was on his feet, madly scrambling for his pants. He found them on the floor and pulled them on, socks next. In less than a minute, he was fully dressed.

The sound of the water changed as Mary stepped under it, and there were whumping waves of it as she slicked it out of her thick hair. Ray kicked the feather duster under the bed and went to the bathroom door.

"I'm going downstairs for a minute," he called.

"What for? Get us food. I'm starving."

"Me too. What, uh, what are you in the mood for?"

"I dunno!" There was a pause. "Something with lemon!"

Ray flipped her off through the door. "Back in a sec."

Once he was in the hallway, he moved quickly. He'd seen her blue Taurus when they'd left the bar; it was parked around the corner and one block down. In the lobby, he paused briefly by the pay phones and made one call, to Jay's Garage. Little Jimmy answered on the first ring.

"Ray?"

"I'm bringing in a new Taurus for five minutes. I need you to access the GPS and get me a map of everywhere it's been in the last ten days. How fast?"

"I'll set up now. Have you in and out in less than two minutes. Bay one."

II

CHAPTER SEVEN

T he ten-minute drive to Jay's Garage would have taken five if Ray had been sober. His caution behind the wheel of the newly stolen Taurus was seriously rookie by his standards, but there wasn't much he could do about it. He pulled into bay one just as the snow started.

"What the fuck are you doin', Ray? Drivin' wit da fuckin' window down? Jeez, man." Little Jimmy was short and skinny, with amazing acne and advanced black-market automotive skills. He was one of the three big brains behind Jay's Chop and Shop. Ray got out, and Little Jimmy's eyes narrowed. "Aw, I see. You'ze fuckin' wasted, dog."

"I had to fuck my way into this ride, Jimmy. Sometimes—I mean, holy shit. I was just in this porno situation, man. Make a weak man want to cut his own head out by the root. Then I had to break into the car, too, because the bitch is a stone-cold player. I never even touched her purse, much less those keys. . . . Just read the GPS and hit print. Two weeks of where this car has been, and fix this fuckin' window. She thinks I'm out buying a lemon. Whole thing is a huge fuckin' mess."

"Sancho!" Little Jimmy screamed. A Puerto Rican stuck his head out of the office. "Fix this window! 'S a goddamned crisis!" He popped the hood. "Be three minutes, Ray. You want coffee or a breath mint?"

▶ VIVA LAS VEGAS, ZZ TOP

Ray walked outside into the cold. The ten-minute drive with the window down had been bad enough to make the squatting night freeze feel warm. After that freakish encounter, it was hard to tell if Mary was a gifted wreck of a woman or a next-level screwball gunning for the Oscar-in-Hiding. He wanted to wash his dick off in the filthy garage sink, but there wasn't time. Instead, he took a deep breath and turned his face up to the falling snow. He tried to think of something that wasn't contaminated, something other than a massive, utterly filthy city pregnant with murderers and wasting poverty and used bandages and bullet casings, where he wasn't standing in the fresh snow with his face to the sky, having just gnawed into the front end of a reverse burn by brutally sodomizing a hysterical psychopath for a pile of extra-dirty money—and that's when it hit him, right then. His eyes clicked open.

Abigail.

"Ray!" Little Jimmy yelled. "We'z done!"

Ray went back in, and Little Jimmy handed him three sheets of paper. He folded them and put them away and then turned to the window, which was up. Sancho opened the door for him, his face a portrait of worry and fear.

"So, dude," Sancho began meekly. "You wired it wrong, so I unsnarled it and put in a clip key. You park it, just pop that fucker out and toss it—good as new. I assume the car is hot, and that clip is no way legal like fuck, so don't go walkin' around with it in your pocket."

"That it, Ray?" Little Jimmy asked. Ray nodded and handed him five hundred and then got in. Jimmy passed two of the bills to Sancho. "Three minutes, baby. Three. Love doin' business with you, same as always."

"You guys rule," Ray said. "Tell Jay I'll stop by next week. And can you do me one more favor? I don't have a phone. Call Ramone at La Jolie and tell him I'm stopping by in exactly four minutes. Dinner for two, and she asked for fucking lemon. Something with lemon."

"Madre de Dios," Sancho whispered.

"Fuckin' lemon," Little Jimmy repeated. He saluted, and Ray pulled out.

Time was of the essence. If Mary decided to leave and found out that he'd stolen her car, he might be able to explain it away. He was a fixer. He killed people. Stealing a car was low on the male-faction list. Getting food from somewhere other than Casey's in the hotel might go a long way toward something. He shook his head and reached out to the heater control, but then pulled his hand back. He couldn't leave any signs at all. Examining the list in his pocket would tell him exactly how clever her handler was, but at present he didn't know.

La Jolie was a Manhattan expat pop-up foodie destination for the Liberty gentrifiers (his neighbors) and a voyeur's paradise for the locals, who dined there to behold the latest aristocracy mockingly portray TV normal. It was a disgusting place, but the food was *New York Times*: Food Section and Chef Ramone had a bad coke habit Ray occasionally sprayed with disinfectant, and he surely had a lemon or two. He double-parked and honked, and Pepe the busboy rushed out and handed a bag through the window. Ray pressed him a fifty and hit the gas.

The side street by the Kimpton where Mary had parked was half empty late on a snowy Thursday night, and he pulled right into the place he'd evacuated twenty-two minutes before. He got out and chucked the clip key through the steaming black maw of a sewer grate.

The doorman nodded to him as he swept in, and Ray composed himself as he made his way to the elevator. On the ride up to the fifth floor, he checked his teeth and smoothed his hair, scratched his crotch through his slacks. He could smell how drunk he was, but the high-speed Taurus operation had given him a measure of much-needed clarity. The food smelled good, and he realized he hadn't eaten anything all day except a train-station pretzel snack. He paused in front of the door and calmed himself. He was a guy who had just gone for a stroll in the new snow, in that fleeting moment before the pristine white succumbed to the City of Philadelphia, a talented lothario with a bag of farm-to-table goodness worthy of any actress-slash-pervert. He smiled and keyed the door open.

▶ JUST WANNA DIE, PUSSY GALORE

The man standing over Mary wheeled and reached into his jacket an instant before the bag of La Jolie exploded in his face. He took a step back, and in that second Ray popped him in the throat with three fingers. The man tried to gasp, and his hands shot up to his throat. Ray reached into the man's coat and plucked out . . . a cell phone. The door to the hotel room clicked closed behind him in the sudden silence.

"What the fuck!" Mary screamed, rising from the bed with her arms flailing. She was wearing a towel around her from the tits down and had a second one turbaned around her head. Casually, Ray finally kicked her in the stomach. Mary collapsed on the edge of the bed and doubled over, choking. The man with his hands on his throat fell to his knees but was finally getting some air, enough to throw up. Ray looked at the cell phone.

"Who's this dude?" Ray asked. The man glared up at him with wild eyes. Mary looked up and snarled.

"Your m . . . m . . . money," she managed.

"Tragic," Ray said. He looked down and took out his gun, pointing it at the guy's head.

"Wait!" Mary croaked.

"No!" the guy managed. "Please! Please!"

Ray turned to Mary. "What the fuck, dummy. You get this poor guy all tangled up in your shit, and now I'm supposed to let it ride? Who is he?"

"Tom," she whispered, rocking and clutching her stomach. "My friend Tom."

Ray frowned and turned back. "Later, Tom."

"Wait!" Tom screamed. He scrabbled back, and his hand made a fan out of a random slice of avocado. "I'm Mary's assistant! I'm helping her get the new gallery up! That's all!"

"Tom works for me," Mary said slowly. "He's my nonfat double honey latte, goddamn it."

"I'm just dropping off her overnight bag," Tom spluttered. "My god, what the hell is this?"

Ray glanced at the table. The bag he had seen in the same instant as Mary lying on the bed with Tom standing over her might not be a bag of extra-dirty cash. It could be a bag full of panties and personal items, like a toothbrush and hair products. Tom might not be a rogue scumbag horning in on the action. He might be an actual lackey, fresh to professional vice and employed for the moment by a tits-and-ass con artist, or, worse, an actual nonfat-double-honey-latte man.

"Nobody fuckin' move," Ray said. He stepped away from them, and they watched as he unzipped the top of the bag, peered in, and rummaged around with his free hand. The gun pointed at Tom's head never wavered until Ray lowered it and held up a crotchless pink unitard. Then he sighed and put the gun away.

"Tom," he said, "your last job ever for Mary is to clean up the mess you're sitting in. After that, you're fired. You hate Mary for almost getting you killed, and you really, really hate her for introducing you to the kind of guy who will definitely shoot you on sight if he ever sees you again. Get to work. Mary, get in the bathroom. We need to have a little chat about common sense and the gravity of this situation."

They both stared at him for the span of a heartbeat, and then Mary got up and Tom began looking around at his last job. Ray stepped back and let Mary pass, followed her into the bathroom, and then shut the door. He took his gun out again and casually leaned against the sink, pointed it at the door, and looked Mary up and down.

"You're lucky," he began. "For the moment. Right now, fifty-fifty chance I open the door, shoot that poor kid, step on his hands to make it look like he was beating you, then beat you to death and make it look like you shot him."

Mary's eyes widened. In truth, Ray would never have done anything like that. Making a mess at the Kimpton would mean cashing in years of goodwill, and reversing a burn on Tim just wasn't worth it. But there was no way she could know that.

"Look," she began, "I can understand that a man in your position is—"

"Don't try to put yourself in my shoes, lady. I'm tired and I'm hungry and I have a ton of shit to do tonight. Don't make me add two murders to the list. That guy know anything about the trouble you're in? Lie to me and die."

"Yes," she whispered. "He knows everything."

"He know my name? What I do? What I'm doing for you?"

She looked down. Ray put the gun back in his jacket and walked out of the bathroom. Tom had the wastebasket and was just finishing picking dinner out of the carpet. His vomit was covered with Kleenex and napkin squares from the minibar. He looked up and stopped.

"So, Tom," Ray began, "I guess you can keep your job until tomorrow. Tomorrow, I want you to meet me in Reading Terminal with a bag of cash Mary is going to give you. Two in the afternoon. I'll be sitting somewhere around the piano. Good?"

Tom nodded.

"Okay then. Don't bring anyone or do anything fucked up. Put the money in a duffel bag, black or brown—any color but red. You sit down at my table, and we chat. You leave without it."

Tom nodded.

"You're fired right after that. If you knew your boss was in a hotel room getting nailed by the animal she hired to bail her shit out of this mess and you showed up armed with a fucking pink tutu, you're the kind of cretin who will get us all killed. I want you out of the picture for your own good."

Tom nodded a third time. Ray reached out and patted him on the cheek.

"Dummy."

Tom jerked his head away and looked down at his shaking hands. Ray walked to the bathroom door. Mary was standing there with her arms crossed.

"You get all that?" he asked. She nodded and frowned.

"Good. You know where my office is, right?"

Mary nodded again, drew a breath to say something, and changed her mind.

"Saturday. Noon sharp. Do not bring anyone."

Without waiting for a reply, he left.

▶ FIRE WATER BURN, THE BLOODHOUND GANG

Pepper greeted him at the door. Her tail wasn't wagging, and there was something in her big, soft eyes that had an edge of coal to it. She sniffed and tossed her head haughtily and then showed Ray her backside and wandered away, the picture of who cares.

"Unbelievable." Ray closed the door and locked it, hung up his coat, and headed for the kitchen. Pepper walked under the dining-room table and dropped into a curl, and then watched him pass under her eyelashes. Ray opened the refrigerator and took out a Cactus Pulp, twisted the lid off, and drained it with the door open. Then he washed his hands and took the wok down off the bamboo hanger, turned a burner on under it, and poured in a splash of peanut oil followed by some sesame seeds. While it heated, he went back to the fridge and took out some leftover roasted pork tenderloin and some kale, chopped it all and dumped it into the wok, stirred, and then wiped the counters back to pristine. While it cooked, he drank a glass of water and stared at Pepper, who stared back.

"You better lose that shitty attitude," Ray said. Pepper just stared. "We're having a guest tomorrow. Not Agnes. So I want to see your cute-dog routine, not this . . . whatever you call this shit."

Nothing. Ray stirred the kale and rinsed his glass out, put it in the rack, and took down a plate.

"You're vibing the wrong guy, kid. Yes, I've been drinking. True, I stole a car. Yes, yes, there were naked shenanigans—way bizarre, true. But my job is way harder than lying on the couch all day, which you aren't even supposed to be doing, by the way. And I did beat up that kid and kick his boss in the guts, but you are one miserable little monster if you're gonna hold that kind of shit against me."

Pepper reared her head and yawned. Ray turned the heat down, splashed in a little soy sauce and a spoonful of Jerusalem plum preserve, and went upstairs to take a long, scalding shower. When he was done, he threw away his underwear and, for no reason at all, the pants and socks he had worn too. Then he put on jeans and a T-shirt and went back downstairs to eat.

Dinner was better than whatever coke-inspired art-food-night-mare-with-lemon Ramone at La Jolie had assembled for him in the four minutes allotted to him. While eating and leafing through *The Physiognomy*, he mostly thought about grocery shopping, a clean thought. He'd never envisioned a woman eating before in passing, just toyed with images of her chewing, handling her fork, that kind of thing, but he allowed himself free rein. He felt like he deserved it.

When he was done, he washed all the dishes and turned the lights out and then crawled under the dining-room table with the dog, who was still shunning him. He turned his flashlight on and took out Little Jimmy's printout of where Mary's car had been. Tim's office down the street from the anarchist café was there three times, but the rest of it didn't mean anything—not yet. He turned the flashlight off and put his hand on Pepper's little head.

It was an interesting list.

ll

CHAPTER EIGHT

▶ RHYMIN & STEALIN, BEASTIE BOYS

At six in the morning, Ray washed the dishes from his coffee and eggs Benedict (lox sub ham) and checked his street guns. The next few hours would be necessarily crappy, but there was nothing to be done about it.

The two Berettas he was taking were loaded with mixed clips. On top were quiet low-grains, two in each clip. Next up came the hollow-points—fast and loud, four each—and then three cross-tops. An ammunition prediction was a daily advantage. First, he might have to quietly shoot someone. A low-grain subsonic held right against someone's stomach or shot through something soft at point-blank range was what he considered a "public bullet." If those didn't work after four shots, it was time to blow the hell out of everything while making a fast exit. The hollow-points would make an entry wound as big around as a number two pencil, an exit wound the size of a navel orange—the fastest way to lose a pound of gore. The cross-tops were etched and carved to the point where they would fragment in the barrel and turn the guns into shrapnel fountains, ruining them if he got that far, but useful for blowing out plate-glass windows, etcetera.

He strapped one clip to his lower back and shoved the other behind his belt buckle and then looked at the rest of his stuff. The

GPS history on the Taurus, wallet and keys, five hundred in cash, one bicycle spoke, a lighter, a grocery list, and four SEPTA tokens. He was wearing construction boots, old jeans, a T-shirt, and a bomber jacket with duct tape on the elbows, and he hadn't shaved or combed his hair. Pepper was done with breakfast and watched him in disappointment. Two guns meant no car ride, and she knew it.

There was no point in trying to bust whoever was tracking him after he left the house. He took the Camry downtown to his office and parked in the spot reserved for him in the parking garage and then rode the elevator up with the other silent people, just another silent worker. Agnes was an early riser, and he was betting she was already in the office, listening to NPR and having her morning coffee and playing with her tarot of contact cards. She was.

"Good morning, dear," she said, eyeing him. "Off to Kensington to see Skuggy?"

"Powwow with the Skug," he confirmed. "Messages?" He took off his jacket and sat down in one of the reception chairs.

"Two. A woman called yesterday, didn't leave her name, but she came in later and left her message in person. Mary something or other—Tim's unpleasant pussy creature. Did she find you last night?"

"At the Kimpton. She followed me around all morning, so I scraped her off in Chinatown. Had to bone her last night, and that was some ugly business, but the game is officially afoot. I'm getting the extra-dirty cash today at two. Message number two?"

"Dr. Abigail Abelard, confirming your dinner date tonight. I gave her your address. She wanted to know if she should bring something, and I suggested wine or possibly a small gift of poetry."

"Cool." He scratched his stubble.

"What's our cover for this case? Please don't tell me it involves my going with you this morning."

"Nah." Gruben Media always made up some kind of project to work on that covered Ray's movements. Over the next week, he had to visit all the places Mary had, murder Tom Latte, launder the extra-dirty money and replace it with extra-dirty money of a totally different kind, set Mary up to take the fall for everything she was setting him up for, and then kill every last one of them, starting with Tim Cantwell. "Tell you what. I'm going to clock lots of drive time, all over the city. Call Toby King and tell him to set up a production company. Television, something with no track record. One-page website, something in development on the IMDB. I can say I'm location-scouting."

"Can Nicolas Cage be in it?"

"TV, Agnes. Maybe that guy from *Firefly*. Anyway, premise is a rogue detective tracking down a Chinese endangered-animal racket. Snakes, testicles, parrots, that kind of thing."

Agnes was writing. He waited until she was finished and poised to continue.

"And we have to do some side work for this idiot project. Find out how to build a bomb out of local ingredients, memo that and put a big red question mark on it like it confused the fuck out of us. And also we have to do some preliminary extras casting—skeeby black dudes, Ricadelphians with tattoos on their hands and faces."

"Chinese kill kill boys?"

"Yep. Good."

"And the production company is out of . . . ?"

The Feds knew as well as anyone else that a movie or television production company out of Delaware or Colorado was a front, usually for Z-list crimes like petty extortion or backdoor grease for dealing with the Teamsters. Sometimes they were pill shepherds. But California and New York were hard, because anyone could call around and ask reference questions. Ray thought about it.

"How about Michigan? They have a huge film incentive."

Agnes wrote it down and then looked up. "So. Dinner."

"Ah, yes." Ray got up and walked into his office. "Abigail likes seafood, so I'm going to center it around dill. Makes sense, right?"

"Hmm. Salmon poached in white wine with capers and dill was yesterday's news ten years ago, dear. Have you considered that oysters are just now in season?"

Ray sat down at his desk and took a metal clipboard out of the top drawer. It was a contractor's version, a stainless-steel folder that opened and closed from the top. He began writing out the fictional production-company goals, giving it a customary flair of crisis, emergency, panic, and above all cheap, cheap, cheap, as in don't spend a dime and always be on the lookout for one.

"Check it out," Ray said. "A scallop sauté on a bed of heirloom tomato, those crazy black Russian ones, artichoke and minced shallot with shaved perigord and you guessed it, dill. Hot top, cold bottom, chilled plate."

"Have you been stealing from menus again?"

"No shit I have. So we start with oysters. I'll have to see what looks the best when I go to Reading Terminal. Then maybe . . . maybe. . . ."

"Let me guess," Agnes said, appearing in the doorway. "You're going to see Skuggy about a rental car so you can go find out a little more about that woman you had to bang last night. Then when you make the pickup in Reading Terminal, you're going to immediately get the money out of the bag and have Skuggy deposit it while you use the same bag for groceries. You're trying to multitask on every level. You're trying to figure out the probable dimensions of the cash so you can make a guess as to the size of the bag you'll be carrying your groceries in."

"Exactly correct. I'm making dinner for a physicist, using the dimensions of twenty grand to calculate elements of said dinner. I think she would appreciate the amount of math going into this. Not that she'll ever know."

"Lovely," Agnes said, meaning it.

"You're so much more understanding than Pepper, Agnes. I bet she poops in the house before I get home."

She went back to her desk and took out the contact cards for the production front. "Did you talk to Cody last night?"

"He says he might be coming, might be bringing the girl, might be staying at your place, and might be staying at mine. College has obviously ruined him."

"We warned him."

Ray walked out with the clipboard and put on his jacket. "I'll check in from a pay phone around five to get the name of the front."

"Good luck, dear. Tell Skuggy I said hello." She picked up her phone and started dialing as he walked out.

▶ THE BIRTHDAY PARTY. MR. CLARINET

The Craft Building was the perfect place for Gruben Media. There were twelve exits, and most people knew about only seven of them. Ray rode the elevator all the way down to B2 and then got out and used a special access key to take the service elevator down to B4.

The fourth basement level was given over to Select Storage, meaning about an acre of chain-link cages, some of them full of unmarked cardboard boxes, some of them half-full of unmarked cardboard boxes, and most of them empty, with a random piece of office furniture here and there. In two years, he'd never seen anyone else down there. One of the janitors had told him that all the cages were leased by the same company, a name with no personnel locked-door outfit on the eleventh floor. That was so creepy, it convinced even the Deadbomb Bingo Rays of the world to mind their own business. He moved without pause to the stairwell in the southeast corner, a narrow emergency exit that led up two flights to a corridor that let out in the lowest level of the parking garage in the next building over.

Once he was on the street, he headed on foot for the Thirteenth Street SEPTA hole that led down to the subway. The snow on the street had been churned into black sludge in the night, and garbage was poking through the two inches of remaining white, new garbage sticking to the top. The sky was dark, but it wasn't quite cold enough to snow again, so there was just seasonal sleet. He pulled his collar up and kept his head down.

SEPTA had its own smell, one unlike any other subway system on Earth. In New York, the subway smelled like sweat and popcorn and occasionally used diapers. The Paris Metro smelled like perfume and BO and bad teeth. London just the bad teeth. Tokyo was all about paper, Osaka plastic, and flowers. SEPTA combined the ripe, oversweet smell of a dead foot with the essence of a thousand electrocuted mice, in a Mephistine noctuolent that provoked in many an unwary rider the third reliable tang: beer vomit.

▶ I TURNED INTO A MARTIAN. MISFITS

A blood-temperate wall of it smacked him as he hit the SEPTA hole and descended. The wet crowd all kept a careful foot of free space around them, the violation of which could provoke anything from a grotesque come-hither to a knife. He didn't look up until he finally hit the Market-Frankford Line. From there, he had a solid hour of escalating racial tension until Tioga Station and the surrounding posturban wasteland.

Ray rode in silence, lost in thought. Around him, the other riders avoided eye contact with both him and each other. After a certain point, anyone white left on the MFL was a junky and everyone who was black knew it, so all hunter/prey calculations were color-coded. The white people wanted each other's drugs. The black people wanted to be left alone unless they had the same bad habits as the white riders, in which case they more enterprisingly went after each other's drugs, money, weapons, and women, and sometimes their shoes and coats as well. Ray knew it was a microeconomic modeling experiment under the magnifying glass of economic think-tanks, altered and tweaked by outside forces to study the reaction ripples.

He'd tortured some of the data out of one group for another twice, but he had no idea how advanced or devolved the current iteration was. He did know his presence would register as a blip in the monitoring metrics, but he also knew there was nothing anyone could do about it.

The pointless desperation was irritating anyway. The political-correction meme had destroyed any articulate mouthiness about the whole thing, which of course was its objective, but sad facts were sad facts. The black population had no hope at all, and they knew it. A decade ago, there had at least been the pretense of trade schools. You weren't going to make it, but you might be able to fix toilets or air conditioners. Now those schools had closed as they were defunded, and what was left was a state of hand-to-mouth combat with ever-changing factions and alliances monetized by welfare and drug money. So, of course, useful business data galore spun off of the kings of the gladiator pit. Ray didn't see how this house of cards and its rules of jungle conduct should apply to him in the least, so when he found himself in the hard headlights of the ghetto monster across from him—a big, bent white kid with "RESPECT" tattooed in prison soot over one eyebrow—he flipped him off with flat ozone in his eyes.

The kid hissed and looked away and picked at the top of his filthy jeans.

Tioga spilled right into a park with garden-variety three-man crack teams, beat-down whores in five colors, and high-temperature solo operations. Ray stuffed his hands in his jacket pockets and walked with his eyes on scan. The snow was still mostly clear, amazingly. He passed the benches, where a few people were sleeping and a girl of maybe sixteen was rocking back and forth and staring into a nightmare only she could see. Eventually he made it to the far side of the park without incident. As he hit the first street west, he saw a couple of ten-year-old boys fistfighting. A block later another boy, sixteen maybe—no coat and an eye infection—hurried past, making kissing sounds and chanting "brown, brown, upside down." Two more blocks of old gray row houses, with front yards decorated with abandoned mattresses and the black skeletons of things that burned and rusted things that rust. He came to Skuggy's and went up and knocked on the door. There was a complex resulting sound: bare feet approaching, ratchet of a shotgun, clearing of a phlegmy throat, the scrape of a mirror unfolding ten feet away at the edge of the porch.

"Skug," Ray called, "it's Ray. I came on behalf of Human Services, to see if you're alive and, if you are, to make you take a fuckin' bath."

Skuggy opened the door. He was a skinny old black man in a bathrobe, with wild eyes and a shotgun cradled in his withered right arm, which was itself cradled in a filthy sling made from a pillowcase. The fingernails on the withered hand were Indian freak-show long. He glared at Ray and bared his yellow teeth.

"You brang Skuggy his fuckin' Chrutmas chicken?"

"Fucking sure didn't."

"Then fuck you!" Skuggy slammed the door.

Ray stood there for a minute. The pulley on the mirror whispered, and it folded back to the wall. He didn't hear any more movement, so he walked back down the stairs and looked both ways. There was a bodega sign a few blocks to the left, so he stuck his hands back in his jacket pockets and headed in that direction. A block down, he passed three black guys in a doorway who gave him territory eyes, but he made it to the little convenience store without incident.

Inside, it was ghetto standard. Candy, cigarettes, processed food, and, even at seven in the morning, a bulletproof plexiglass-fronted stainless steel toaster full of wings. Ray made eye contact with the assassin on the far side of the scratched-to-shit safety glass and pointed at the Chernobyl box.

"All the chicken and a pack of Newports, menthol."

The guy put everything in a box and maneuvered it out after Ray paid, all without a word. He carried it back to Skuggy's and knocked on the door again.

"Skug, it's Ray," he repeated. "I'm here on behalf of Human Services, who want to burn your house down with you in it. Your daughter, the super-young one you're sure is yours, came to my office with a kind of herpes that made Agnes faint, and I called the CDC, so—"

The door flew open and Skuggy gave him the same look as last time.

"You brang Skuggy his—oh." He grabbed the box with his good hand and Ray followed him in.

Skuggy's house smelled like motor oil and solvents and mothballs. It was dark because of the security plywood on the windows, but tidy. The living room had a recliner and a sofa, both covered in clear protective plastic, a coffee table, and a big flat-screen on a TV stand. The dining room had an actual dining-room table, covered in newspaper and clock parts for as long as Ray could remember.

"Want some?" Skuggy held the box out. Ray took a wing and sat down on the couch. Skug crashed down on his recliner and dug in. He ate voraciously, stripping the wings to the bone with his big teeth in expert ripping motions, one stroke per bone. Ray nibbled and waited for Skuggy to speak first.

"Need a car?" Skuggy asked after wing number six. Ray nodded.

"A car, and I need you to come with me to Reading Terminal to deal with this cash problem."

"Kinda problem?"

"Long story, but the short version is the cash comes from a bank robbery that went crazy fucked-up wrong. Feds are watching for the numbers. The bag will definitely have a tracer in it, so I need you to put pants on so you can empty the bag in a stall in the men's room. I have to carry it out, but I can't risk the cash being in the bag because I have to kill the courier. Plus, I have to go grocery shopping."

Skuggy nodded. "When?"

"I gotta run errands in the rental, so I need you to meet me there at one."

"Kinda errands?"

"All the fuck over the place. I have a list from a car I stole for a few minutes last night, have to find out where it's been." Ray got up and dropped his chicken bones back in the box and then wiped his hands on his pants. Abruptly, Skuggy was done. He licked the fingers on his good hand loudly and burped.

"Want some company?"

"Sure," Ray replied. "Make it snappy, man. Faster you get ready, the more places we can hit."

Skuggy grunted and rose. "Be just a sec. I'ma bring me some them Amish donuts home. Blueberry." He tottered off toward the back of the house. "You like them blueberry ones, Ray?"

"I do. My favorite is the apple fritters."

"Crispy," Skuggy called. "Touch of vinegar."

A few minutes later, Skuggy emerged wearing an old brown suit, well cared for, with his withered arm in a clean brocade sling. His old wing tips were polished, and his hair was wet with afro sheen. He'd even brushed his teeth. He took a pair of huge sunglasses out of his jacket, put them on, and then pointed his face at Ray.

"Cold?"

"Not especially. Bring an umbrella."

Skuggy took a tall umbrella from beside the door and tapped along with it like it was a cane. Outside, he inhaled deeply as he locked the door. Then he took the Newport Ray offered him, and they both lit up.

"Car's right down there. Cutlass with the old-school negrodellic rims."

▶ SAMSON ET DALILA, OP. 47, MARIA CALLAS

"Once upon a time," Skuggy began, "all this shit was different." He gestured with his cigarette at the entire world as they turned onto Chester. "Cash—like crazy bad bank bills with blood on 'em—we used to mail that shit. Mail it, Ray, as in put that shit in the fuckin' mail. In 1972, I mailed seventy-eight thousand dollars to myself, from Atlanta to Houston, one box. Just showed up at the post office, stood in line, stick! Yo, baby, gotta mail my mama a spellin' book and some eight-tracks for the crazy bitch's Camaro. Not anymore. But damn, Reading Terminal now. Philly be a criminal hot spot, even people in Toledo know that shit, but Reading. . . . You ever hear of a boy name Winslow Green?"

Ray shook his head.

"Green was a smart negro. He dead now, I know you ain't gonna tell nobody anyway, but he so bright he pull off the first iPhone 3G crime in Philly. Right there in Reading Terminal."

"No shit? What'd he do?"

"Some genius shit is what he did. So Green is in there gettin' some kinda fat-man sandwich—he was skinny, but you know what I mean, some kinda guinea with broccoli—and he sees one them boys take the cash out the register. All the cash. Green take note. He just got this phone that day, so he look like an everyday phone dum-dummy. Anyway, the kid go back by the big stove and open a safe, put the money in. Green look at his phone. Now see, he ain't never seen no safe in Reading Terminal, ain't never really seen what the 3G doin' either. He walk this way, he walk that way. Then he get all clever and do some geometry on a napkin. The 3G got wide augmentation system, Cell Hunter, openBmap. Green use his GPS to triangulate exactly where that fucking safe is."

Skuggy paused to light two cigarettes. He handed one to Ray and looked out the window again, recollecting a little slower as he savored it all.

"Now, everyone lookin' at those new phones, and Green? He just another everyone. Next two weeks, he finds fifteen more safes in there, does his napkin triangulation, inputs it into that phone of his. Forty-two businesses in Reading Terminal, and by the end of that first month he know where every single safe is, right down to the inch. Guess what he did with that fancy phone after that?"

"Robbed the place."

"Not just robbed the place, Ray. He conducted a *criminal opera*. So the whole Terminal got a crawl space under it. He make these squares out that shitty det cord you score off Chino Chang back in the day, crawls under there one night and sets 'em all in place. Next night, he goes back in with like a million miles of cable, sets a big-ass electromagnet under each safe, and every magnet's attached to that cable. Now that last night, that's a Saturday night, busy as fuck. Them safes be full as shit. Two a.m., BOOM, he drops every last fuckin' one of them through the floor. Sixty seconds later, they come out on the tow winch he hooked up in the back of this old taco truck. Close the back doors, and he gone. From det to two blocks away is two minutes tops. Then he spend a fuckin' week cuttin' 'em all. Two mil an' big change, baby. Two mil an' big change."

"Aw, man!" Ray slapped the wheel. "How come I never heard of it?"

"Like anybody gonna talk, dingdong? That much cash? Ain't no way. That's big white money, the old kind. Kind with the blessing hush-hush. You maybe heard Reading Terminal closed one Sunday for renovation or busted toilets, but you ain't never gonna hear no total on no Saturday numbers, no sir."

"Winslow Green. What happened to him?"

"The cocaine."

They drove for a while in silence, closing in on Germantown. Eventually Ray handed Skuggy the printout.

"See what you can see, man," Ray said. "Should be right up on the next corner."

Skuggy consulted the paper and adjusted his sunglasses, looked up, and pointed. Ray followed his finger. An aquarium store, a real estate office, and a pizza place. They pulled into the parking lot, and Skuggy lowered the paper and turned to him.

"Me or you?"

"I'll scope out the first stop," Ray said. "Maybe you do the next one."

"Leave me them cigarettes."

▶ DIG, LAZARUS, DIG!!!, NICK CAVE & THE BAD SEEDS

By the time they parked down the street from Reading Terminal they'd hit more than half the list, and they all had one thing in common: real estate.

"This Tim a money man. Maybe he be spreadin' it around," Skuggy theorized.

"Maybe," Ray agreed. "You head on in and get a donut. The swap is at two by the piano. I gotta go change."

"Inta what?"

"I keep a suit at the dry cleaners over on Eleventh. I'll pick it up and change in the bathroom of the Korean place next to it. Gray suit, blue tie." He parked in a one hour space and cut the engine, handed him the keys.

Skuggy pocketed them and set off for Reading Terminal, tapping along with his umbrella, just another old criminal. Ray peeled off toward the dry cleaners. He kept a dozen suits in rotation across the city for just this kind of situation. Once he got there, he picked it up, went to the restaurant next door and ordered a beer, changed in the bathroom and transferred all his weapons around, slicked his hair back with hand soap, tossed his Kensington garb in the trash, and left a two-dollar tip. A block down, he swapped his shoes out for loafers. It was time, he thought, to do some grocery shopping. He'd been looking forward to this part all day long.

Reading Terminal was packed on any Friday at two in the afternoon, and this Friday was no exception. The one-foot provocation zone edict didn't apply inside, and the Philadelphians mingled in an uneasy truce as they maneuvered through the maze of artisan deli stalls. Stately businesswomen brushed past the ubiquitous *Sopranos* extras. Suited banking samurai neatly dodged the chunky workers with stooped shoulders. There was a noticeable absence of children. Ray glided like an ice-skater with his hands behind his back, ticking off the items on his mental grocery list. He still had twenty minutes, so he picked up some smoked trout and two halibut cheeks. Once he spotted Skuggy, who stood swaying next to the piano player and drinking a Coke. Then Ray went through the produce section and got everything else. He'd get the oysters on the way out.

Tom Latte had secured a little two-top, five tables away from the piano, by two o'clock. Ray set his grocery bags down next to the overhead-compartment-sized gray duffel bag beneath the table. Then he beamed down at Tom and held his arms wide.

"Tommy the honey latte," he said warmly. "Give us a great big hug for the audience."

Tom rose uncertainly and gave Ray a chaste hug. Ray slipped the tracer into Tom's suit pocket and then patted him on the butt. Tom jerked and Ray stepped back and then sat, still smiling. He gestured at the other chair, and Tom sat down.

"So, Tom, it's all there?"

"Yes," Tom replied, smiling nervously. "Yes, sir. Yes, it is."

"I like this place," Ray said. He leaned back. "Got time for coffee?"

Tom's nervous smile spasmed a little before he got a handle on it, so Ray toned it down and looked away.

"Easy, man. We're almost done. We sit for a minute or two, just a couple guys from the same office or whatever. Chitchat. So Mary, your boss—you like working for her? She got you all emotionally off-balance?" He looked at Tom then, and it was all as clear as day. "She made you fall in love with her. It's all over you, kid." Ray sighed. "It happens in this line of work. If I was you, I really would just take the fired thing seriously. Cut and run and never look back. You can do that, man. You can just shut it down at the pump and dry out, take a plane to New Mexico and see where the chips fall. Leave your ride, call no one, go straight to the airport."

Tom's nervous smile faded. Gradually his eyes hardened. Ray gave him the kind of sad smile you make at the bad part of a story with a mediocre ending, picked up all the bags, and split.

Everything that happened next was like a choreographed dance. Tom stood up and would have followed Ray or signaled other watchers, but in that instant, right when Tom rose high enough to raise a hand over the heads around him, Skuggy spilled his entire Coke into the piano keys. The pianist was a sweet old lady with a wig and bizarre clownish makeup. She screamed, an inhuman wail, and several people rushed to her aid. Tom turned and Skuggy expertly backed out of the confusion, bent to pick up his umbrella, and his head vanished from Tom's view. When Tom turned back, Ray had been swallowed by the crowd.

Ray quickly went to the oyster place and ordered two dozen Kumamotos. While he waited for the guy to bag them up, Skuggy breezed down a different aisle and stopped at the Amish donut place. The line was ten people deep but moved with great efficiency, so after he ordered a dozen blueberry donuts and two apple fritters—with an extra-double bag because it looked like rain and it was his "walking day"—he entered the men's room ten steps ahead of Ray.

From there it was a cakewalk. The bald patch in the bathroom herd was by the trash can, an abandoned no-man's zone, and Skuggy conquered it further by approaching it, leaning over, and loudly blowing his nose, one nostril at a time, shooting the contents of his sinus directly into the used paper cups and wrappers in an outdoorsy move that was totally inappropriate in a confined space. Ray entered, penetrated the reinforced perimeter, and set the cash bag down. In thirty seconds, anyone who had witnessed the two men step up to the trash can had rotated out of view. Skuggy picked up the cash bag and went into a stall. Ray went into a stall two doors down.

Cell phones would have come in handy for the last part, but a purist in no way required one. Signaling each other with clicks and grunts was fine. Skuggy sat on the toilet and transferred the extra-dirty cash to his extra-double donut bag, sheaving through each stack of bills. He removed two tracking wafers and put them back in the duffel bag. A third, more powerful tracking device was sewn into the cash bag's handle. When he was done, he flushed his toilet and kicked the stall door open.

"Toilet in this one be broken!" he declared loudly. He went to the sinks around the corner with his bags, and a moment later Ray appeared and started washing his hands. Ray picked up the empty cash bag and quickly put his groceries inside. Skuggy examined his teeth in the mirror above the next sink over and straightened his tie, standing casual guard. He would drop the money off at a laundry later, but while he was downtown he'd said he might as well get some pussy.

Ray left Reading Terminal and headed for Chinatown, which was less than five minutes away. He walked like he was in no particular hurry, and at one point stopped and got some poblanos and a head of cilantro at a sidewalk vendor stall. He walked into Emerald Alley. The same old man looked up at Ray with the same deadpan expression.

"Cixin," Ray said, holding up his bag. "Running errands." The old man stared back at him, waiting. Ray set down the bag and peeled five twenties off the roll in his pocket and handed them over. The old man vanished them.

"Watch my bag for five minutes?"

Cixin gestured that Ray should move it to his side of the register. Ray did and then looked toward the far end of the store.

"Back door that way?"

Nod.

"'Kay. I'll come back in through the front."

Ray went out the back door into the alley, walked two slippery blocks back toward Reading Terminal, and then took a side chute back to the street. He found Tom in a white four-door half a block up, parked in a loading zone with his blinkers on, watching the entrance to Emerald Alley. Ray walked up behind the car on the street side. When he got even with it, he opened the back door on the driver's side and slipped in, drawing his chest gun in the same move. Tom looked into the rearview as Ray shot once, point-blank through the seat, and then Ray got out and left.

Back at Emerald Alley, he picked up his bag with a nod. He walked four blocks up, caught a cab to Thirtieth Street Station, and lost himself. Half an hour later, he took a second cab to his office to pick up his car and find out the name and address of the production company front. It was closing in on four o'clock.

Date night.

II

CHAPTER NINE

▶ LA CUMPARSITA. STEVAN PASERO & RICHARD PATTERSON

At exactly eight, there was a knock at the door—five medium raps, perfectly spaced. Ray looked all the way through the house from the kitchen and for a fleeting instant wondered if he'd overdone it. The lamps were on, and a cheery fire was burning in the fireplace. The two dozen stargazer lilies he'd picked up on the way home were scattered in vases throughout. Pepper was positioned in the center of the couch, a pink bow in her hair, picture-perfect after her bath and blow-dry. He was wearing casual slacks and a black Armani V-neck, his hair slicked back with gel.

Pepper looked from him to the door and barked once, sharply, holding position.

"Enter!" he called. He'd unlocked the door a minute and thirty seconds ago. He opened the drawer at his waist and dropped the towel he was holding on top of one of the last Berettas on the first floor.

Abigail opened the door, and her eyes went instantly wide at the tableau. Ray raised his wine glass and beamed. It was the exact reaction he'd designed the moment to provoke. Even saluting with the wine glass was part of it.

"My goodness!" Abigail declared. Snow was gently falling behind her and, framed against it, she was perfect, like a forest elf or a supernatural creature from the art section of the Metropolitan Library. She was wearing a beige overcoat over a brilliant green sweater, jeans, UGG boots, and a checkered scarf and holding a mesh bag of clementines from the Italian Market. She looked up from Pepper across the ocean of house, her big eyes wide and glittering with firelight, her skin a startlingly creamy white, flushed at the cheekbones from the cold, a little snow in her hair, and Ray looked down to pour her a glass of wine as his poker face failed.

"Welcome," he boomed. He carried two glasses out of the kitchen. She closed the door and took off her coat, accepting the wine with a smile that seemed to come from her entire body. He draped her coat over the back of the armchair next to the door, and they instantly made wild, passionate love.

Ray had no idea how it had happened. He'd leaned in to give her a peck on the cheek, and her head turned just so and it landed on the edge of her unpainted lips. Then she leaned into it, and their teeth clicked together. Her arm touched his waist, right above the shotgun scar, and he pulled back a few inches and looked into her upturned face, her searching eyes. She made a curious peep—part hunger and part bird—and rose on her toes and stuck her tongue in his mouth. He circled her waist with his free hand in a crushing embrace and lifted her. Seconds later they were tearing off each other's clothes and trying to make it to the couch, trying not to spill the wine, trying to eat each other alive and live forever as a unique hybrid organism with a single skin, far from everything, on one of the moons of Saturn.

Afterward, they lay panting in the bed upstairs, having made it up there at some point. Ray felt a blissful peace. He'd forgotten how comfortable the bed was, for one thing. He hadn't slept in it in almost two years. Plus, the lovemaking had thrilled him in a way that he'd hoped to experience early in high school, when he'd had no idea what to expect except for what he found in the romance of movies and his own dramatic imagination, before he became aware of the conjugal-visit-in-prison variant that had become the dominant practice, the Era of Pornography element of everyday boning.

No, this was far, far different. Abigail made love with everything she had, staring into his eyes far past his name. The way her hips arched back, her small butt, her cold hands clutching and eventually hot and slick with their sweat. . . . Beside him, Abigail let out a deep breath and rolled over to face him. He glanced sideways at her, and they stared into each other's eyes.

"Gracious me," she said, that love-fuck look still filling her eyes.

"No shit," he agreed.

She stroked his chest, slowly, and then draped a leg over him and snuggled in. "It's been, what, three years for me," she said softly.

"Huh," Ray said, suddenly uneasy.

"That was fantastic." She stretched, and it went all the way into her voice. "It's hard to believe we just went from lunch dating to whatever this is in . . . I guess less than one minute."

"Mnn."

"What's your dog's name?"

"Pepper? Her name is Pepper."

"Cute. How old is she?"

Ray had no idea. He kissed the top of Abigail's head, and she looked up at him.

"You hungry?" He kissed her nose.

"Yes, I am," she purred and kissed his chin. Then they were kissing again. He disengaged and rolled out of bed, stretching. She watched him, smiling at his naked body. He looked around the room as if for the first time in ages. It was a decoy room, really, but he knew there were robes in the closet because that's where people put them. He took out two white terry cloth Kimpton robes and put one on, tied the waist, and laid the other one on the edge of the bed. Abigail sat up, holding the sheet to her chest with one hand, still smiling. Her tousled hair was perfect.

"I have some cooking to do, Doctor Abelard. I can bring up your wine, or you can come down and watch me. There are oysters for an appetizer—Kumamotos."

"You carried me past a library," she said, pulling the robe to herself. She got out of bed and tightened it around her. "But I'd rather watch you shuck oysters while I drink wine."

He couldn't stop his smile if he tried. His poker face had retired for the night. "C'mon then."

▶ CHRISTMAS ON TV. CHRIS ISAAK

Ray took the oysters out of the fridge and put them in the sink. Abigail settled on a stool at the island, wine in front of her, watching him work.

"I love your place," she said, cradling her chin. "This kitchen is amazing." Her eyes played over the rack of copper-bottom pots, the wide ceramic urn of utensils, the glass vase of skewers (bicycle spokes—Ray had a flash of Fat Rocky Roy staggering backward with one sticking out of his eye in the bathroom of a motel in Atlantic City), the potted herbs on the windowsill.

"So, how was your day?" she continued. "Gruben Media man . . ."

"Good," Ray answered. He got out his oyster shucker and took down a plate. "How was yours, Doctor? Nerd out like a mofo?"

Abigail laughed, a good, clean noise that drew Pepper out from under the dining-room table. Ray smiled at the sound of it and started popping, covering the oysters with a towel from a different drawer. He glanced up and scanned the snowy back yard for footprints for the third time in a minute, but not nervously. Just habit.

"I did indeed nerd out. We played simulations all day."

"That like video games?" He paused to sip his wine.

"In a way. Modeling electron ellipses in postreaction enzyme cones. Variants in water-molecule hyperstring halos. Maybe more like playing a piano with an infinite number of keys, I suppose."

"I'll be damned," Ray said. She gave him an odd look. He took a lemon out of the crisper and sliced it, plated the oysters, and set them down in between them. The odd smile faded, but the one she pointed at the Kumamotos was noticeably dimmer.

"So your day?" she prompted, picking up her first oyster. "I never did understand what you do either."

Ray slurped one down and considered. "Well, right now Gruben is under contract with a television production company out of Michigan. Wellesley Productions, pilot for a cable thriller about exotic animal trafficking. They have all kinds of requests, so I spent the day palling around with a friend of mine doing location scouting. Have to visit real estate offices all next week to skirt some permit issues, that kind of thing. Oh, and get this—I have to start recruiting extras out of Kensington."

"I see. I might know some people, if the production company pays." She ate her oyster and smiled in earnest again and then picked up a second.

"In Kensington?" Strange.

"I volunteer at a shelter there every Wednesday night, six to ten." She slurped it down and watched his reaction play over his face.

"Amazing," he summarized.

"What?" She liked it. He liked saying it too.

"You. A physicist who does volunteer work in Kensington. It's almost religious, but I know it isn't, so. . . ."

"In my way, Raymond, I am the most religious person I've ever known. But I don't believe in God, per se."

Abruptly, his poker face came back into play. "What . . . what do you believe in, then?"

"You," she said shortly. "Me. I believe in the future."

▶ BALL OF CONFUSION. THE TEMPTATIONS

They ate in relative silence after that, two hungry lovers. Ray had pulled together a feast, distracted as he was. Poached halibut cheeks on cold papaya with garlic and clementine skin, julienned and seared crisp; more oysters; and kale with a pistachio-avocado dressing. When they were done, he made frozen blueberries with milk and honey and clementine juice, stirred together into something different and better than ice cream, and he watched her spoon it up until she caught him.

"Wish we had some pumpkin seeds," he said. She smiled into her bowl.

"I knew that got you. You're a closed book in many ways, Ray. Such a complicated mind. But I saw a page in the middle of your thriller right then."

"I bet you did."

"It's getting late." She gave him a closing-time kind of smile.

"You should stay, Abigail. It must have snowed three inches tonight. The roads will be clear in the morning." They stared at each other shyly, which was strange considering how the night had gone so far, and then they left the dishes and went back upstairs. Later— much later, when she finally fell asleep—Ray lay awake for a long time, thinking. He thought about the advice he had given Tom Latte in Reading Terminal, about how it was never too late to cut and run. He thought about the little oranges. He thought of Abigail's tonsils, which he had seen much of that night. He also thought of the guns he had left fixed up under the table they had eaten on, because he had killed the messenger again, and there was no telling what the Piper would look like.

But mostly he thought about the smell of Abigail's hair.

II

CHAPTER TEN

▶ TAKE FIVE. RODRIGO Y GABRIELA

After energetic morning sex—different this time, and full of tickling and athletic pounding and saliva—followed by breakfast, they parted ways. Abigail was off to her office lab and Ray to the kitchen to clean up and take the guns back out of the garage. He was going to pick her up tomorrow morning at her work, for a day in the park followed by a night on the town. They kissed lingeringly in the doorway, and he could still taste her entire body in his mouth, like a warm peach, as he took the rifle out from under the dining-room table.

Skuggy would be dealing with the extra-dirty cash that morning, converting it from a bank-robbery take with numbers on the federal watch list to assorted low bills from the Kensington drug mess, themselves on all kinds of watch lists; easy enough to deposit if you did legitimate business there, but crazy bad to have in your possession if you were a hedge-fund manager who had recently squeaked out of a bust. Agnes would be in the office, even though it was Saturday. He had to meet Mary Chapman at noon. She would either be late or early, and he would have to explain why he'd killed her assistant. Ray sighed. He already hated all other women. When that happened in literature, he'd always been so sure it was bullshit.

After he shaved, he dressed in a suit and tie and had one final cup of coffee while Pepper peed in the back yard. Snow had fallen all through the night, six inches of it, and the little Pomeranian wore herself out charging through it, her inner fox made playful and snarky by all the recent commotion in her den, no doubt. When she came back in, he dried her feet and checked his guns one more time. Just after ten. More than an hour to check out the two nearest places on his list.

He took the black '16 Mercedes something-or-other because he didn't want to ding any of the good cars. Philly drivers were among the worst in the nation, a statistic possibly linked with the number of uninsured drivers, which hovered around 40 percent. He backed out of the garage and watched the garage door close and then headed for Sansom Street.

The snow had given the scowling metropolis of doom a temporary smile. No one could see the trash they'd thrown out the window the day before, and it was like it had never happened. The world had a bright glow to it with the light reflecting off of the snow. He rambled around looking for a tail and finally pulled in at the real estate office on Thirty-Eighth. Turner Realty was open, and a woman—blond, with a turtleneck sweater—was sitting at the front desk working on a computer. Ray parked and went in with his metal clipboard. The woman looked up and frowned instead of smiling.

"Hi?" She was in a hurry, and he didn't have an appointment.

"Who the fuck are you," Ray asked with no question mark, not smiling at all. "Where the fuck is everybody?"

"I'm sorry, Mister . . ." She was almost incredulous, but there was something underneath it—fear, with a measure of anxiety that had been riding her before he ever walked in. It smelled like paydirt.

"Christ," Ray spat. "No one gets paid with this kind of . . ." He sat down in a plastic chair across from her and stared out the window. "It's sunny in Vegas right now." He snapped his eyes at her. "Did you know that? Did you?"

"Maybe I should call someone," she suggested, worried now. She cautiously reached out for the phone on her desk.

"Do," he said shortly. Then he opened the metal clipboard and took a ballpoint pen out of his jacket, clicking it. She hesitated, and he looked up.

"How long have you been working here, lady?"

"I don't see why——"

He slammed the folder down on his thigh, and she jumped. He pointed at her, and she drew a breath. He was onto something and he knew it, so he threw the dice.

"Let's see how fucked up we are. Right now you're going over everything you need to buy in to this deal, but about half of it is bullshit. 'What the fuck,' you keep saying to yourself. 'We're faking assets to buy into a fraud. I'm breaking all kinds of laws, and I don't even know how I get paid!' And la de da. And now this. Now this! You're in with the big dogs, and here one of them shows and you didn't even know I was coming. You didn't even know! Now why is that, you're asking yourself. Is it because someone forgot to tell you because it's so . . . busy here?" Ray made a twirling gesture with his finger. "Or is it because you're a low-rent glory hole with legs who's gonna take the hit if the shit hits the fan?"

He watched it compute.

▶ TAKE EVERYTHING, MAZZY STAR

Taffy hemorrhaged the whole story in a forty-minute confession that crossed the line between panicked and foaming, so Ray took his time on his way to Gruben Media as he considered all the new details. Tim had recruited eleven investors for a riverfront condo project, but only one of them had a majority stake. Pontiac LLC was Indian, with a hundred and twenty-two million in gambling assets they were poised to move out of a tax shelter. When they did, the investment group would buy the property, and then the deal would promptly fall apart. Pontiac LLC would wind up with six acres of plague dirt and rotting landfill, and the seller's consortium of fifteen real estate brokers would disband and quietly hang out new shingles. Tim's cut was unknown, but he was the mastermind, so it was big enough to get his long ride back and set up on the top floor of a tall, tall building, high enough up so that he couldn't see what his friends and colleagues had done to the economy. And it was sure to net enough extra to buy a serious yard shank for Deadbomb Bingo Ray. This was the crime he was being set up for.

The anarchist café was hopping when he drove past, so he parked and went in, got a coffee, and stood around with two skins and a chunky little woman with a partial beard. They must have thought he was someone's father and shunned him in a polite way, which was sweet. He didn't have his earbud or the transceiver, but that wasn't what he was there for. He'd noticed a bulletin board outside the door with announcements on his first visit. Band fliers, student housing, lots of angry lesbian potlucks, art swaps, and the like. He blew on his coffee and sipped as he read them all, and eventually he took two of them down: a handwritten flier for a thing called Chaox, which appeared to be an artist collective with classes in "blowtorchin'" and "weldification," and a slick notice for something called !RIGHTS!, with a fist on either side. !RIGHTS! seemed to be comprised of deep left-wing psychos, furious about everything from GMOs to Chinese smog. Potentially useful in just the right way, two crusades headed for what they didn't yet realize was not the same promised land. It gave him an idea.

The drive to the office was uneventful. He doubted he had a tail. Tom Latte's sudden death would have thrown a newer operation for a loop; he'd changed cars; and they already knew where he was going to be anyway. He pulled into the parking garage of the Craft Building and parked without incident, made it through the lobby and up to his floor with nobody behind him, and walked through the door of Gruben Media at fifteen minutes to noon. Agnes was at her desk, arms crossed, waiting for him with a scowl on her face.

"A Miss Chapman is waiting," she said sourly. "I showed her to the bar, and she's appreciating the view." The door to his office was open. Ray peeked in, wincing. Mary was seated in front of his desk with her back to them, staring out the window with a tumbler of scotch dangling from one hand. She turned, and it was instantly obvious she'd been crying.

"She's extremely upset," Agnes confirmed.

Ray swept into his office and closed the door behind him. He went right to the bar but changed his mind, took his jacket off, tossed it on the couch, and then sat next to it. Mary faced him, and he gave her a sympathetic smile.

"What's the story, mornin' glory?"

"Tom is dead," she whispered.

Ray sat back and looked out the window. "Tell me what you know." It came out slow and even.

"He was in Chinatown. He gave you the money, right?"

"Yeah. Reading Terminal, just like we planned. By the piano. I left. So he went to Chinatown and died. Poor devil."

"You killed him." She started sobbing again, quiet convulsions of grief that seemed confusingly real.

"Mary, think about it. Usually in this kind of thing, people get killed for *not* delivering the money. Did, ah . . . is there any way the guy who's blackmailing you could have figured out what you're up to?"

"I don't think so," she breathed. "Hold me!" And with that she lurched to her feet and fell into him. Ray struggled to get out from under her, but she'd turned into an octopus. Instead, he wrestled her into a sitting position beside him and took a deep breath.

"Then it's the money," he said. "Who gave it to you?"

Mary stopped crying. She looked up and sniffed.

"I got it from my bank." She looked away.

"I don't think you did. Someone knew you had twenty grand floating free, and they came looking for it. Just lousy timing. Happens." Ray stood up and went to the bar, sloshed scotch into two glasses. "Poor fuckin' Tom. I feel bad about throwing that food at him now."

"You're a monster," she said a little louder. On the other side of the office door, Agnes Capsule snickered. Ray handed Mary her tumbler of scotch.

"For the moment, I'm the only monster you have, Chapman. So let's get down to it. With Tom killed like this, the clock is ticking double-time. You want this blackmail over with, we have to move fast. Someone knows what you're up to. A dead bagman in Chinatown is a message, pure and simple, and the message is stop your shit or you're dead, dead, dead. Got it?"

Mary took the drink and drained it. She took a minute to think it through; and while she did, Ray went to the window and looked out. More clouds were moving in.

Something was wrong with this confession. He could feel it. Mary was a little too authentically scared. It wasn't him, he was sure. For the moment, she thought she had as much control over him as she needed, even though it wasn't much. No, it was something else.

It couldn't be Tim Cantwell, either. He was a banker. A mark. Even a vengeful, petty, bloodthirsty hedge-fund manager was still just a numbers man. Mary Chapman was a killer of some kind, so she wasn't afraid of Cantwell. Ray frowned at his reflection.

Mary was working for Tim Cantwell on the bigger deal, taking down real-estate money in the kind of complicated shuffle hedge-fund managers were known for, defrauding Indians in this case. Framing Deadbomb Bingo Ray was part of a bigger picture. If all blame for his past crimes could be shifted onto someone else, the microscope Tim was under would shift its focus right at a critical time for a huge, multimillion-dollar move. Ray had thought it was a complicated revenge fantasy being acted out, but it was more than that—and Mary knew it. Someone had to take a fall, and Ray had been close to the crime that had almost taken Tim down, close enough to be the logical target. The real goal had to be the Indian money. Ray would take the hit for it. The Indians would pony up for the prison shank. Tim Cantwell would be rich. His people would be free. The plan was a little bigger than Ray had thought. Mary was better than he'd thought, too.

Mary also knew that Ray might have killed her assistant Tom, but the logic behind it was hard to divine. She was attempting to figure it out behind him, at this very moment, but it was coming up snake eyes again and again. There was no angle in Ray killing anyone in broad daylight with a shit-ton of filthy money on him, no angle at all, except the total confusion of this very instant. Which was why he'd done it. He turned and cranked the knob on her paranoia to eleven.

"This guy who's blackmailing you. Money always goes somewhere, and it's always up. Your man with the plan is getting fucked around, Mary. Think about it. Someone bigger than him is yanking his chain, just like every fucker in this entire world. Who's above him? Think or sink."

Mary's eyes went wide. Whoever she was thinking about, and there *was* someone, had a grip on her. She shivered, and goose bumps appeared on her arms. Cornered. And he could see the player she was envisioning too, the worst kind there was, a faceless silhouette pulling the strings. The best kind of all—the nameless ghost who scared everyone. The butcher boy, he called it. The player he still didn't know. The one who terrified her.

"This person have a name? This . . . person who killed that poor fucking latte kid? Did you even like him?"

She looked up at Ray, and he leaned down and stared hard into her eyes, looking for a truth he already had. "Did you . . . Oh, you did, you dirty fucking whore. You fucked him."

Mary slapped him. He had her. The confusion was far bigger now, and darkly flush. She couldn't trust Tim Cantwell anymore. She certainly couldn't trust Ray. She couldn't trust anyone. The only person she'd ever trusted had died in Chinatown.

"I'm going in to get those files," Ray growled. "Call your man and set up a meet. Somewhere in public. Then I tell him that the game is over and if you ever see him again, he's gone."

The fix was in if she took the bait. The Feds would be waiting for Ray to meet the blackmailer. And the blackmailer would be Tim, who would sing a different tune. And no one would ever believe Ray, especially after they discovered the red bank money that they thought was in his house.

"Deal," she said. She handed him the empty glass, picked up her clutch bag, and stormed out. Ray followed her into the doorway. After she was gone, he and Agnes looked at each other.

"Well," Agnes said, "that was easy."

▶ LONG TRAIN RUNNIN', THE DOOBIE BROTHERS

"Sort of was," Ray agreed. "I mean, there are always layers and layers of shit to this kind of thing, but Mary . . . I can't exactly tell what layer of scum she's wiggling through."

"Yet." Agnes looked at the door. "Think she's maybe playing it deep? Hired to play your nads for Tim, and now she's playing everyone for the big score?"

"Possible," Ray said, "but I still don't know. I think we might have a problem."

"We'll find out soon enough. We always do."

Ray went back into his office and sat down on the couch. It still smelled like Mary Chapman—her minty dick mouth and her hair, her mascara and her Chanel juice. He wished he had one of the pine-tree deodorizers cab drivers hung on the rearview mirror.

"You going location-scouting?" Agnes called. "Still early."

"I don't feel like it," Ray complained. "I already gave this lady a nervous breakdown this morning. The real estate woman was in bad shape when I left."

"Maybe go catch a buzz somewhere. Blow a doobie and shop for that watch you keep talking about."

"Shopping." He put his hands behind his head and stared up at the ceiling. "Maybe I'll see if Skug wants to get out of the house. He got all dressed to the nines for Reading Terminal."

"He probably has the new money ready. Maybe you two could go out for lunch."

"Call him, will you? From emergency burner to emergency burner. I'll meet him in Little Bell. And call poor fucking Freddy Hobbs. Cody says he might be getting his sack twisted by some Thai massage tranny today. Tell him I came across some money, that I'm in a super-great mood. And I wanna place a big bet."

"Neat." Agnes pondered. "He'll want an amount and a location."

"I guess tell him I'll meet him at the Pelican. He hangs out there and plays pool. Make like it's a good sign, so his guard will be down."

"Good idea." Agnes took a new cell phone out of her desk and went through her cards for one of Skuggy's phone numbers.

▶ TRANSFUSION BLUES. JOHNNY CASH

Little Bell was a micro plaza/park a block away from the Liberty Bell. Ray liked it because it was an oasis of quiet in a perpetual ocean of tourists. It was presumably for the employees of the office buildings to either side, but in the three years he'd been using it, he'd never seen anyone else sitting on the benches. It was clean and modern, and the signs declaring it a nonpublic space were sufficiently menacing for everyone except lifestyle criminals. Ray was drinking coffee and reading the paper when Skuggy sat down next to him with a paper bag full of money and the box of leftover Amish donuts.

"Day old," Skuggy said. "Wanna get down on this?"

"Right on." Ray took out the apple fritter and bit into it. Skuggy took out the remaining blueberry donut, and they ate for a moment in companionable silence.

"That the money?" Ray asked eventually.

Skuggy nodded. "Yeah." He was wearing a suit that surpassed in splendor the one he'd worn to Reading Terminal. This time he also wore a mohair three-quarter-length overcoat and a black cravat, enormous sunglasses with gold rims, and a hat tilted at a rakish angle. Ray took it all in, smiling.

"You look like Iceberg Slim's Ethiopian cousin."

"Fuck you."

"Any problems?"

"Nah." Skuggy laughed. "Yeah, but no. I guess kinda. Made the money change just fine, but I was on the hunt for a certain kind of lady last night, you might recall."

"Don't tell me. These kinds of personal details invariably disgust the shit out of me, Skug."

Skuggy snorted and scowled at him. "You a prudish man for a maniac, Ray. Always found that kinda fucked up about you."

"Whatever." Ray wiped his hands on his pants and took his cigarettes out.

"So, minus the squirtin' and all the smells, I skip right to the teeth. See, a wise man be on the lookout for just the right number, mostly 'cause—"

Ray cut him off with a raised hand. Skuggy flared his eyes and nostrils.

"Save it," Ray said. "I was prepared to cringe my way through it, but we're meeting Freddy Hobbs at his bar office in an hour and one of us has to find a car we own. You drive here?"

"Took the long way."

"Me too."

"Catch a tourist cab over by the bell?" Skuggy suggested. He patted Ray's arm with his good hand and pointed at the cigarette. Ray took the pack out and shook one loose for him.

"Mary Chapman came by the office."

"She pissed you killed her pet dummy?"

"Not really." Ray told him about the entire thing, how he was beginning to suspect that Mary might be gambling for the big prize and how something way bigger than Tim Cantwell had her on the fence about the entire operation, which was larger than expected. Skuggy listened and smoked, nodding occasionally. When Ray was done, he thought for a few minutes before he said anything.

"My guess is this," Skuggy said finally. "Step sideways and go down under it all, and look at it from there. Tim Cantwell, his defect be the key to the whole thing."

"Roll with it. Let's hear what you got."

"Okay. First time we hear about Tim is two years ago. He frauds out on a bunch of investors, takes 'em for everything—life savings, retirement, the whole nine yards. Legal for the most part, leastwise he got away with it. So the investors hire you. With me so far?"

"Keep going."

"Right. Now, twenty Gs. That's all these broke-ass people have left. Twenty to take Tim Cantwell down. Make him pay, whatever. You say no. Not even close to enough. Hard fuckin' news."

"They weren't happy."

"'Kay. Then it's ten. Ten Gs to look at him. One day. Now you say okay. And in that one day, you figure out how to blow his operation apart, get half them fuckin' shitheads put away, and clean up with eighty Gs to boot. Even hundred now, so you say yes. One week later, we got rent and Tim's pod is in county lockup waiting trial."

"Point?"

"Point is this. Tim, he's back now. New plan, halfway decent one it looks like—got this pussy after you, got the dollar signs in his crosshairs, et cetera. But some things don't never change. Tim, he's a numbers man. Good one. But the root, the window we have to look through here, in the same window we came in through last time. The man is a fuckup in one serious way. He's a shitty judge of character."

"Ahh." Ray sat up out of his meditative slouch. "Let me run with the ball for a sec. So you're saying that Tim Cantwell and his hedge-fund guys fucked up the first time because they ripped off the wrong people."

"Keep runnin'."

"And now, he might be ripping off the wrong people again."

"Keep runnin'."

"And he might be hiring the wrong people too."

"Bingo, Bingo, Bingo. See, a straight-up numbers man always gonna marry the wrong woman. He always gonna think his neighbor the serial killer be a fuckin' sweet little homey. Always think the crazy man just fucked his momma is the UPS guy just lost his coat. Tim don't dream in songs and stories, Ray. He dream the ticker tape. Boy knows as much about people as he do about kiwifruit."

"Jesus."

"I know." Skuggy shot his cigarette at the nearest EMPLOYEES ONLY sign. "Ain't no way to live. Nah. We punch his ticket, we be doin' him a solid."

Ray shook his head. "I wonder, Skug. I mean, me and you . . . I never said I was a good person to anyone I wasn't lying to, know what I mean? But Tim? How the fuck did people like that ever peck their way out of a uterus? I mean, there are so many kinds of pieces of shit anymore, it's hard to sort them out."

"I feel ya, baby. We got us the big souls, them little ones too. Some be greasy, some be sticky, some shiny, and there be all kinda shapes an' sizes an' whatnot. But Tim be kinda spooky ta me. Boy just a body walkin' round. I mean, all empty like that? You know what goes right on in." Skuggy gestured with his good hand at the world in general. "All the little things creep through his cracks an' his keyholes. The greed that's on the radio. The pussy fear what eatin' the world alive. All the hatin' on every last fuckin' thing. Tim pretty much a sponge, I guess."

"Sponge," Ray repeated. He considered. "In that light, I think it's safe to assume that his entire plan is backfiring from top to bottom."

"We also ain't the only players probably figured this out."

They thought about that. An imperious yuppie with a briefcase walked out of one of the office buildings. He glanced at them, and Ray and Skuggy both hit him with ten-mile stares. He kept going.

"Shit," Ray said.

"Aw, yep."

"Let's go shake down that dipshit Freddy Hobbs for twenty and the vig before he gets in too deep." Ray got up and Skuggy did too, a little slower.

"You got a plan, I assume." They started walking. Ray hailed a cab when they got to the sidewalk, and one dropped out of the passing traffic almost immediately.

"I do. Hobbs is a different kind of money man. He has enough of a soul to feel fear. Like real, real hard."

II

CHAPTER ELEVEN

The Pelican was a run-down bunker of a bar in Manayunk, where a small segment of Irish Philly aged disgracefully over glass after glass of watery beer on tap in the bad light, a mix of Christmas-tree twinkle of lottery machines and free advertising neon. There was no music, just the industrious clink, shuffle, whisper, belly-laugh slurry that probably started just after nine in the morning and got messy as the clock face staggered in lazy circles. It smelled like sausage, even though they didn't serve food, and the floor was eternally sticky. Ray and Skuggy stood in the doorway for a beat until their eyes adjusted. Skuggy didn't take his huge sunglasses off, so Ray beat him to the punch.

"You're the only black dude, Skug," he said loudly. Mouth traffic stopped, and heads turned. Skuggy flipped off the entire room with his good hand and beamed.

"Black boys be in back," Skuggy said, loud himself. "Where they keeps all the pussay."

Heads turned back to tables. Freddy Hobbs rose from a table in the back and motioned them over. Eyes traveled back and forth, and Freddy took it the wrong way entirely, somehow oddly proud that the two dapper nightmares were looking for him, that somehow their evident potency transferred power to him in some way. He mistakenly puffed with pride. His demeanor said Freddy Hobbs was a player, moving gold, slumming, and for the moment, just for the moment, his cover was blown and the lesser bookies and shit jungle transfer wads could shudder in awe of his might.

"Aw, ding," Skuggy breathed. "We got a run on somethin' sparkly, Ray. You check your horoscope?"

"Nope."

"Me neither. Now, we had us a chicken right now? We look at them innards, and I bet you a blueberry donut them bird guts tell us Freddy gonna play T-ball like a sissy."

"C'mon," Ray said. "Let's go do our thing."

▶ FIRE DOWN BELOW. NICK CAVE

"Mr. Ray," Freddy said, beaming. He gestured at the other side of his personal booth. Freddy looked like he'd been grown in the Pelican. His comb-over was thin and oily, over a head made round by cheesesteaks and pastrami. His tie was too short, and the seams of his clothing were close to popping in some places. The teeth in his smile were extremely small, little more than nubs, and he actually had the chewed-out butt of a cigar wedged between two of his stubby fingers. "Mr. Deadbomb Bingo Ray," he said a little more quietly. "And Mr. Skamander. Please, please. . . ."

He sat and raised a hand at the bartender. "Three scotches, Tony. Top shelf."

Ray slid in across from him. Skuggy pulled up the nearest chair and positioned it at the end of the table, slow and graceful, and that's when Freddy's smile began to fade.

"So, ah, Ray. Your secretary calls me, tells me you're, like, happy . . . you wanna place a bet, that kinda thing. 'M I reading this right?"

Ray didn't say anything. Skuggy didn't either. The drinks came courtesy of Tony the bartender, a younger, beefier version of Freddy, except with track pants instead of big & tall slacks and a Philadelphia Eagles T-shirt. He didn't seem too happy, and that made Freddy all the rest of the way panic. Skuggy looked up and then picked up his drink and sniffed it.

"Go wash yo hands, funny boy," he said. "You gettin' beat cream on the glass." He turned away. "Cain't stand this fuckin' town, days like this."

Tony made a long, offended "yo," much like a cow, and Ray drew his first gun and pointed it right at Tony's crotch, point-blank. It was so casual that no one noticed except the four of them.

"Just fuck off," Ray said. Then he looked up and squinted. "You look familiar. What's your mother's name?"

"Tony," Freddy said, spluttering a little. "We'z all good here. C'mon now, guys."

"Him's momma name Toodie," Skuggy said. "Now we circle all the way back to the teeth, Raymond. Told you I would. See, dentures be one thing—"

"Skug," Ray snapped. "Dude. I'm not saying I'm Catholic. I'm not. You know that. But cut me some slack. Shit's like a virus, leaves scars in your head. I mean, you only hear about the perverts. The priests and the kids and all that. Teen butthole girls can't give it up any other way. But you never hear shit about the masses of former Catholic non-freakazoids who feel strange talking about sex for an entirely different reason. It's just kinda scummy, man."

"What the fuck you sayin', Raymond? You saying getting' slapped around by nuns messed up your boner? That it? 'Cause I can see it. You take little Ray, he fuck up spellin' maybe, wicked big woman come 'round with a ruler—"

"Not it, Skug. Not at all. It's a privacy kind of thing. The booth confessional. That kind of shit. Makes people secretive."

"Oh, there you go." Skuggy turned to Freddy Hobbs. "You hear this shit? Prude is prude. Man has to compare notes. That's how we learn. Ray here get his tricks out women's magazines, I guess."

"Maybe I do, Skug. But garden-variety blabbermouth kiss-and-tell, I mean that shit inspires people to get all kinds of impressions that—"

"You funnin' on snakes?" Skuggy's tone was flat and full of awful wrath. The horror level in Freddy Hobbs and Tony the bartender soared to new heights at this. "Muthafuckin low muthafuckin—"

"Snakes, fish, whatever. I just don't want to hear it, man." Ray shifted and pulled the hammer back on the Beretta, wormed the muzzle deeper into Tony the bartender's package. "Makes me mad. You know, the other night at the hotel, I had to do some grisly shit in the name of the game. I'm surprised it didn't rain five-legged frogs that night. Now, did I go into graphic detail about it?"

"First I heard." Skuggy stroked his withered hand. He gave Ray a piercing look. "That what this about?"

"Yeah, man. I kinda have a girlfriend right now. Shit is disgusting is all I'm saying."

"Damn." Skuggy picked up his glass and drained half the scotch. "Man can get his feelings hurt. Women don't realize that. They just think we ready ta get up to any old perversion, but a brother got ta close his eyes ta sleep. My second wife was like that. Some nights, I just wanna lay in the bathtub an' have me a good cry."

"No shit?"

"Yeah, dog. Woman had all kinda wrong fire." He shrugged with his face and toyed with his glass, spoke slowly. "I thought maybe I get used to it, but naw, dog. I did and she up it some, like she wanted me all sad and twisted up inside."

"What a bitch."

"My bitch, though." Skuggy sighed. "The raw queen."

They sat in silence like that for a moment, Skuggy at the edge of dreamland, Ray thoughtful with a gun pressed into Tony the bartender's crotch, Freddy Hobbs on the verge of a heart attack. Eventually, Ray cleared his throat.

"It's that same feeling for me, Skug. Maybe I just feel it more often, I don't know. See, I can dig that you have this thing with women who have a certain dental profile. But the how and why, the gnarly brass tacks of how all that fits together. . . ."

"I feel you, baby," Skuggy said solemnly. "I shoulda put it all together." He sighed and stared into space. "I love the stories is all. Maybe too much, sometimes. Like what we was talkin' about with the numbers man, what hired that woman done hurt your feelin's. The woman Freddy here sent your way."

"Right." Ray picked up his scotch with his free hand and drained it, smacked his lips, and held up the empty to Tony. "Another round, scooter. Make it snappy."

Tony took the glass with a shaking hand. Skuggy held his up too. Ray leaned back and put his gun away. Tony walked away with pinched, tiny steps, like a crippled dancer or a clubfoot. Ray and Skuggy regarded each other.

"Glad we had this talk, Ray."

"Me too."

"This girlfriend, we talk about her maybe tomorrow," he suggested. "In a nice way, I mean. This be new territory—can't get this nasty Pelican shit all up on it."

They nodded to each other and turned to Freddy Hobbs, who had turned fire-engine red. Skuggy's good hand wandered over the table and plucked up Freddy's glass. Freddy stared straight ahead, trembling, and pretended not to notice as Skuggy slowly raised it to his lips and sucked the scotch out, little sip after little sip, his lips pursed out as far as they would go, his yellow stare on Freddy's face. Ray stared at Freddy, too, with no expression at all. The next round came, and this time Tony the bartender almost ran backward to get away.

"So, I'm here to place a bet," Ray said. Skuggy picked up the paper bag of money next to him and dropped it into Freddy's lap. "How much is in there, Skug?"

"Sixteen Gs. Cost four to clean the brains off."

"Cool," Ray said slowly. "Cool. Take six out for Skug, will you, Freddy?"

Freddy activated and looked at the bag, unrolled the top. Carefully, he took out six banded bundles and handed them over. Skuggy took them and gently tucked them into his sling.

"Before I tell you what I'm betting on, why don't you tell me about Mary Chapman," Ray said. "All of it."

Freddy nodded. "The woman, right. I . . . I'm sorry as a mother-fucker if that went sideways, Ray. She seemed all right to me. I mean more than all right—like, clean and desperate and kind of dumb."

"You the dummy," Skuggy said quietly. "Dummy."

"Right, right." Freddy drew a shuddering breath. "See, I . . . it started with this guy Tom. I don't even know how we crossed wires, me and that guy. Nice fella. Placed bets on horses, mostly, said he used to live in Chicago. Art hustler, got hooked on the ponies. Anyway, he comes to me a couple weeks ago and says he has this bird with a serious fucking problem, like way outta my league. I mean . . ." He picked up his drink. "I mean jeez, I can squeeze a guy, but this was big. I meet with her, tell her I might know somebody who knows somebody that might help for the right kind of change. First I hook her up with this guy Calloway. Aloha Calloway. She meets, says no, needs the big-time. Says she kinda heard of a guy, just rumors, used to work out of Vegas. I put it together."

"That didn't raise any flags for you?" Ray sat back. Skuggy's stomach gurgled, loud and sudden.

"Naw. I mean, you met her, right? Sides, I just tell her where your office is, that's all. Everyone knows where your office is, Ray. You're in the phone book, see?"

Ray picked up his drink and sipped, thinking. Freddy kept talking.

"So I guess, I guess she bummed you out, man. What can I say?"

"How much she pay you, Freddy?"

"Aww." Freddy drained his scotch, wiped his lips. "Twenty Gs, Ray. Swear to God. Twenty Gs cash to point her in the right direction. I had to, man. That kinda money is ridiculous just to drop a name and an address."

Ray and Skuggy looked at each other. Ray shook his head. Skuggy scowled.

"He telling the truth, Ray," Skuggy said. "Maybe he get a partial pass. But if we killin' this ninny, we make him swallow that cigar first?" He turned back to Freddy. "I just curious if it possible."

"Maybe." Ray finished his drink. "Okay, Freddy. Here's what we're doing. One—you owe me money. That crazy bitch is trying to set me up to get shanked in prison. I killed that guy Tom. It's time to straighten the blankets on the bed here. Twenty Gs and the vig brings it to, say, twenty-five. Cash. Before we leave. Snuffing the candle on that Tom guy is going to cost you too. Chinatown. There's a junk store called Emerald Alley, little old man named Cixin works the register. You go there and drop off five Gs in twenties and a 1979 quarter, tell him Coug Rollins says 'what up, homey.' Got it?"

"Five Gs and . . . and . . . a 1979 quarter." The last part came out slathered in horror.

"And you say?"

"Wh . . . what up, h . . . h . . . homey?"

"Good. Now that money. You put that aside and give me a ticket for it. Name on the ticket is Tim Cantwell. That's crazy Mary's boss. You keep those bills separate. They're special poison from the ghetto, kind of money a piece of shit like you can pass easy, but those numbers will trip Cantwell hard if I need 'em to. Week from now, I don't need this ticket, I get my money back. Good?"

"Okay." Whispered.

"Then we're friends again!" Ray said it like he was talking to a kid at a party with clowns and balloons. Skuggy looked around and then tossed his chin at Freddy.

"Go on get that money, dingdong. I'm hungry."

Freddy scooted, but before he was all the way out of the booth, Ray grabbed his wrist, hard.

"No shit, Freddy. Money and the receipt, or I swear we will kill every single person in this bar except you. Because that's just the beginning."

"I know," Freddy said quietly. "I know."

Ray let go, and Freddy slid out and trundled at speed back toward the poolroom, where the bookies kept a checkout safe in the table by the coin slot. Skuggy surveyed the bar. They were being ignored, but in a polite way. Ray watched for Freddy with one hand close to the gun he'd just had on the bartender. He didn't expect any trouble, but he wasn't taking any chances.

"You wanna take a cab to that Russian place?" Skuggy suggested. "One Agnes goin' on about? I could use me some borscht."

"Sounds good." Ray scanned the room and settled back. "Tomorrow we have to go check out the guy who's holding the blackmail material."

"What kinda disguise?"

"Your favorite. You play the rich weirdo, and I play the driver."

Skuggy tittered.

"Our boy," Ray said softly. Skuggy's good hand drifted to the gun at his waist. Freddy had gone from red to gray and moist, but he'd managed to pull it together on some level. He slid back into the booth and hesitantly passed a paper bag to Ray, who rolled it tight to feel it for hardware and then put it on the seat next to him.

"Cleaned me out for the moment, but it's all there," Freddy said quietly. "Receipt is on top." He tried for a smile. "I'm sorry as hell this didn't work out. I just had no fuckin' clue."

"She's good," Ray allowed. "I can see how she could burn you like this."

"Okay, I drop the Chinaman his money and his coin, like, later? I feel like shit right now." Freddy looked down at his drink. Ray took his wallet out and tossed a hundred on the table.

"Get drunk, Freddy," he advised. "Week from now, it's business as usual."

Freddy nodded and drained his glass. Ray slipped out of the booth and adjusted his coat, tucking the money under one arm. Skuggy rose too, and gently put his chair back.

"Be seein' ya," Skuggy said quietly.

They left Freddy staring into his empty glass. No one looked up as they strode through the Pelican. Tony the bartender actually turned away. Outside, the sky had gone a deeper gray and the wind had picked up. Ray lit two cigarettes in the lee of the doorway and passed one to Skuggy. They smoked and watched for a cab. Eventually, Skuggy turned to him.

"You ever had an aquarium, Ray?"

"Nah. Never had a waterbed, either."

Skuggy nodded. "I'ma get me some piranhas."

"What the hell?" Ray laughed.

"Jungle fish," Skuggy said. A cab finally stopped, the third empty one to pass. "Freddy got me thinkin' on it again. Seen it on Discovery last night. Strip a man in front of a bathtub with a few of 'em freakin' out in the water, he talk. Be scary as you are."

▶ APACHE. THE SHADOWS

The late lunch at Abe Fisher was quiet. Skuggy was tired after borscht and pierogies and the awful pickled herring he so enjoyed. Ray ate sparingly, and when they parted ways outside, Skuggy cabbed home and Ray went back and picked up his car.

It was dark by the time he got home. Pepper greeted him for a change, their battle over the couch momentarily forgotten.

"I smell like herring, you gross little fox?" he asked, kneeling and petting her. She licked his hand, so he guessed that he did. After she'd gone out and then eaten her dinner, he poured himself a glass of wine and carried it around the house in the dark. Around midnight, he took a fast shower and changed into jeans and a T-shirt and then crawled under the dining-room table. Staring up into the darkness that hid the weapons above him, he tried to think of the sky, which he imagined was clean above the soot and car exhaust. He wondered how far up you had to go to get past it all, even past the litter in orbit. That's how he fell asleep.

II

CHAPTER TWELVE

Hydrogenesis was in the Hammerstein Plaza, a single-story sprawl with a dozen other start-ups with names that could mean anything. Only half of them were working on a Sunday, so the parking lot was mostly empty. The Lexus belonging to Anton Brown was parked right in front, next to a Volvo with a Bernie Sanders bumper sticker. Ray parked in the next row back, with open spaces to either side, and got out and looked at his car. The Mercedes was impressively obnoxious. He glanced at Abigail's Volvo, frowned a little, and started walking.

Ray had a pretty good day planned, but as always he was prepared to wing it. He was running through the variations of a snowy weekend romance when he went in. Anton Brown was at the desk in what would normally be the reception area, bracketed by three walls of a cubicle festooned with sticky notes. He looked up and forced a smile.

"Hey," Anton said flatly. "You this Ray guy?"

"I am indeed this Ray guy," Ray replied. "Abby around?"

"You mean Doctor Abelard?" Anton's Early Man eyebrow curled into a wad in the center. Ray didn't answer, just took his gloves off and glanced out at the parking lot, ignoring Anton entirely. Anton waited petulantly until it became clear that Ray was somewhere else, that he wasn't up to sparring with the help. Then Anton rose and disappeared through the door behind him, fussy and pigeon-toed. Ray looked back and put on his best smile.

A moment later, Anton emerged and sat down at his desk. Abigail peeked out and flashed Ray a smile.

"Raymond! Come in here. I want to show you something positively nerdy. You'll love it."

Anton looked up and mouthed the word "nerdy" and then looked back down. His hairline lowered and his heavy jaw muscles flared. Ray could smell the love, the lust, the lonesome disappointment, and the bitter betrayal rolling off of him as Ray smiled over his oily head.

"Hey, baby," he rumbled. He brushed past the front desk on a contrail of tasteful cologne, confidence, and dick pheromones. "Nerdy is the new juicy." It was only his imagination, he knew, but he felt a sudden flare of heat at his back as he followed Abigail through the door into the lab.

"I'll be damned," Ray said, taking it all in. It was not what he expected at all. There were four large whiteboards, the modern kind you wrote on with dry-erase markers, a table with four big computers, a little stand with a coffee machine, and a pool table. Abigail watched his reaction with a huge grin.

"I certainly hope not. That's part of why I wanted to show you this."

Ray walked over to the pool table. There were ten cue balls, ten ping pong balls, eight golf balls and no sticks. They were scattered around two oranges and an apple that were in a tight little triangle in the center. Abigail appeared at his side and put her arm around his waist. He looked down at her upturned face, and they kissed.

"So," she said. She took one of the cue balls and bounced it off the far rail. "Physics." She caught it on the bounce.

"Physics," he repeated.

"How much do you know about neutrons?"

Ray bounced one of the balls off the rails, sending it ricocheting down the table, and then caught it on the return. "Water. H_2O."

"Ha! Good!" That pleased her immensely, he could tell. And surprised her. She slapped him on the butt, and he stiffened and smiled down at her.

"You told me you were working with water molecules, so …"

"Still good! Means you were listening. Now, the protons and electrons, specifically the ones in the human brain, that's where it gets interesting."

"I guess give me the dummy version."

"Since I'm hungry, I will," she replied. "Water. We have a great deal of water in us, as you know. In the brain alone, the number of water molecules is upward of two hundred times greater than a billion times a trillion."

"I'll be," he said.

She giggled. "Good one." She walked over to one of the boards and gestured at it with her chin. He followed her, and together they stared at the gory strings of nonsense. "The basis of memory is in that billion times trillion. The record of who we are, what we think, and how we do it. Our memories. Our essence."

"You're trying to prove that our souls are in the water in our heads," Ray said slowly. She reached out and took his hand.

"No, Ray. We already know they are. They're encoded in the quantum resonance, in the orbits of electrons." There was a measure of awe in her voice. He shook his head.

"Where are all the little electron balls? Got a bag of marbles in here somewhere?"

"They're too small, plus they aren't even here sometimes. But you're on the right track."

"So what is this, then?"

She turned to him and gave him a searching look that lasted overlong. Then she stepped into the orbit of his arms. "Heisenberg. Heard of him?"

Ray's *Star Trek* book was no help at all. He shook his head.

"Those little guys—our electrons—when I say they're so small that they aren't here all the time, I mean they're sometimes particle, sometimes wave."

"I totally don't get it," he admitted.

"Our souls are moving in and out of this reality all day long, Ray. Here in the particle, elsewhere in the wave. I'm trying to look under the Einstein-Rosen bridge to find out where our Heisenberg copies are."

"Our . . . souls, you mean."

She smiled the perfect smile.

▶ REVENGE OF THE NUMBER, PORTISHEAD

The drive to Clark Park was quiet. They listened to music and enjoyed each other's company. Abigail exuded a postconfessional bliss after revealing the odd nature of her work, and Ray was content to let her enjoy it. As he drove, he thought about his interpretation of the nature of the human mind, which mostly came from crime and dealing cards, and how strange it was that anyone would try to learn anything about it by looking at the very small, when the very large was so much easier to cut into. In some ways, he and Abigail were conducting parallel investigations. She was looking for a recording of her being, one so perfect that it was in no way different from the original. She was looking for herself, in the least corny way imaginable. Ray, too, was a student of the human soul. He lived and breathed the disgusting science of it all daily, and he also endeavored to be better at it than anyone else.

"Coffee?" he asked.

"Please." She snuggled into her big sweater. "I just love the snow, especially on days like today."

"Just before the ice? When the ground is brighter than the sky?"

"Exactly." So exuberant. It made him want to kiss her on the nose, so he did at the next light.

"I packed us a snow picnic," he informed her. "Borscht, dark rye with caviar, smoked trout, and this fabulous Portuguese goat cheese. A few clementines. And a thermos of coffee—lots of cream, lots and lots of sugar."

Abigail gave him a long, appraising look, and when she finally blinked she turned to the snow again. "You are a terrible, terrible man."

"I never said I was good, Doctor. Press rewind and fast-forward through me, check for yourself."

"I'm having too much fun," she declared. "Our day has just started, and I already feel like my belly button is smiling."

Ray laughed. He liked that. There was a parking place right along the park's divide, by the bend in the road just up from a lonely hot dog vendor. Ray pulled in and got out. He didn't think Abigail was the kind to wait for him to open her door; she wasn't, and sprang out at the same time and danced right into the snow. As he unlocked the trunk, the snowball she'd tossed at him exploded on his shoulder.

"Hey!" he yelled. She turned and ran. Ray paused to watch her. She moved like an athletic child, full of jumps and spins, her mittened hands raised in glory. There was a row of benches, and she stopped at the first one and turned, beckoning him with one hand.

Ray took the picnic basket out. There were other things in the trunk. Under the spare tire was five thousand in cash, and there was a pointed bicycle spoke under the lip of the trunk by the lock. He slammed it closed and made his way over to her, scanning the area as he went, outwardly admiring the view.

"Hang on," he said as he walked up. Abigail was dusting the bench off with a mitten. Ray set the basket in the snow, opened it, took out the two pads he'd put on top, and held them up. "You sit in that snow, and your firm little apple of a butt will melt it, Doctor. Then you get what we laymen call 'redbottom.'"

She wrinkled her nose at him. "I think my bottom is still red, mister," she chided and then hugged him. "You can check later. Top-to-bottom inspection." She wiggled her eyebrows.

He kissed her nose again and set the pads down, patted hers, and she sat. Then he took out the thermos and poured coffee into the blue porcelain cups he'd brought. Steam rolled off them in an impressive way, and Abigail *oohed* and accepted hers with both hands and took a sip. He sipped as well and sat down next to her.

"Did you bring poetry?" she asked.

"Nah. I already got in your pants."

She slapped him on the arm and sat back. There were birds moving through, mostly Franklin's gulls and cave swallows.

"So, where are you from?" she asked. "I mean originally."

He glanced over at her. "How do you know I'm not a local?"

"No accent. Plus a million little things. You eat like a Californian. Lots of fruit and veggies. You know wine. Your skin looks like it's taken a beating in this life—in a good way, in a way that lets me see your most common expressions in the lines around your eyes."

"You little detective," he said admiringly. "You're right, I'm not from here at all. Grew up in Arizona. We moved to Mexico City for a few years when I was a kid, then L.A. Lived in Vegas for a while."

"Las Vegas? What in the world did you do there?"

"Dealt cards, mostly."

"No! That must have been a magical time." She took that as a good thing, which was nothing short of amazing. "All those numbers skittering around in all those lights, and the stars in the sky in the desert at night. . . ." She shook her head.

"You're a rare bird, Abigail Abelard."

"And you are a snowflake," she said. They looked into each other's eyes. "I still don't know what to make of you. A man of secrets and passions and desires. Like a French spy, except effective."

"Huh." He didn't know what to say, but it occurred to him right then that if he kept falling in love with this woman, he was eventually going to fall all the way in without noticing—and then he'd have to spend the rest of his life lying to a genius.

"Family?" she asked. Her attentive eyes stayed on him, not like she was looking for anything, but like she was paying attention because she actually wanted to know.

"Standard. My father was in sales. Aerospace."

"Were you two close?" She sipped.

Ray shrugged. "Not really. He had a lot on his plate while I was growing up."

"Hmm. A child of science. Interesting. What about your mother?"

"She was, ah, I guess she was a housewife, mostly. Active in the Shriners, that kind of thing. Collected spoons. I think I still have the one from Montana."

"Hmm. Brothers? Sisters? I bet you have five sisters, don't you?"

Ray laughed and sipped his coffee. "Two brothers, both older. Freddy was a few years older than me. He was in real estate when it was big, before Fannie Mae and Freddie Mac took it all down, maybe five or six years before that. He would have shit if he'd seen the recession. But he . . . ah, he didn't. Car."

Abigail's face fell, and she touched his knee. "I'm sorry."

Ray shrugged. "Long time now. Buckle up. It's the law."

"Your other brother?" She seemed to be hoping for a better story.

"Lives in upstate New York."

"Well." She sat back, looking relieved. "What was Mexico City like?"

"Super fun," Ray replied, smiling at the memory. "I was in the sixth grade, and my parents signed me up to do volunteer work at this radio station after school. We had a sort of company tutor, and I guess they were worried we weren't socializing enough. Got my first kiss." He winked. "I even tried *la marijuana.*" He let "marijuana" roll off his tongue in a heavy Spanish accent, and Abigail laughed like a bell.

"I've never been to Mexico. Always wanted to go," she said.

He picked up the thermos and topped off their coffees. "So you've traveled? Tell me your tales of adventure."

"I have not traveled," she clarified. "Not really. I did a year in Switzerland during my PhD program. When I was there . . . let's see. I went to Paris a few times. I've been to London twice for conferences, one time to Hong Kong. But mostly I've been here. Did my undergrad work at UC Davis and then got my Penn grant."

"Family?"

"Only child, raised by my dad. He's at Yale, so I'm a Yankee born and raised. Fantastic professor. Linguist."

"A linguist," Ray admired. "What languages do you speak?"

"English and mathematics," she replied. She gestured with her coffee cup at the trees. "Not sure if he's disappointed, but I don't think so. He'd never say." She turned to him. "He's a man of secrets and passions, just like you. I bet you'd like him."

"I bet I would." He smiled warmly. "Ready for a snack?"

"I am."

Ray took out the bowls and spoons and the bigger thermos with the borscht, filled the bowls up, and then took out the rye and put it between them. Lastly, he twisted the lid off the caviar and stuck a small spoon in it.

"Good," Abigail said, blowing out steam. "You make this?"

"Got it at this little place I went to yesterday," Ray admitted. He found he was hungry after the first bite. The steaming red against the snow was perfectly picturesque. Abigail took a slice of bread and smeared it with caviar and then chewed with enthusiasm.

"Read the news this morning?" she asked out of the blue. Ray was suddenly embarrassed. He never, ever read the news.

"Why? Something catch your eye?"

"These people." She ate and watched the birds. "Sometimes the world seems broken, like it's a giant opera with a deaf audience. If we're right, then a recording of every last thought, every action, is somewhere."

"Hmm." He didn't know what to say, so he covered it with eating.

"When I was working at CERN in Switzerland. . . . Our understanding of the subatomic world is growing by leaps and bounds. Some estimates put us less than a century away from being able to unfold a proton and redescribe it in two dimensions. Or four, or six—or nine. Imagine, a two-dimensional proton, a gossamer string light-years long. Or a proton the size of an egg, or a football. The moon. Then we can scribble on it, etching the surface with enough computational power to house all of the minds in creation. Refold it, and form an entanglement for instantaneous interaction, oh. . . ."

"Ah." He put his spoon in his bowl and gave her an appraising look. "Abby, you sound positively superstitious."

"I am," she agreed. She didn't elaborate. Watching her, he knew that the almost girlish glee she was exhibiting was no front: Abigail was happy. But she was conceivably so complicated that she had ascended to a level he'd sensed in the greatest of poker players, and in the royalty of his own profession as well. Abigail was so complex that she was actually pure, in the same way as the birds she was watching. She looked at him, drawn by his watching.

"That look makes me feel beautiful," she said softly.

They finished their borscht and bread and caviar, and then they had some of the cheese and split one of the oranges. After that they held hands for a while, until they were good and properly cold, until the fireplace at Ray's was the next logical thing.

▶ FROM HER TO ETERNITY, NICK CAVE

The new tail picked them up two blocks south of Clark Park—a black sedan with tinted windows and no snow on any of it, like it had been sitting for two hours with the engine running. Like the driver had been watching someone. Ray glanced from the rearview to Abigail, who had taken off her mittens and was alternately blowing on her cold fingers and holding them out at the heater. She smiled back.

"Buckle up," Ray said, fastening his seat belt. She did, almost apologetically.

"I read a review of a new Mexican restaurant out in Cranberry. Isn't that an odd place for one?"

"There's a great little bookstore out there," Ray said. "Maybe a colony of West Coast expats is forming." He drove a little faster than he had on the way in, in the general direction of Liberty. Scraping a tail off with a passenger was going to be a problem, so he needed a plan. They hit the University City limits, and Ray detoured left, into the quiet residential zone off of Forty-First.

"So, tell me about Pepper." She sat back and played with the condensation on the inside of the window. "You strike me as an admirer of cats, Ray. There has to be a story to go with your little Pomeranian companion."

"She's a rescue dog," he said honestly. "The previous owner wasn't good to her. I guess he used her as a prop to pick up chicks, if you can believe that." Anton Brown had used Pepper—just Dog then—as a profiling tool. People walking tiny dogs were not immediately identified as bank-robbery suspects. In that way, Anton had been able to operate freely in the aftermath of a heist, inside the search grid directly after a job. "She was a little underweight, minor eye infection, that kind of thing. First pet I've ever had, and I tell you what, I've learned all kinds of surprising things."

"She charmed you," Abigail said. "And being charming yourself, you came to her rescue. A perfect loop. Those are always instructive."

They came to a stoplight. The sedan was directly behind them, shifting from tail to something else. Ray winked at her and undid his seat belt.

"One more cup of coffee for the drive," he said. "My hands are freezing. I'll grab it from the picnic basket."

"Oh, me!" Abigail exclaimed. "Me too!"

"Just a sec."

Ray got out and quickly popped the trunk, obscuring the sedan behind them from her view. He opened the picnic basket and took out the thermos and the two coffee cups, clean after the scrub he had given them with snow. He hooked it all in one hand and then took the sharpened bicycle spoke out with the other. Ray turned to the sedan and smiled in a friendly, slightly confused way. Then he walked over to the driver's side and used the thermos to tap lightly on the window, the spoke hidden along his side.

The window zipped down halfway, and a big, bald man with hard blue eyes glared out at him, his lips curled in a mocking smile. He was alone in the car. Ray stabbed him in the neck and left the end of the spoke sticking out and then walked back to his Mercedes and closed the trunk. He got back in and handed the thermos and cups to Abigail as the light turned green. He fastened his seat belt and drove.

"I haven't had a snow picnic since . . . I must have been ten or eleven," Abigail said. She set one of the coffee cups on the dash and the other in her lap and unscrewed the thermos. Ray glanced in the rearview. The sedan was still sitting there. He accepted the coffee cup and sipped.

"Me neither," he said honestly. "You bring out the romantic in me."

"Sweet."

▶ WALK DON'T RUN. THE VENTURES

Pepper greeted them from the couch with a look that was part vacationing guardian and part knowing guilt, but even so Ray could read in her body language that no one had come to the door or been in the back yard.

"It's a little early for wine," Ray said, taking off his coat while Abigail unwound her scarf.

"Scotch?"

"You read my mind."

"You be in charge of that, and I'll apply my PhD to the fireplace. We should have a roaring hearth in . . ." she paused midway through taking off her coat. "Somewhere between a few thousand seconds from now and never."

He hung her coat for her. They took off their wet shoes and socks, and once again he was struck by her lack of toenail polish. She seemed unaware of the mani/pedi phenomenon. While she busied herself with the logs and kindling, he went into the kitchen and looked out at the back yard. No new prints, and nothing in the neighboring yard either. While everyone knew where he lived, it was widely known that to approach uninvited meant certain death and that he would kill everyone even remotely associated with the first person to die. His reputation was holding.

He opened the liquor cabinet and took down the Oban, poured two fingers into two Polish crystal tumblers, added a drop of water to each, and carried them out to the living room. Abigail had the beginning of a perfect little fire going, as he knew she would. He set down her scotch on the coffee table within reach and then sat down next to Pepper and patted the little dog's head. Pepper thumped her tail once and closed her eyes. Ray had no idea how old she was. The vet had guessed between five and ten, though she'd confessed that she had no idea either. Rescue dogs came with so many question marks.

"What should we do for dinner?" he asked.

"We could try that little place in Cranberry if you want." She added another log. She didn't want to go out, the extra log said.

"We could order in," he mused. "Or I could make us something."

She sat down in front of the fire and took a sip of her scotch. "I'm up for anything. Just no meat except from the deep ocean blue."

"Mexican?"

She turned. "I haven't forgotten about the Mexico City part of your résumé, mister. What can I do to help?"

Ray smiled. "You can sit by the fire, maybe pick out some music."

"A picnic lunch in the snow, and now you're making me Mexican food. Are you trying to seduce me again, Raymond?"

He got up. "You started it." He took his scotch and headed for the kitchen. Pepper followed him.

"I did not. I mean, I did."

"You did. First, the whole playing-with-balls thing at your work was more than suggestive, Doctor."

"I'm speechless."

"Then there's your general charm factor. Something about you always reminds me of a ballet in progress, or a song that started before I entered the room and will keep playing when I'm gone."

"I'm impressed," she said, rising and walking to the island. "Not much gets past you, Ray. I make a great effort to be what I consider . . . good. It's a long story."

Ray took a bag of dehydrated ancho chilies out of one of the cabinets and quickly pulled the stems and seeded them. Then he dropped them in a one-quart pan and turned the heat on low.

"Okay, junior cookie," he said. "Pick a bottle of port from the pantry and open it. That's your whole job."

"I quit."

While she looked through the bottles, Ray chopped up an onion and skinned five cloves of garlic, added this to the pot with some olive oil, and shook in some salt. Abigail padded over with the port. He pointed at the drawer with the opener, stirring while she inexpertly dug out the cork. When she handed it to him, he leaned in and they kissed, and her breath was hot on his face as he pulled away. Her eyes were wide and full of invitation in a look he had begun to recognize. He smiled and turned to the pan.

"Check this out," he said. He cranked the heat and they watched side by side as everything began popping and crackling. Just before smoke appeared, Ray dumped in a cup of the port, and they stepped back from the flash of steam. He turned the heat down and put a lid on it, and when he turned back toward her she hugged him.

"That smells like the edge of a miracle," she whispered and then looked up at him with that look again. And just like that, it was on.

▶ SUPERSTAR, SONIC YOUTH

Afterward, she watched him cook, both of them wearing stolen Kimpton robes again. He moved efficiently as he filled flour tortillas with the vegetables he'd lightly seared in olive oil and cumin seeds and then poured the port and ancho enchilada sauce out of the blender over the top, finishing it with the shredded remains of the Portuguese goat cheese. He could feel her eyes on him and moved with an economy of motion in an attempt to please her. It worked.

"What a—" She stopped and he turned.

"I know. Total show-off."

What had started in the kitchen had moved to the dining-room table and then the stairs, and then in stages into the bedroom, and then been repeated in the bath. Ray's entire groin hurt, and he felt lightheaded. He put on an oven mitt and put the tray of enchiladas in to bake and then leaned back against the sink and sighed.

"Fifteen minutes," he said. "I'll steam some kale to go with it. Want some of this port?" He held up the bottle.

"Let's save it for dessert," she suggested. She got up and hobbled toward the fireplace. "What goes good with enchiladas?"

"Margaritas, but I'm afraid the effort might kill me. So shots with extra lime."

She settled down in front of the fireplace. "Just like my . . . ninth year of college."

Ray took two shot glasses down and poured Herradura. The lime was already on the counter, so he cut two wedges and carried them out, joining her by the fire. Pepper was nowhere to be seen, probably hiding somewhere upstairs.

"You went to school for a long time," he said, handing her a shot.

"I sure did," she agreed. They clinked their glasses together and drank. She smacked her lips and turned sideways, lying down with her head in his lap. He leaned back and stroked her hair. "It never ends, actually. I'll be in university in one form or another for the duration of this life-span."

"Somebody has to do it."

"Hmm. This feels good." She closed her eyes and, after a moment, asked, "You like what you do, Ray?"

"What, the whole media thing?" He thought about it. "I suppose. It's interesting work, in its way. No two days are the same. Travel is nice. The people."

"Huh."

"What about you? A lifetime of school. . . ."

"I was born for it. When I was a kid, I used to spend the summers with my grandfather in New Brunswick. He had this little farm. He was a physicist too, mostly Cambridge, but he was at Oxford for a while. But the work he did contributing to the orbits of protons and electrons—dry stuff, I know, but on those long summer afternoons, it turned the world into something else for me."

"Sounds nice."

"It was."

They sat like that, with Abigail remembering her first steps down the road she was on, just as he had earlier, her clean face relaxed and her eyes closed as Ray stroked her hair. He thought about the guy he'd shanked in the throat earlier. Who the fuck was he? If he was Tom Latte's replacement, then Mary Chapman needed a different talent scout. Two for two was lame. It occurred to him that it might have been a second-party tail, one that had been on Tom Latte and had shifted into the foreground after Chinatown, but he doubted it. He still knew the number of people and their general descriptions from their lunch at ENOS; his memory was that good. He would have picked up a solo second tail earlier. It was so unlikely, it bordered on the impossible. No, the most likely scenario was that he'd shanked a guy working for Tim Cantwell directly, outside of Mary Chapman's operation, or that he'd tapped an employee of the hypothetical third player. But what mattered in the end was the message he'd sent. It was sure to shake any remaining players loose. Ray smiled.

"What a day," he said. "You ready for dinner?"

Abigail opened her eyes, and there was still dreaming in them. She reached up and caressed his throat. "Yes."

▶ YOUR HEART IS AS BLACK AS NIGHT. MELODY GARDOT

That night in bed, Abigail held him like she had weird news. He could feel it, and she could feel him feeling it too. She was curled against his side with her head on his chest, playing with one of his chest hairs. He waited, tired, hoping it wouldn't be too bad. Eventually she spoke.

"Ray, we haven't known each other all that long. Not really. But there's a passion I feel with you. I don't know. When we make love, it's not like it normally is. For me, I mean. I don't normally scream like that. I . . . what I'm trying to say is that . . . that, I don't know how to put it, but what you make me feel is important to me."

Ray didn't say anything.

"Remember this morning, when I was telling you about the basis of memory? It's important for me to, ah, to have these kinds of memories. To know carnal passion. To know—and I mean *know* know—this feeling of abandon, to hear the music inside of me. It's enriching, in a critical way I've been missing. Transformative, even."

Ray still didn't say anything. She pulled away a little and looked at him. He tilted his head and looked back.

"A hundred years ago," she breathed, "the speed limit in most cities was ten miles per hour. The average life expectancy of a man was forty-seven years. Seventy-five years ago, no one thought a man would walk on the moon in their lifetime. No one." It was important to her, he realized, that he pay extremely careful attention to what she was saying. Her mind was working in that instant in the same way as when she studied the cue balls on her test table. "Twenty years ago, no one would have believed we would have Netflix on our telephones." She smiled. "Maybe some people. But my point is this.

If memory, identity itself, is recorded in the orbits and telemetry of water's quanta, like we were talking about earlier—"

"You're not worried about God," Ray said, realizing where she was going. "You're worried about the scientists of a hundred years from now cracking into the minds of history and looking for—"

"Looking for everything. Everyone. Me. Us."

She watched him think about it, and he did.

"It's like a lottery, Ray. We have to be as perfect as we can be to get a ticket to the afterlife. Billions and billions of people, but only a handful will have a glowing card. . . ."

Half of an hour passed before he finally smiled and closed his eyes, and she kissed him on the chin and nestled her head under it, draping her leg over his stomach. And like that, they fell asleep.

II

CHAPTER THIRTEEN

▶ AIN'T NO WOMAN (LIKE THE ONE I'VE GOT), THE FOUR TOPS

L ike some kinda fuckin' Fu Manchu juju invadin' my mother-fuckin' hairpiece," Skuggy exclaimed, patting his afro.

"Jesus." It was all Ray could think to say. It was just after nine in the morning, and they were in Skuggy's Ford Bronco making a preliminary run at the building holding the blackmail material. A crippled old black man in a seersucker suit was the ultimate in Philly surveillance work. Plus, Skuggy was a savant genius when it came to impersonating a rich weirdo, chiefly because he was borderline bipolar and he actually was a rich weirdo. Additionally, the costume brought out the side of him that was dangerous in a next-level way, beyond angry beehive and well into biblical-serpent territory. There was a fifty-fifty chance that the morning would end in bloodshed, and Skuggy had a .38 in his sling and a sawed-off twelve-gauge under the seat. Ray had just told him about Abigail's theory of the afterlife.

"She be right, you dingbat ninny," Skuggy declared. "They been fuckin' with atoms since the bomb, baby. Ain't no reason to stop. Now, say she right about this timetable, an' she probably is, then we talkin' 'bout maybe thirty, forty billion people the science men motherfuckers o' tomorrow gonna be lookin' at. Best try to stand out, is no-shit strong advice."

"She's crazy, Skuggy. I've been fucking a crazy woman. Again."

"Man, Raymond. Just when I think you smart, you change my mind all by yourself. All women's crazy, an' you know it—an' men jus' like 'em or worse. I'm crazy, and so are you. Too fuckin' bad, you fuckin' sissy. This one just be a complex nutjob, but it sure as shit don't mean she's wrong."

"How so?"

"People been lookin' for God forever, man! They always will be! But people always find what they lookin' for if they look long enough, Ray. Negros found Europe, and they found Asia too. On foot. Then the brand-new white-and-brown Negros they made found the whole rest of the world. Read a book, dummy. All this looking with starvation an' fire an' peyote and fuck-all crazy shit, that ain't be workin', 'cause we ain't found one fuckin' thing. Now all she sayin' is that someday we gonna become the thing we lookin' for. You know how an automatic transmission works?"

"No."

Skuggy glared at him, fierce. "Then fuck you."

"I can't believe you're taking her side, man. I mean, if—"

"Ray!" Skuggy turned the radio down. "I can't believe you think there is a side! She don't have one! You don't either! What, you become a priest last night, or some kinda superhero can say when the whole greedy fuckin' world gonna stop learnin' and say 'Aw, I guess that good, we go ahead stop now'? Let me the fuck out this fuckin' ride!"

"It's your—ah, shit." Ray pointed. "Here we are."

Skuggy smoothed out, instantly. "Huh. Well." He squinted and scowled. "Dat ain't good."

Gordon, Pritchett & Hughes was on the fifth floor of the Pearl Building, an imposing turn-of-the-century Gothic throwback with sooty gargoyles and a sweeping congressional staircase. The law office occupied the entire fifth floor, which was the second bad sign. Skuggy made a sucking sound, like he had a matchstick in his mouth.

Ray's eyes narrowed, and he adjusted his tie. Traffic came to a stop, and they looked at each other.

"That right there is a buildin' full of raw daddy." Skuggy looked down and picked a piece of lint off his sling.

"They probably have donuts," Ray said uncertainly. "Scones."

"I'ma get me a brandy inna sniffin' glass. Jus' you watch." He looked back at the building. "Fore they kill us both."

Ray parked, and they got out. The sky was heavy with the possibility of more snow. He was wearing one of his more expensive suits, funereal black with no tie, and Armani's heaviest coat. Skuggy turned his thin face into the wind. His checked Holland fields coat blew open, but the scrawny old man showed no sign of being cold.

They walked the block to the steps in silence. If there was a metal detector, the plan was for Skuggy to have a coughing fit and they'd retreat in feigned medical confusion. Their appointment was in fifteen minutes, which gave them enough time to enter the building and scope it out and then wait in the office and establish their presence. Agnes had used a cover story they'd played through a few times already, so the stage was set. Skuggy was Mozine, a seventies-era local disco maven and the architect of numerous sketchy contracts and some flat-out extortions. Ray was his nameless assistant/driver/thug/medic. Together they represented the kind of cloudy operation that could be talked about only under the umbrella of attorney–client privilege. Once they were in the office and in front of Eugene Gordon, Esq., their story would change, but crooked music was their ticket in.

Like so many of the older buildings in Philadelphia, the Pearl had an early-prison vibe. It was strangely empty, like an abandoned hospital. There was no real front desk, just a buzzer; and when they pressed the button for the law office, the door buzzed back with no greeting or questions. Ray and Skuggy didn't look at each other. They were on camera and they knew it, so they entered with hard all over them, in character.

The cameras were everywhere, and that changed the plan to some degree. There wouldn't be any roaming around. They went straight to the elevator, and Ray pressed the button. Skuggy kept his eyes forward, but Ray knew the old man was counting their steps and making calculations. Ray identified as many of the cameras as he could, under the guise of cautious bodyguard. They stepped into the elevator and turned to face out. Ray pressed five.

"Remind me to call the Zebra on the way home, James," Skuggy said in the voice of James Earl Jones. Ray almost laughed. Skuggy used monitored moments like this to try to make him break character. Ray nodded and stabbed back.

"Right, sir. The cat testicle harvest from the Humane Society. Your therapeutic lotions."

Skuggy said nothing, just stared forward, a regal African disco warlord who dabbled in witchcraft.

The doors opened on the lobby of something like the CEO audience chamber of a major corporation that had been taken over by librarians. It was utterly quiet, with old law books from floor to ceiling on every wall. Two potted palms bracketed the desk of the only person in the room, a blond runway model in a blue dress, who greeted them with a cool stare and returned her attention to her computer. Skuggy led the way.

"Miss," he began when they were in front of the desk. She looked up and pointed at the door to her side.

"Mr. Gordon will see you without delay."

▶ PITBULL TERRIER. DIE ANTWOORD

Eugene Gordon rose from behind his desk as they entered. He was trim, in his early seventies and without any stoop, with an iron crew cut and Germanic cheekbones above a tailored gray suit. His hard blue eyes looked brand-new.

"Gentlemen," he said, without offering to shake hands. He gestured instead at the chairs across from his desk. "Please."

Skuggy sat first, giving Gordon his x-ray look. The lawyer was unfazed and waited until Ray was seated before he spread his hands in an invitation to speak. Ray put a photo of Mary Chapman on his desk. Gordon glanced at it and then looked at Ray and waited for more.

"You know this woman?" Ray asked evenly.

Gordon said nothing. He had no reaction at all. He didn't even move. Ray continued in a conversational way.

"She hired me to lock you in the trunk of a car with a hundred sewer rats and a can of gas and some matches. Sort of a pick-your-own-death type of thing."

"This," Skuggy said in James Earl again, "is Deadbomb Bingo Ray. Know how he got that name?" Skuggy's hard eyes narrowed. "Wadn't from runnin' no bingo game. Dummy."

Sometimes a moment is so frightening that it has the opposite effect of the engineered intent. Sometimes a man immediately cracks at freakish bad news and goes stone-cold crazy. Sometimes they go rude granite hard, and in the sudden reptile it becomes apparent that they are planning something unimaginably bad. There was almost never no reaction at all. But it did happen.

"You stabbed one of my employees in the neck yesterday, Mr. Ray. Talk to me about that."

Ray and Skuggy looked at each other.

"An' you was on a picnic date wif da pussy apostle," Skuggy admired. "Dat be points for style, baby."

"You first," Ray said, turning back to Gordon. "The woman."

"She calls herself Mary Chapman." Gordon glanced at the picture again, made a small grimace of distaste. "Mrs. Chapman retained my services to hold documents for her. If she falls under duress, I am to release them to a third party." He got up and went slowly around his desk and then sat on the edge of it. "I was unaware that she wanted me . . . eaten or burned alive. Hardly surprising, I

129

suppose. My firm naturally examined her cover identity. Mrs. Chapman, as you know her, leaves a trail of bodies behind her wherever she goes, many of them spectacularly . . . disfigured." He smiled slightly, and right then Ray had him pegged. It wasn't a good puzzle piece, either. Eugene Gordon had everything in common with the coldest calculators in the pit-boss arena. And he was an order of magnitude richer. Philadelphia was an old city, and its old lawyers were occasionally the hardest kind of player—as in Eugene Gordon.

"Well." Ray sat back. "I guess you know who I am too."

Gordon didn't nod. "Down to the size of your molars, Mr. Ray. Now, exactly what did Mrs. Chapman hire you for?"

"She claims that you're blackmailing her over an insider trading deal. The money was running out, and you'd told her some pervert action would do until she got funded again."

"My my my." He got up and walked to the window. Just then it started to snow, almost like he'd made it happen. "One hundred thousand dollars, Mr. Ray, and the documents are yours. If not, we let this play out, except someone other than me will be in the trunk of that car with the rats. I like the idea. Let's not let it go to waste."

He stood immobile while Ray considered. He had the money, it wasn't that. But he was being played and he knew it. He couldn't trust anyone who would sell out the other side over rats and a trunk fire, and Gordon knew it. He was waiting for Ray to come to the same conclusion.

"A deal, then," Ray said. "What do you want me to do?"

Gordon turned and showed an expression for the first time. He smiled. "There is a man named Manny Trujillo. You know him, correct?"

Manny was a Cuban killing machine holed up in Atlantic City, working a small crew, scooping up the crumbs that fell out of the big casino crime rings. Ray nodded.

"I need to get a forceful message to him and his people. A client of mine is moving on something in that area. He needs a clear theater of operations."

"So Manny and his crew take a break?"

"Correct."

"When?"

"Tomorrow to Monday."

Manny owed him a huge favor and was terrified of him, but the potential for blowback was unknown if he had no idea what Gordon's client was up to. He sensed that it was a question he wasn't supposed to ask, so he didn't.

"Done."

"Excellent." Gordon returned to his desk and sat down, opened the top drawer, and took out a file. He'd known they were coming. He slid it across. Ray picked it up and opened it. Three sheets of numbers. Code. He looked up.

"Bank accounts. Transaction data. Find a good accountant, one who works in the shade." Gordon knew more. He knew the story of Mary Chapman. He knew all kinds of things. But right now they were even. Every additional question would come with a price tag.

"Pleasure," Ray said, rising. Skuggy rose as well. They made to leave, and Gordon stopped them with a raised hand.

"I might be curious to learn how this plays out—but not especially curious. You're an interesting man with an interesting résumé, Mr. Ray. We could use someone like you if you ever get tired of the scab under this lovely new snow. I'm told the cherry trees in London are. . . ." He spread his hands.

Ray nodded.

They walked out into the snow without a word, down the street past the Bronco, to the neon STEAK sign two blocks down. The place was just opening, and the bartender wore a bow tie. It was the kind of place where Ray's escorts did most of their work, an upscale old-timey dive, where gentiles swanned through each other's cologne and hundred-dollar cigar contrails and Cialis was available under the counter.

"Maybe not, Ray," Skuggy said pensively. Ray looked at him. "Maybe you just walk the fuck out on this one. Kill that crazy bitch and have done with it. Keep her money. Kill Tim Cantwell and all his people. Just kill 'em all and walk away."

Ray patted his skinny shoulder and opened the door for him. "I kill only the newly destitute, Skugs. You know that. Let's see about your brandy."

▶ FRIEND OF THE DEVIL, GRATEFUL DEAD

On the MFL train on the way home, a man overdosed on something right out of Tioga, like he'd been waiting to get out of the junky swarm huddled below the platform, as if the last miracle of the score had been the two dollars and twenty-five cents he needed to shoot up someplace warm, where he was sitting down, even if he had no idea where he was going. Ray watched him nod and then go blue and die, and he knew there was a lesson in there somewhere, but for the life of him he didn't know what it was.

He thought about Abigail as the body started to cool. Her skin. The intelligent light in her clear blue eyes, the way her eyes smiled when her lips did. How perfect she was, dancing her way through a life of quantum inspection, down to a defining obsession with thinking perfect thoughts and having perfect memories. The three pages of code in his pocket were associated with a specific crime—the hedge-fund asset shuffle that had fucked Tim somehow—and the best candidate for interpreting them was none other than Abigail's assistant, Anton Brown.

Full circle. The instructive loop again. Ray got off at Thirtieth Street Station thinking about that, neatly scissoring his way through the sudden commotion erupting around the latest Kensington cadaver to take the nowhere ride. Perfect circle. He wondered if there was any way Abigail could appreciate that.

||

CHAPTER FOURTEEN

It was still early when he got home, not even eight, so he took a shower to sluice the SEPTA off and then put on a fresh suit, no tie. Pepper followed him around until he gave her a tin of kippers, and while she ate, he drank a glass of red wine and considered his next move.

There was no telling what kind of interesting business was piling up at the Kimpton, plus it would be good to depressurize at the bar after dealing with Philadelphia public transit. A walk through the snow would be cleansing for the hard-to-get-to spots, like the backs of his eyes and the inside of his tongue. And besides, he needed to use the pay phones in the hotel lobby.

Abigail was working late, he knew, alone in her lab playing with cue balls and running simulations. He wanted more than anything to be the guy who didn't take any of it seriously—the carefree penis machine who showed up unannounced with a bottle of wine and oysters and fucked her into a delirium on the pool table—but that wasn't how it was playing out. It was hard to tell what to do when it came to her, now that he knew she was fixated on having what she considered the perfect mind. Did sex and physics go together? If he was eating pussy on a level that made her transcend normal human consciousness, what might she see when she looked through that rapturous ecstasy at the massive whiteboards? Could she possibly glimpse some part of what she was looking for? He shook his head.

"Pepper!" he called. Pepper looked up from licking her food bowl. "Perimeter check." He opened the back door after checking the yard again, and Pepper tiptoed out into the snow, immediately peed, and then ran back inside and jumped up on the couch. He was losing control of her, if he'd ever had any at all. He went to the door and checked his guns and then put on his boots, coat, and scarf and headed out for the bar.

▶ ESTUDIO BRILLANTE DE ALARD, EDUARDO FERNANDEZ

The snow was almost a foot deep, but the sidewalks were clear. Ray walked with his head down, listening and watching without giving it away. He took the long way to the hotel, avoiding the busy streets and cutting across parks and plazas when he could. The snowflakes were big and slow, quieting the world. He paused from time to time, letting his mind wander, listening to his thoughts as they came.

It would be interesting to see what was about to happen in Atlantic City with Gordon's client. Putting the brakes on the biggest working crew there would have an odd effect on the place. Atlantic City was a broken version of Las Vegas, with a lurid sieve of a strip—unreal in how loud and tacky it was, like something from a horror movie—with a patch of dirty beach and smelly, lagoonal water on one side and hard criminal ghetto on the other. The economic divide was incredibly pronounced, and in that narrow gap a fire was burning inside the walls of the buildings. It was an interesting place for crime. The legal criminals in towers occasionally crushed the crackheads in the ghetto in unreported bloodbaths when they went too wild, but for the most part either side was occupied with warring in their own economic bracket. Money burped and farted out of the groaning behemoths on the neon intestine, and everyone waiting in the darkness to suck it down was arrayed in rows, with the most productively vicious and effectively intemperate vying for front-row status. Manny Trujillo and his crew, the ones Gordon wanted to take a one-week vacation, were first-string center forward in the twilight zoo.

As he got closer to the Kimpton, he recognized several cars. Tessa was tending bar. The Wheelers, Phil and Miranda, were done with yoga or whatever it was they did on most evenings and were drinking Bloody Marys and yammering about stocks and boats and how much Phil hated his cakewalk shithead career. Mary Chapman's little blue Taurus was parked half a block down from where she'd parked the last time. The car had an inch of snow on it too, so she'd been drinking for at least an hour. Stanley the doorman nodded in recognition and moved to open the door, but Ray stopped him by flashing the cigarette he'd been hiding in his coat.

"Pickin' up bad habits, Mr. Ray?" Stanley was young, enormous, African black, and one of those naturally happy people. He was fun to talk to, so Ray always paused and took a minute when he was working. He stepped away from the door and lit up.

"Tell ya, Stanley, I'm just one bad habit anymore. Gettin' real fuckin' good at it too."

Stanley laughed. "'Spirit that won the West, Mr. Ray."

Ray had to smile. Stanley opened the door a few times and garnered a few bucks on a luggage pick-up. He had a deal going with the cab drivers on the side and made out like a bandit. In the next lull, he hopped a little to warm his feet and turned to Ray again.

"Busy in there tonight. Germans in the house—convention, I guess. Now, the Europeans, they got some nice-lookin' women. I won't complain, no sir."

"I will," Ray said. "One time I was in Belize, wall-to-wall Euro-kini. But Stanley, those women are hairier than either of us." Stanley made an "ouch" with his face. "And you think you can hold your booze? Dude, pack an extra liver if you're going down that road. Americans stopped drinking properly at some point, and as a people, as a culture, we should be ashamed."

"Liquor and hair, baby, shoppin' at the same store." Stanley laughed again. "What you doin' in Belize, Mr. Ray? Other than helping rid the world of European bikinis? Eurokinis, you call 'em? Dog devil."

He'd been in Belize for seven weeks gathering information on two gay guys who'd robbed a tech company in San Francisco and then moved there to start a restaurant on the beach, a little place that served French food and rented scooters and Jet Skis. Paulo and Mike. Nice guys, and the place had a great bar where Ray, over the course of several weeks, became a fixture and met many hairy but otherwise beautiful women. In the end, he learned that Mike had actually made a legitimate transaction, selling his stock at just the right time, and had split with a head full of knowledge that made him potentially dangerous competition. Mike knew it and so did Paulo, so they severed their money trail through the Caymans and blew town. They were happy. They didn't want to do anything more than hang out and get sunburned and gossip. Ray reported that he'd found them and they were posing no threat at all, but the order to pull the trigger had been given anyway.

He'd been sent there as a detective, to locate and then gather information. The trigger work wasn't part of the original deal, just implied. But of course, that also meant the killing floor was open for bidding. He told Paulo, the more vengeful and pissy of the two, and then flew back to San Francisco and gunned down Mike's old boss for double the money.

"I was there tracking an investment potential. But you get a chance, go. Check out the bat caves. Spearfishing if you're into it."

"I do my fishing at Trader Joe's, man. But I dig it."

Ray flicked his cigarette out into the street and steeled himself, and then went inside.

▶ DNI. MAN OR ASTRO-MAN?

Casey's was mostly full, and the volume was high and festive, loud enough to have a private conversation right in the middle of it. That was a good thing, because Mary Chapman was sitting alone at a two-top facing the door, waiting for him, and she wanted to blab about something so bad, she almost jumped out of her chair. Instead, she waved frantically. Ray sighed and took off his overcoat as he made his way to her table.

"Fancy meeting you here," he said sourly. He draped his coat over the back of the chair and sat. Mary stared at him, hurt and then cold.

"That rude biddy you call a secretary said I'd find you here again. She refused to call you. Said that you don't even have a cell phone."

"What do you want, Mary?"

She leaned in. "Your report!" she hissed. Ray could smell the gin on her breath. "I paid you to do something, and I want to know what's being done!"

"Easy." He leaned back and signaled the waitress. "Jesus, lady, you'd think I was your house painter. You stalk everyone you hire, or just the ones who stick—" The waitress appeared, smiling and blond. Kim.

"Maker's for me and . . ." he passed the ball to Mary.

"Martini," she said pleasantly. "Gin, two olives, drop of scotch in the glass."

"One smokey and a double. Extended happy hour for the Germans." She winked and spun off. Mary wheeled on Ray again, and her smile vanished.

Ray sat back and watched her fume. There was something so fake about her. Of course, she was a hired piece of ass setting him up to take the big fall, but it was more than that. It was almost as if she was faking being phony, like she was an actress hired to play an actress. He wondered if Abigail and her obsession with perfect honesty was throwing his radar off, if seeing bullshit doubles and bad news inside of bad news was a hallucination.

"I can't stand you, Mary," he said honestly.

She reeled back like she'd been slapped.

"I tell clients that all the time, so don't think I'm singling you out. Wait until I've had a drink. For now"—he raised a hand as she took a breath—"keep your mouth shut. Wrong kind of anything comes out of your fucked-up head, and I will punch you in the throat right across this table, right here in public. And I like this place. Don't make me do it."

Her mouth slammed shut, and she looked to the side. He watched as her jaw started working. A moment passed like that before she shot him a glare that would kill hornets. Ray realized he was hungry, but there was no way he was eating anything. It would make everything take too long, and there was something about Mary Chapman being close to food that didn't seem right.

The drinks came eventually, and Ray picked up his glass and carefully studied it as she watched, just to piss her off more. Finally, when it seemed like she was going to explode, he drained it and set it down and then wiped his lips.

"So here it is." He leaned in and beckoned her with one finger to do the same. "I have a guy who has the blueprints to everything ever built. I have another guy who has the schematics of every alarm ever installed. I have another guy who can remove entire safes from the basement of the White House. Just takes time to set it up."

Mary said nothing, but she was thinking fast. He could see it. Ray frowned.

"I'm not using any of those guys. I already cased the building. Been in and out. I know right where your shit is. I can get it. After I do, I'm going to his house in a car with a trunk full of sewer rats, and then I lock him in the trunk with 'em. With the gas can and the matches. I ever see you again after that, I blow your nasty head open and dig your address out of your little purse, burn your house down, and kill everyone you ever liked, that kind of thing." He sat back.

Mary Chapman sat back too. She was impossibly beautiful in the wash of neon from the window, and she knew it. She'd picked that table intentionally to frame herself just so. She lightly touched her throat and then pointed her eyes at him.

"Questions?" he asked. "Go ahead."

"How did you find out where Gordon lives?" Ray's poker face held, but it was startling. It would have been his first question too.

"None of your fuckin' business is how."

Mary clicked her tongue and sipped her martini. As she thought, she scanned the room behind him. He watched for her eyes to catch on something, but they didn't. She was deep in thought.

"So," she said eventually, eyes back on him, "how did you find my documents? I mean, are you sure they're the ones?"

"I'm sure. Still my business."

"What, ah . . . what do they look like? So I can be sure."

"My source tells me it's three pages of numbers. Not even locked up, which is why this is all so easy. Gordon, what happens with him, that's the hard part. We'd be done if I didn't have to—" Ray looked back and forth. No one was listening. He ran his finger across his throat. "The rats and whatnot."

Mary thought some more. She finished her drink and waved for the waitress but soon gave up. It was too busy. Ray tossed a fifty on the table and started to rise.

"Wait," Mary said, startled. She'd lost control of the situation entirely—just like Ray often did with Pepper—and she wasn't used to it. He stood and took his overcoat off the back of his chair and draped it over his arm. Then he leaned down as if to give her a peck on the cheek and whispered in her ear.

"Drop some flowers at my office tomorrow for Agnes, you worthless bitch. That old lady means the world to me, and you ruined her day twice. Don't send them delivery. You drop them off. You. Ten a.m. And then stay way the fuck out of my way. I'm working on other shit, and if I see your face I'll remove it. Anybody follows me dies bad. The next and last time we see each other is the day after tomorrow at five thirty. Don't ever come here again, and don't forget the fuckin' flowers."

There were two exits, one leading outside and the other into the hotel lobby. He left Mary sitting there stunned and went through the lobby exit and then took a left to the pay phones. Cody answered on the third ring.

"Ray! I'm glad you called. My mother is going to need meds if we don't hammer out Christmas. My chick is thumbs-up. So I'm saying that I'm inviting us to your place."

"S'fine, Code. Listen. When I get home, I'm going to use one of the Colorado burners to snap three photos. Classified."

"Hang on."

Ray waited while Cody figured out the number to send them to, also a Colorado number. After he reeled off the digits, Ray filled him in on what he thought they might be.

"So . . ." Cody said slowly. "Skuggy and you both think these are transaction records, but you can't tell what for. I can do my thing, but no promises."

"Right on. So, Cody. Kinda weird news, but I met a chick."

"You meet chicks all the time, Ray. She a tranny or something?"

"She's a physicist."

Cody laughed, and Ray smiled at the sound. It washed the grime of Mary Chapman away and replaced it with menthol. "I guess she has no idea how much calculating you do? Or does she. . . ."

"Not a clue. I'm running Gruben Media around the clock, dude."

"Hmm. What's Agnes think?"

"They talked on the phone. I guess that's good. No one said anything about Woody Allen or the afterlife yet. Come to think of it, it's maybe a good idea they don't meet for drinks."

"Whatever, man—good news is good news. Deadbomb Bingo Ray hears a love song and doesn't try to rewrite the tune. Never thought the day would come."

"Well, fuck you and the—"

"No, no! I just mean, I dunno. Surprises me is all."

"Whatever. I'll call the number I'm sending the pics to at five tomorrow. Good?"

"Check. How's the Kimpton?"

"Swarming with Germans. I'm headed home. Mañana, dude."

"Yo."

Next he called Skuggy, who still didn't recognize the Kimpton numbers.

"Fuuuuuck you," the old black man growled.

"Skug, it's me. Listen, man, sorry to call like this, but the clock is ticking. I need you to get me a guy with a halfway decent car service to tail this Mary bitch. Starting tomorrow at my office, ten A.M. Blue Taurus. Agnes will have some photos off the security camera."

"Hakeem be available. Him an' his boys tail the secret fuckin' service, baby."

"Good. What's up with you answering the phone like that?"

"Pakistan be callin' me, baby. So, Ray." He took a deep breath, the prelude to expressing one of his more forceful thoughts. "Ray, you and Queen Proton of the Tomorrow Heaven, you been fuckin', right? Now, I been thinkin' 'bout our sensitive man talk, an' I wanna run this past you. What if—"

Ray hung up. Last, he called Agnes and told her what to do, and to make sure she got Mary's phone number, e-mail, everything. The address would be a fake, but the rest of it wouldn't. Agnes dutifully took notes. In the background, he could hear the movie she was watching—*Sunset Boulevard*, same as always.

"Your Abigail called," she said when they were done.

"She did?" In spite of himself, Ray felt a thrill in the center of his chest.

"She did. Just confirming your dinner date tomorrow." She tittered. "Raymond, she smells your magic. I'm sensitive to these things, especially after that bus ride through Moab in '69. It was like being on Mars, Raymond. This man, I think his name was—"

"Agnes, I gotta pee."

"Before you go, did you talk to Cody about Christmas? I left several messages, but—"

"Tomorrow." He hung up and turned to go, but then on impulse turned back. He picked up the phone again and dialed a number, let it ring once, and then hung up and walked out. Stanley was busy with the cab drivers, so Ray stuck his hands in his pockets and headed away from the hotel lights.

Patches of starry sky were visible between the clouds, and the snow had settled and the wind had died. He hummed a little, snips of "Gone Daddy Gone." When he finally got home, Pepper greeted him at the door with a four-hundred-dollar shoe in her mouth.

"My rebel," he said, smiling. She did a tight circle and ran for it.

He hung up his overcoat and then went to the kitchen and poured himself a glass of wine, carried it upstairs to the library, and sat down in the recliner. The Colorado burner phone he had just called from the Kimpton lobby was in the stand next to it. He took it out and checked the numbers.

Two missed calls. Mary had gone to the pay phone after him and hit redial to get the last number. Ray looked up.

It was exactly what he would have done.

❚❚

CHAPTER FIFTEEN

▶ HELLO. THE CAT EMPIRE

The educational arc of the criminal mind was a surprisingly conventional one, though the graduation points were often marked by murder, and diplomas and advanced accolades were distinguished by things like large-denomination cash, big fire, radical pussy overload, and other people's gold teeth. But the underlying momentum, the measure of professionalism, was the same in every field. This is what Ray considered as he drove aimlessly through the gentrification ring around University City, unfolding the origami of his current situation. There was a setup inside this current setup. He could feel it. One of the tricks to divining the true nature of any given game was to theorize on résumés alone while for the moment disregarding all the cards in play. Ignore the table, and read the players' histories. People lied about everything, which made the examination of their actions so key. Nobody could be expected to tell the truth about what they wanted, and not a single player in this kind of game, with the possible exception of the lawyer, was any kind of exception. Résumés spoke loudly in this respect. What had everyone actually done?

In the language of the résumé—itself a collection of graduations, advancements, and accolades—an equally important consideration was what they *hadn't* done. The number of players at the table was growing, but he could retain his objectivity as the dealer if he could read all the faces in time. Part of the Deadbomb Bingo Ray persona was his uncanny ability to guess, and his accuracy stemmed from mental judo just like this.

Since reading the fine print on Pepper's flea and tick medication, Ray also liked to think in terms of biological parallels. It was the instructive element of pet ownership he had mentioned in passing to Abigail. The worm pills were really interesting too. It all came together in the way he evaluated situations like this.

The first player at the table: Tim fucking Cantwell. Tim had the money sickness, so he fit right into the flea-and-worm philosophy. People worked, bought shit, got sick, got well, eventually died anyway. Along the way, they generated money. The money changed hands, as in it moved. Up. It hid places along the way. It got lost. It clumped together with its own kind. In these respects and more, money was alive, in the same way as a migraine or a toothache.

Tim was more than just a parasite on that already warty, sweaty organism. The bulky, heavy-duty parasites were easily identifiable; they were banks and, in the modern era, government, which openly worked as an agent of commerce. Tim was a parasite on a parasite in this case, like a mite on a flea, or a bacterium in the gut of a tapeworm. He made his money much like his parasite host, but it was essentially by stealing some of its stolen food and then shitting in its bloodstream.

So everyone on both sides hated the motherfucker, which didn't mean shit unless someone killed him. Ray had decided on day one, right there in the anarchist café, that Tim was eventually going to die a creative death. The only reason he was still alive was that his scam had to be disassembled—piece by piece, block by block—or one of his fellow pieces of shit would just pick it up and run with it once he was out of the picture. And there was his fee to consider. Fixing anything was never free, no matter who the client was, even if it was Ray himself.

Next up was Mary Chapman. She appeared to be a virus that had entered the bacterial thing that was Tim Cantwell, and straight through his inner pussy too. A coward and consummate backdoor operator, he'd actually hired a woman with a feather duster sticking out of her ass to run the ballsy part of the show. Eugene Gordon, Esq.—yet another player at the table—had suggested that Mary was a killer. All well and good. Of course she was. But she hadn't killed anyone yet. She was doing her job, stringing him along, paving the way for Tim to graduate into the Bahaman big time.

Unless she was playing everyone, which was looking more and more likely. There was only one reason she would trash the résumé that opened the door for people like Tim to offer her employment in the first place: she wouldn't need a résumé when the smoke cleared. Whatever kind of score she'd potentially uncovered was big enough to change her face and her fingerprints.

It almost added up, but not quite. Not yet. If that was the case, Mary Chapman was one of the greatest players he'd ever met, and by extension of logic would have nothing to do with any of them, or even Philadelphia. She seemed in so many ways to be exactly what she read like—a cog with flared holes. Ray shook his head and realized he had unconsciously driven all the way back to the café where everything had started.

Paranoia was part of the job. There was a functioning pay phone outside a crap store on Forty-Ninth, so he wheeled into a parking spot. It was time to check in on everyone. Skuggy picked up on the first ring, anticipating him.

"Bubba, this Chapman woman be a dingdong."

"How so?" The snow around the phone was flattened out in a little circle of frozen trash and ice phlegm. He stood in the middle of it and tried not to touch the crusty brown edges.

"She went straight from your office to Chinatown. Got out and wandered around like she lost for an hour, and now she headed outta town on the freeway."

"Which way?"

"Hakeem say she goin' north. He got a cell phone, see."

Ray rolled his eyes. "Okay. I want a list of everywhere she went in Chinatown."

"Now? Hakeem be headed north. On the freeway. You want me ta start over again?"

"I'll check back in a few hours."

He considered his options on his way back to the car. He could break into Anton's house. He could follow Tim Cantwell around. He could go to the office and listen to Agnes bitch about Cody and the Christmas plan while she fished for juicy news about his relationship with Abigail. Or . . . he could go build something he was going to need in the very near future. He decided on the last.

The drive out to Chesterbrook was faster than he expected. The freeway was clear but people were still avoiding it, and the promise of more snow would keep it that way until rush hour. Dinner wasn't until six. Plenty of time to build a few bombs.

Hiding a miniature bomb-building factory in the Age of Terror was both easier than ever and hugely profitable. A year after 9/11, Ray and Skuggy had tracked the first chemical sniffer rigs that rolled out of the outlying federal buildings in a crazy ten-car relay for six weeks, charting their routes and meticulously developing an understanding of their search metrics. They later sold the information on the black market dozens of times over, including to three government agencies, until the data got too hot and they dropped it. Skuggy bought a third and fourth house that year and paid for his first mother-in-law's chemo in cash. Ray bought five acres of grapes in southwestern Washington State.

Edison Direct Marketing was a three-room office in an L-shaped business mall, surrounded entirely by Caucasian-owned flops: The Yarn Barn. An architecture firm that specialized in gazebos. Eddie's Fish-N-Tackle. T-Mobile. The giant, dirty parking lot was never more than half full, and the distressed, going-out-of-business feel was palpable the day they moved in, three years ago. No one ever moved, because the plaza would never sell. In a city full of abandoned buildings, rent was close to free, and most of them probably hadn't paid in months.

Ray parked, walked up, and peeked in through the grimy window. Mail all over the floor in front of the door, a desk with an old monitor, four orange plastic chairs, and two fake plants. The plants had been Cody's idea. He said plastic plants perfected the picture of going nowhere, least of all anywhere like up. Ray unlocked the place and went in, kicked the junk mail into the corner, and went right to the next room, locking all the doors behind him as he went. When he was inside and the door was secure, he turned on the lights.

Sixty-two boxes of Philadelphia Eagles hats, two spray canisters of pesticide (roaches and bedbugs), the plastic jumpsuit and mask and gloves worn by bug workers, and an outboard boat engine that was partially disassembled. The life of an innocuous loser, writ large. He moved on to the third room with the adjoining bathroom. Janitorial products, none of which had made it into the bathroom, and an old folding picnic table.

Once his jumpsuit was on and he was masked and gloved, he uncrated the boxes at the bottom of the janitorial inventory. Five sticks of dynamite, two standard fragmentation grenades, a bag of one-inch-diameter ball bearings, det cord, fuses, triggers, timers, aluminum foil, iron wool, four boxes of screws, five digital thermostats—the works. He looked it all over and then took out four sticks of dynamite, two timers, and two digital thermostats.

▶ BLOOD OF THE LAMB, BILLY BRAGG & WILCO

It was a simple thing to build a bomb. Idiots did it every day. Across the world at that moment, dozens—if not thousands, if "legal" bombs were included—were being constructed by intellects that ran the gamut from the bottom up. But few of them were designed to be what Ray fondly thought of as comfort bombs. He finished wiring them up and then sat back on the floor and looked at them. All of them were practically works of art in so many ways.

The way it worked was straightforward enough. Tim's office, for instance, was the most likely place for the entire gaggle of Tim's cohorts to be assembled for the Friday take-down. All Ray had to do was break in that morning and plant one of the bombs and then turn off the thermostat. Once everyone was assembled, someone would crank the heat. When the ambient temperature reached the comfort zone, everyone would take off their coats, and moments later the dynamite would flatten the building. The thermostat activated the trigger when it hit a certain temperature, so it could also work in reverse. Set it for sixty-five, and it would go off an hour or so after everyone went home.

He needed four at the moment, but built extras just to be safe, which appealed to his sense of irony. One for Tim's office, one for Tim's house, one for wherever Mary Chapman lived, and one for Anton Brown. Four explosions in one night. He decided to expand the investigation profile to include nonlinear targets, things outside of any possible ATF connection. There were so many candidates. Ideally, collateral targets should be selected to shift the line of inquiry, but there were a few people he wanted to blow up on general principle. He built two more and shelved the secondary-target consideration for later. It was getting close to rush hour, and he didn't want to be late for his date.

After he had put everything away and stowed the bombs in a box with some prison-grade toilet paper and a bottle of carpet cleaner, his burner buzzed. Skuggy.

"What up?"

"You at the office?"

"I'm at the other office." Meaning I already hate cell phones, but be extra-super cautious.

"Mary's headed back. Took a dump at the rest stop and turned around."

"Huh."

"Yep."

Ray hung up after Skuggy did and then thought. Hakeem didn't think he'd been spotted, or Skuggy would have reported that he'd called it off. So there was something in the rest stop. He thought about that as he went back to the car with his box and headed for downtown. Slick, whatever it was.

▶ TOMORROW NIGHT, PATTY GRIFFIN

They met at Salvador's at exactly six o'clock, both of them walking up to the door at the same instant. Ray was resplendent in his perfect suit, with his chiseled face and fetching scar, his hair the poster of World War II aviation, his hands in his pockets, his red scarf trailing in the wind. Abigail was beautifully disheveled, wearing jeans and another oversized greenish sweater and a raincoat. Her hair was touched by a hurricane, and her bright, piercing blue eyes might have glowed, or seen through fog. Without a word, she wrapped her arms around him and hugged him hard, and he hugged her hard back and rocked on his heels, lifting her a little and then setting her down. She looked up into his face and smiled in a comfortable way.

"Hi, Ray."

He kissed her forehead. "Hey, baby." Holding hands, they went inside.

Salvador's was Spanish and popular, booked a few weeks in advance if you weren't Deadbomb Bingo Ray. They were taken immediately to a booth with a view and left with their menus. A waiter took their drink order—scotch for Ray and red wine for Abigail. Both of them could barely pay attention. Ray couldn't believe her hair. It looked like art. She appeared lost in the scar under his eye.

"Tell me about your day," he said. "The media version."

"Friedmann and Hagen at the University of Rochester found the number pi in the upper limit of energy for each orbital of the hydrogen atom. Gamma functions and the unlikely rise of the Wallis formula."

"Those guys."

"It's . . . fascinating, Ray. It represents a reversal in the variational principle in the hydrogen atom alone. And *pi* is a transcendental number—no repeating pattern ever occurs. Ever. It's been calculated to 13.3 trillion digits. Why hydrogen, Ray? One of my two atoms. The infinite number, in the quanta of our most basic atom." She was clearly excited. Ray liked watching it, and his smile grew.

"So, an infinite number in your eternity. Smacks of progress, Abby."

She sighed and nodded, and for an instant her eyes were somewhere else, looking down a huge corridor into a place too big to have walls, looping, and the look transfixed him. She snapped out of it as their drinks came.

"And you? Promising leads on the locations?"

"I drove around some." He sipped his scotch and tried to think of a way to tell her about his day without lying. "Friend of mine was researching this and that. I went by my other office. It was mostly a day of planning and meditative construction." He opened his menu. "And it made me hungry."

"Me too!"

They read the menus like they wanted to get it over with. Ray didn't care what he ordered. He wanted to watch Abigail eat. She was so good at it. She looked up and caught him watching her.

"See anything good?"

"Oh, yes."

She snapped her menu closed. "Paella, clams and all."

He snapped his closed too. "Pulpo a la gallega."

"Ohh. Octopus." She picked up her spoon. "We can share again."

"My thoughts exactly."

"Ray," Abigail said, toying with her spoon, "do you hear music? When you're alone, thinking?"

"I do." He liked watching her think, so he did.

"The music inside of us, the soundtrack, is a memory of a song. When a song is sung the very first time, when the writer of that piece of music feels that electric thrill the first time it's played from start to finish, that's the only time the song ever existed."

Ray nodded.

"Everything that happens in us is just like a song. The melody is gone, lost in history and only played once, and so often just for the music maker, alone with an instrument in that moment of alchemy, creating magic from the inert zero of the silent world. Everything afterward is a copy."

"If that's true," Ray said slowly, "then memory is nothing more than a wet cemetery."

"Yesss." She smiled playfully. "Full of ghosts, waiting for a chance beam of light."

"I see."

"See this too." She reached across the table and put her hand on his. He looked at it, a small pink glove over his manicured war hammer, and then looked up into her bright eyes. "When I'm with you, sometimes I feel those moments of that first song. I don't know why." He felt it too, and understood that she was talking about love, in the way that only a physicist would. And, like her, he didn't know why either.

"I'm feeling that moment right now," he softly confessed. Abigail's eyes watered.

"These instants are ornaments for a God that might be, maybe, if we prosper as a people long enough to create the science."

Ray didn't believe in anything bigger than the reality of the world around him, but he found the concept of walking next to someone who did appealing for the first time. It was as if part of Abigail's personal journey to perfection was like the sun or the moon, rising and setting on a path far beyond his comprehension, but welcoming just the same.

"I dig your shit, baby," he said. Abigail laughed and slapped his hand.

▶ ROCKS AND WATER, DEB TALAN

After that, it was their on to their ritual, one of looking for each other's true quantum resonance and sharing food, drinking and tasting what was in the other's mouth, feeling the heat of each other's skin across the distance of the table, and the rest of the restaurant vanished for a time, folded away. The next thing Ray knew, the check was on the table and they were holding hands outside.

"I have work in the morning," Abigail said.

He drew her into his arms. "Me too."

"I'd invite you back to my place, but I live out of boxes and suitcases." She smiled into his smile. "You might have a thing for futons, I don't know. Mine is small and kind of hard, but that might—"

"Are you asking if I have an alarm clock?" He kissed her. "So you don't miss any of eternity?"

"I am."

"I do."

They started walking, hand in hand. The world was black and white and cold, with clean snow under the pools of light spilling from signs and street lamps, under a dark, clear sky with a handful of stars. It was below freezing, but Ray felt warm after eating whatever he'd eaten, and the thought of Abigail naked under her raincoat and sweater, the thought of her curling toes, it was all like fire to him.

"Which way's your car?" he asked.

"A block down. Meet back at your place?"

"I beat you there, I'll get the fire going."

They walked to Abigail's Volvo with their fingers intertwined. Ray saw her look up at the stars and wondered again what she was thinking, what she saw. He looked up himself and saw what he always did—burning balls of whatever was flammable in all that darkness. It was big, to the point of having no size at all. And common knowledge held that at some point it would all come to an end in the same kind of titanic explosion that had started it. Fire and explosions in dimensionless darkness. He smiled at how personal it was.

"What's that I see you thinking there?" Abigail had looked from her stars to him.

"Nothing," he replied honestly. "You?"

"I see a man getting ready to start a fire," she said, and kissed him. They'd arrived at her Volvo. She unlocked it and hopped in and then looked up before she closed the door. "Want me to stop for anything?"

He shook his head and closed her door. She blew him a kiss through the window, and as soon as she was out of sight, he took his phone out and punched in the latest number for Skuggy while walking fast toward his car.

▶ BRING DA RUCKUS, WU-TANG CLAN

"Even wif a fuckin' phone, you still ain't got a phone," Skuggy answered.

"Don't bust my vibe, Skug. Give me good news."

"Bad news is we got a player, baby. Hakeem had to call in backup, Little Elijah and Bobo G."

"Three cars for one bimbo?"

"Ain't no bimbo is what I'm sayin'. Hakeem don't think he got made, but she come back in the city an' she start drivin' Evasion 101, straight from the hard-girl handbook. She do the slowpoke, whole nine yards. Now she got three shadows, and she rollin' like she know someone back there."

"Shit."

"Hakeem think she picked up a package at that rest stop. Something small."

"Send a woman out there, tonight, with a flashlight and fuckin' tweezers. And as soon as she stops and it's all clear—as in Hakeem is on foot, and she's somewhere inside playing with dicks or washing her head off—have Little Elijah bust into her ride and look around."

"On it."

"Good." Ray got to his car and unlocked it. "If nothing else, we get to see how good she is."

"I gots a bad fuckin' feelin' we in for a surprise, Ray." He hung up. Ray looked at the phone and then took the battery out and skidded it across the street and tossed the phone itself into a sewer grate.

On the drive home, he thought about Mary Chapman, driving around out there on the salted roads just like he was. He didn't care for the notion. At the last stoplight before his street, he looked up at the sky again. Skuggy had the kind of predictive powers that allowed one-armed criminals a long life, a desperate form of superstition with deep roots tangling and feeding on the voluminous bog of his psyche. It paid to listen to him. Ray used his sleeve to wipe away the condensation on the windshield and stared up. If Mary Chapman saw the same thing in the night sky that he did, then making sure she was dead when the show was over was the only play.

‖

CHAPTER SIXTEEN

He had the fire going and was sitting in front of it barefoot when Abigail arrived. The lights of her car panned over the walls as she pulled up front, followed by the sound of her car door opening and closing. He'd had time to sweep the back, put his guns away, and let Pepper out to take a leak. The neighborhood had been quiet when he scanned the streets on the way in, but he still felt a pang as she crunched up the ice to the front door. He'd never worried about a sniper's crosshairs on the back of any of his visitors until now. His life was changing.

"Goodness gracious," Abigail said, bustling in. He'd unlocked the door two minutes ago.

"You need something better than that raincoat," he observed. She hung it up and smiled at him. Her nose was red, and her cheeks were flushed. As she took her boots and socks off, Ray padded into the kitchen and got the wine and a second glass. Pepper looked up from her dinner, glanced through the house at Abigail, and went back to eating.

"Most of my stuff is still in storage," she called.

"How long have you been here?" He joined her by the fire, where she crouched with her hands out. They kissed, and her cold nose felt wet.

"Two years." She smiled and took the glass of wine. "But my stuff has been in storage pretty much since grad school."

"You live a life of sacrifice, Abby."

"I do." She settled cross-legged and raised the glass of red wine to him. "The road is long, full of trials grim and harrowing." She sipped, rolling the wine in her mouth luxuriously before swallowing. "But I will not falter."

"Atta girl." He settled too. Abigail glanced down at his scarred foot.

"What happened there?"

"Trials. Grim and harrowing."

"And here?" She reached out and touched the scar under his eye with a cold finger.

"Purely cosmetic. I use it as a charm device." He took her hand and kissed it. "Sort of like De Niro's mole. Adds character."

Abruptly, Abigail climbed into his lap. Her butt was on the bony side, and she wiggled and pressed it hard into him. "You certainly are a character."

"How long you wanna sit by the fire?" he breathed into her mouth.

"The fire in you is warmer," she breathed back.

▶ VALERIE, AMY WINEHOUSE

"Where would we wind up, if indeed our souls are writ in water?"

"That's the question, isn't it?" Abigail turned over and swept some blond aside. "Think about it like I do. The same computational power that could tap into the record of our minds could be used to engineer almost anything. Our souls would be stored according to metrics we can only guess at, but humanity has a long available history of speculation on the afterlife."

"You mean heaven and hell."

"Oh, heaven, hell, all of it. Nirvana, the final point of light, you name it. I guess Hitler and Stalin would be placed in the same general area, but then again they might not be placed anywhere.

All the Dalai Lamas, well, I wouldn't mind joining their club, with Keats," she slapped his chest, "and Bowie and—"

"The afterlife." Ray ran his index finger down the divot above her upper lip.

"I wanted to ask you something about your work. At Gruben Media."

That wasn't good news. His poker face held. "Shoot."

"What I was telling you about earlier? The discovery of the number *pi* in the gamma functions of hydrogen quanta is sort of my thing, and my grant here is up for renewal." She bit her lower lip. "I got . . . I sort of got a job offer today. The California Institute of Technology in Pasadena. Better than Harvard or Stanford or Cambridge. It's. . . . Have you ever been to Pasadena?" She twirled her hair with one finger; a tell. She was nervous. He'd never seen it before.

Seven years ago, he'd tracked two deadbeats from Inglewood to Palmdale. The woman was driving without her seat belt on, so she died when he shot the tire out. The guy lived long enough to make bubbles while Ray pulled the briefcase he was after out of their car.

"Yeah. S'real nice. Why?"

"Want to go check it out with me? I mean, if you can get away." She climbed on top of him. "Palm trees. And sun, Ray. It was seventy-eight degrees there today." She kissed him. "I checked. On the Internet."

He kissed her back, hard. He didn't know what she was asking him, but it sounded like an invitation to more than just a sunny place. It was hard to tell how long it would take to tear apart everything he was currently tearing apart, so he didn't answer right away. Abigail must have sensed how pleased he was with the invitation, because she came alive again. The passion engulfed them a second time, longer and with even more energy and nuance, like they had been transformed into priceless violins, with hands of their own to play each other.

Afterward, she lay on her back in the center of the torn-up bed staring at the ceiling, sorting her memories before his eyes. He got up, and her eyes drifted to his form, far away, looking right through him. Gradually she focused, and he smiled.

"Pasadena," he said.

"We can make a long weekend out of it," she said dreamily.

"Abigail," he began softly.

"Ray, when we first met at the café, why were you there?"

An electric surge went through him. Her eyes were closed and it came out sleepy, but the question pierced him just the same.

"I was getting coffee, Abby."

"Mnn." She rolled onto her side. "I was there with my temp, Anton. I can't even remember what he was talking about. All I could focus on was the dark man at the next table, drinking coffee and reading the paper. Those eyes, I thought. Made me want to go swimming."

Relieved, he sat down and put his hand on her hip.

"You mean you felt like you wanted to be naked, or you want to go swimming in Pasadena?"

"Both. But I mostly wanted to inspect your soul."

He sighed at this news.

"It's lonely inside me, Ray." She was quieting. "Who would have thought. . . . That day, I felt like I was looking for something without knowing I had eyes."

And just like that, she was asleep. He watched her for a moment and then took a robe out of the closet, pulled it on, and went silently downstairs. The house was quiet, and the fire had long since burned down to glowing coals. The lights were out, but he didn't turn them on. He padded into the kitchen, opened the refrigerator, and took out one of the Colorado cell phones and called Skuggy.

"We got her," the old man reported in a gravely voice. "Airport Marriott Residency, the same one Ronald Fulbright stayed in. Elijah went in. Took the boy long enough, but the room belongs to the dummy you killed in Chinatown. No one can get in her car 'cause she's in the corner of the complex, parked right in front."

"Make sure they have it covered from two angles. I don't want her sneaking out the back to a second ride."

"Already done. Look like she be sleepin', or sittin' in the dark starin' out the window."

"Creepy. The rest stop?"

"Nothing but wicked nasty."

"Okay. Tomorrow gives her one last day to move around and start folding up her operation. I'll check in early."

Neither of them said anything. Eventually, Skuggy took a deep breath.

"Still enough time to cut an' run, Ray. We ain't got to win every last time. You deal with Tim, we all take a trip to Vegas an' catch a show."

"We have to see how big the pot is, Skug. Dangerous to walk until we do. Tomorrow midnight, say Mary Chapman is just a rent-a-poon and not some kind of serious player, Tim's little group all have names and faces, we reevaluate, see where we stand. I got a feeling something huge is just under the surface. Worst-case scenario, we walk and break even off the bait money. Maybe see what that lawyer wanted with London."

"London," Skuggy repeated in a hollow voice.

▶ SHADY GROVE. LAURA BOOSINGER

Next, he called Atlantic City. Manny Trujillo.

"Tiny's," a voice said over the bar noise in the background.

"Calling for Manny." Ray kept it quiet, and it came out sinister.

"Who's callin'?"

"Guy with his bingo card. He knows me."

There was a rustling as the phone was moved around and muted, moved around more. A door opened and closed, and the bar volume cut to zero.

"Ray?"

"Manny."

Manny laughed nervously. "Deadbomb Bingo Ray. I'll be damned. How's . . . how's it shakin'?"

"Shakin' like disco, dude. I got a small favor to ask."

"You know I owe you a big one, man. Shoot. I mean ask. Just ask."

Ray had worked with Manny over the last decade on a half dozen jobs that blurred into Atlantic City. Two years ago, Manny had stumbled across a motorcycle club working a standard drug-mule scheme up the coast that went through both their territories. The drivers were hicks from Florida who had easily taken better than the minimum wage they were making to rat out their bosses. Manny had found an empire within the empire, as there usually was. When a group smuggled drugs, the lowest-paid people in that organization usually made money on the side any way they could. In this case, it was jewelry lifted straight off bodies at the Greater Sarasota morgue. A small bag of the stones off the wealthy dead was worth much more in weight and volume than coke or heroin. Ray and Manny took the special shipment just outside Philadelphia, but this time the secondary-empire goons came along for the ride. Manny and Ray both had guns, but it was Ray who'd thought to bring the grenades.

"I need you and your boys to suspend operations until I give you the all-clear, maybe a week, tops."

"Done." The reply was too fast. "We already did, a few days ago. Ray, something way fucked up is going down here in AC. Don't know what, but it's big. Like, huge big."

"How so?"

"Check this. We got a kind of convention comin' in tomorrow. It's a charity kind of thing—Kids with Leukemia or African War Whatever—but it's like the whole thing has spiders all over it. This is big money, like Trump money, so security here's through the roof.

Can't even bring a gun to the bar, there's all these checkpoints. Number of cops and Feds gone through the roof."

Puzzling. A faint chill crawled over Ray's scalp.

"So, ah, Ray, you got maybe some kinda new gig? Like a change in income bracket type of thing?"

It was Ray's turn to laugh.

"Nah, I mean it, man! You in on somethin' this big time, you know, I'm just sayin' don't forget the little guys. Don't forget who knew you back in the day."

"We're cool, Manny. Always will be. I'll drop you a line in a day or two."

"Best of luck."

Ray hung up. He stared at the phone until the lights on it went out. Then he sat in the darkness for a long, long time. Then he called Cody.

▶ MAKE IT RAIN. ED SHEERAN

‖

CHAPTER
SEVENTEEN

The money trail led back to the Indians, who were on the hook in Tim's new hedge-fund scam for double digit millions. Though the trail led straight to them, there were so many problems following it back. To begin with, Indian casino money had its own security, scary racist mafia types Ray had steered clear of for years. Word was to leave them alone. Don't rip them off, don't cut them in, don't smile or frown at them, nothing.

He'd already done all that, and the score was still floating. So there was a problem. Three years ago, an associate of Skuggy's had come across a dog-fighting ring sponsored by an unlikely alliance between a group of United Airlines pilots and a washed-out knee job from the nineties Jets lineup. It was big enough to generate in the low millions annually, with the championship bouts held in July every year. Three breeding and training camps doubled as bookie repositories on the big Fourth of July Fight Night, sitting on more than a million in mixed currency for twenty-four hours. It was just too sweet to walk away from.

It had been a blurry night, full of smoke and blood and unseasonal rains. Skuggy, Cody, Ray, and a guy named Bobby knocked over the breeder camp outside of Lancaster at the same time as two other groups raided camps two and three. Bobby was killed, Cody was shot in the foot and lost a toe, and Ray turned the entire place into a fiery hole in the ground on their way out. The death toll on their end was seventeen, with dogs running wild in the madness. And no one could have foreseen that the United pilots were also smuggling exotic parrots, who took to the sky after the C-4 blast, many of them on fire.

One of the repositories had been on Indian land, at the edge of the Mohegan rez. There were many fatalities on both sides. The word came down that the Mohegans had had no idea it was there, that it had been running below their radar. In the aftermath, everyone on both sides of that prong of the trident disappeared. Over the next six months, parts of them were found in four states. Ray had been part of the planning phase on all fronts, and it was anyone's guess if someone had given him up under the pliers and blowtorches, if the name Deadbomb Bingo Ray had been written down in a little black book of scores unsettled. He didn't try to find out, either. There had never been any reason to. Until now.

"Morning. . . ." Abigail stirred next to him, turned over, and put her warm hand on his chest. "Time is it?"

"Five minutes to six." He put his hand on hers. "What, you have an internal alarm clock?"

"'Course I do." She snuggled into him. "Don't want to get out of bed. Is it snowing?" She still hadn't opened her eyes.

"Little bit." He shifted around until he had his arms around her.

"You already awake?"

"Yep."

"Like you made coffee awake? Or lying here with your erect apparatus awake?"

"Awake like I will make you late for work if you tempt me awake."

She rolled away and sighed, and he got up. She rolled back over and opened her eyes and then sat up and her eyes widened. "You always wake up like that?"

"All men do. Part of the whole gig."

She tossed the comforter back and closed her eyes again.

▶ DIRTY LAUNDRY. BITTER:SWEET

"My assistant is going to know something's up." Abigail blew on her coffee and sipped. Ray set her omelet down on the counter in front of her.

"Maybe he'll just think you need to do laundry." He turned back and dumped more egg in the pan. The perfect omelet was a matter of degrees, but making one for an obsessed physicist brought out the best in him. Behind him, Abigail sliced into hers with the edge of her fork.

"He would never guess that last night led to this morning, which then led to this masterpiece."

"The potato gruyère omelet is . . . ?"

"Divine." Abigail ate like it was a performance, just as she always did, but this time for a tutorial on breakfast etiquette. Even her posture was perfect. Smiling, Ray turned back to the stove.

"So, busy day?"

"I have a conference call at nine thirty. Grabbing some time on the big computer at the university."

"Ah, good. You'll have to remember to ask about the weather forecast."

"Have you read much about the pace of scientific development?"

"Can't say I have." He plated his omelet and ferried it to the counter.

"There are so many takes on it. It's generally accepted that, for the time being, the low-hanging fruit in modern innovation has been plucked and that we've entered a market-generated period of stagnation. It takes money to get anywhere further, and we're too busy throwing everything into war. War is expensive."

"Hmn." He took a bite and considered. "Sounds like science needs a criminal consultant."

Abigail laughed in delight. "Go on."

"The pace of innovation. Imagine innovation is a car. You need a carjacker, but you also need just the right kind."

"There's a variety?"

"Sure." He made a circling motion with his fork. "I'm only speculating here, of course, but I read that Bill Gates says he'll always hire a lazy person to do a difficult job, because a lazy person will find an easy way to do it. By the same logic, and I sort of see what you mean by low-hanging fruit, I dunno. Think outside of the box, as in someone who won't go looking for fruit higher up that tree. He or she might light the tree on fire, or make bricks out of the dirt the tree's planted in, maybe build a fake tree and steal the real one. That kind of thing. Revise what low-hanging fruit means."

"So you're saying . . . you're saying that making the leap from theory to applied science has been stymied by the classical architecture of the participant thinkers."

"You said it, not me. In my job, I spend a lot of time looking for things. Sometimes that means walking, sometimes driving. Everyone knows that. But sometimes I sit still, and that's why I find more shit than anyone else."

Abigail carried her empty plate to the sink and rinsed. Pepper came in and sat, staring at Ray in polite beggar mode. He gave her some egg.

"Well. Food for thought." She gave him a reflective look. He gave back a simple smile.

"You gonna be late?"

"I'm the boss," she replied. "And I'm never early, never late. Ray, when you say you find a great deal sitting still, what do you mean?"

He put his fork down. "Say someone asks me to find just the right café, or the ideal riverbank, or the perfect bell tower. They're making a wish. Looking is only finding if you have some kind of hope."

"I'll be."

"There's all kind of hope, Abby. The right kind is like a key."

▶ REGULATE. WARREN G

Agnes was on the phone when he walked into the office. She gave him a sweet smile and pointed at the flowers Mary Chapman had dropped off and gave him the thumbs-up. He went to his office and took out a sheet of paper, wrote "Bugs?" on it and showed it to her, pointing at the flowers. She wrinkled her nose and shook her head no.

He had two messages waiting on his desk, written out in Agnes's peerless old-lady script. The first one was from Skuggy. "Dog, come over this afternoon. Bring chicken or fuck yourself." The second one gave him pause. It was from Gordon, the attorney. "Please keep my office informed as the situation plays out. Also, if your timetable permits, I'd love to discuss London in greater detail, possibly next week, but of course at your convenience. —Gordon." Agnes had made a personal note in the margin: "He sounds fancy."

"That was our producer," Agnes said after hanging up. Ray walked back out, carrying the message from the lawyer. "He says hello. Everything is up and running. Your business cards are in the top drawer of your desk."

"How'd the flowers go? She nice this time?"

"That awful woman is always nice, Raymond. In a sort of cool way, like she's in a Lysol commercial."

"Ew."

"That boy Hakeem who came in to get the security photo was a gem. Skuggy has such wonderful little friends."

"Right on. So the lawyer guy—he say anything else? What kinda hit you get off of him? Other than fancy."

"No hit at all. His secretary called, faint German accent. Polite. Then I talked to him for a minute. He made me think about . . . Donald Sutherland. Sort of breathy like that."

"Hmm."

"So, bring me up to speed. Where are we on the case?"

Ray told her about the dynamite and the temperature triggers, what a hard time they were having with Mary Chapman, his conversation with Manny Trujillo in Atlantic City, and how he needed better reinforcements than the gem Hakeem and his crew.

"Anyway, upshot is I'm picking Cody up at the airport tonight at ten."

"And he didn't call *me*?" Agnes was scandalized. "Is this supposed to be a surprise for—don't you dare, Raymond! Don't you dare tell me that you talked to Cody about Christmas and he told you something mean. Something terrible and awful and cruel, like he wants to bring his paramour home with him and they're going to stay at your house, with all those guns and pointy things, and all because he's afraid I will talk about my life goals."

"Agnes, it's not that," Ray said. "I mean it is, but—"

"I won't be baking cookies this year." She opened her top drawer and took out her stapler. "I just might take the entire holiday season off, go on a cruise of some kind. With Cody home, what would you need with an old woman and all this hassle? I'll take Pepper with me, and the two of us can have a fine old time."

"Please," Ray said. "I think Cody is just—"

"He can explain it to me himself, Raymond."

"Sweetheart, just listen. You're his mother. He loves you, and he's proud of you. Your last name is Capsule. You want to kill a famous movie director for reasons you refuse to share. I don't mind any of that. Cody and I both love that about you. It's heartwarming. But this gal of his is an Art major. I'm sure she's lovely, but that isn't a sturdy breed and you know it. We need to sound her out, see how stable she—"

"And you!" she wheeled in her chair, a hard glint in her eye. "Your Abigail. I suppose the four of you will go to the drive-in on double dates? Stroll arm in arm like those fruitcakes on the television? Laughing, with your scarves and your Dapper Dan haircuts! Talking about trendy restaurants and venereal diseases and the price of monkeys in Copper County? Why, I wouldn't—"

Ray stopped her with a look. "Abby's moving."

"Aw." Her anger melted instantly. "Oh, honey, no."

"Job in California. Pasadena."

Agnes was silent. She put her hands in her lap. Ray got up and walked into his office, leaving the door open so they could still talk.

"Raymond, in all the years you've been in our lives, you've never spent time with a woman like this. Are you . . . did you . . . did you ask her to stay? It's sudden, sure, but so is love. I was in love with Cody's father the instant I laid eyes on him."

"I can't ask her anything like that. She has, like, a destiny."

"I don't have a destiny," Agnes said soberly. "Bless him, Cody doesn't either. Not Skuggy or that beautiful boy Hakeem. Almost no one has a destiny, Ray. But you do. It's part of the reason people are drawn to you. It's like, it's like something magical happens when you're around. You have a presence. That means destiny to me, darling. Can't you just ask her if you can bring your destinies together, to braid them into something, something . . . oh, how lovely that would be."

"I'm not sure it works that way." Ray looked out at the brooding sky. The clouds weren't even moving. "I don't know. I have to think."

"You let me know if there's anything we can do." Agnes sniffed, and Ray realized she was really upset. He went to the office bar and poured her two tablespoons of gin and then carried it out to her desk. She took a little sip and sniffed again.

"One time, Raymond, I was at an Alcoholics Anonymous meeting in Cleveland back in 1971." She took a Kleenex out of the sleeve of her sweater and wiped her nose. "Larry and I had been taking LSD every day for three weeks, and we were convinced we had every problem there was. I was listening to the people's stories, and I became convinced that all of them were sick, and that I was too, though in my case it was different. They all had a version, it seemed to me, of homesickness. But it wasn't a *place* they missed. No, it was a place in *time*. All of them had one moment—maybe a week, maybe a month or a year—when they weren't worried about anything, when they felt full and every sunrise was gentle and bright. . . ." She wiped her nose and sipped her gin again. "And it passed for all of them. The moment passed, and they wanted it back. They hid any way they could from that loss and tried to look for it in a bottle at the same time."

Ray patted her bony little shoulder. She drew a breath and continued.

"In my perceptual abandon, I understood clearly that the journey for so many of the rest of us is to find that moment, even if we're destined to lose it and become drunks or die or go crazy and convert to Republicanism." She looked up and put her mottled hand over his. "Be careful, Raymond. Be careful that this moment doesn't pass away forever. I don't have the kind of imagination to guess at what the time sickness would do to a man like you."

"Agnes Capsule," Ray said softly, "for the thousandth time in a thousand days, I'm glad for your special wisdom. Thank god someone invented LSD."

"Mnn." She handed her cup up to him. "One more—the whiskey this time, I think."

▶ ODE TO THE WIND, MIDNIGHT CATTLE CALLERS

There wasn't time to do the SEPTA sewer-pipe shuffle all the way out to Skuggy's, so he improvised. It was safe to assume that one party or another would follow him from his office. It was an easy place to pick him up, for one thing. His house was much more difficult than an office building with more than a thousand almost identical people and a three-story parking garage full of nearly identical cars. A solid way to scrape off a tail was a trip on foot through Chinatown and then a cab to Thirtieth Street Station, then a second cab to destination X, a place with chicken in Kensington.

Ray hung back and smoked after he exited the building. He eventually took a random cab and gave the guy shitty directions that would have them looking for something vague in Chinatown.

"Jade Alley? You mean like a green alley? Skinny street wit' a green sign? I don't get it."

"It's on Tenth or Thirteenth," Ray replied. "Just get us close and I'll recognize where we are."

"So, like, Thirteenth and what? Help me out here, buddy."

"Few blocks in from Market, maybe five or ten."

"Meter's running, man."

And that was that. As they meandered around in light afternoon traffic, Ray watched for signs of a tail and got them a little more lost. He finally had the guy drop him off a block from the underground SEPTA nest around Eleventh and Market. After he paid, he went down and then came out of one of the ten exits in the area, all the way up on Thirteenth. From there, he cut in a few blocks and caught a stray cab to Thirtieth Street Station.

The sun had come out by the time cab number two dropped him off, and when he walked in, the light had lit the station's interior like a cathedral. The obsidian statue of the angel was spangled with light, and a cluster of Japanese tourists were shooting away with their phones. Commuter traffic was heavy, most of them professionals heading home early to the suburbs. Ray got a coffee at the little café and strolled down the food court, watching the reflections behind him in the thousands of reflective surfaces in the wide corridor of vendors. That's when he saw him.

It was a skater kid, thin, with a pale face and lanky black hair, black hooded sweatshirt, and black jeans—all very standard for a pissed-off kid. But there was something too fluid in the way he moved. He'd been on the sidewalk when Ray got out of the cab in Chinatown, he was sure of it. He wheeled and caught just a glimpse of the kid's face. Maybe not a kid at all.

Ray skirted a small family and rounded the corner, heading left toward the open seating area. Just as he rounded the next corner, he ventured another look back. The kid was still there, the hood up, cutting a clean line through the pedestrians, moving with fluid, predatory grace.

It was a hit.

His adrenaline surged, and the countless escape routes he'd planned appeared in his mind, like a map superimposed in glowing, transparent red. He struck out across the wide area in the direction of the clock kiosk, beyond which was a wide space without pews. There was no defense against a public killing, not if the assassin was willing to risk it all, but there were ways to make it difficult for long enough to get away.

The platforms for the Amtrak trains were below, down the escalators. Up to the left was the wide corridor that led up to the platforms for the commuter trains. He headed for the commuter trains because of the number of people in between, pushing his way through like a man with a train to catch. He almost missed the woman coming at him—business suit, cell phone to her ear, eyes forward, running late. As they were steps from passing each other, she shifted her free hand, and in a random bar of sunlight he caught the glint of something sharp. She seemed to stumble in that instant, right into his arms. He caught her knife hand on the top of her thumb, and with his free hand he reached around her wrist and broke it.

It was all so smooth that no one around them stopped. He pulled the knife out of her hand and pocketed it as he hugged her, picking her up and spinning her like it was a lovers' reunion. Then he put her down and beamed.

"Nipsy!"

She smiled and hissed through her teeth. He hugged her again and this time buried his face in her red hair, his mouth close to her ear.

"I'll kill you right now if you don't hit the brakes, lady. Then I find your hometown."

"My phone," she whispered.

"Do it, and I let you live."

She shifted and raised her phone to her ear. "All stop."

"Good. Who else is there other than the skater kid?"

He felt her stiffen and pushed her away. The confusion in her eyes vanished as she looked over his shoulder. Ray stepped around her and walked out the exit without looking back. Across the street a block away was the queue for Boltbus, running workers and budget tourists from New York and back. Cabs circled the buses for pickups and dropoffs. Ray ran flat out, vaulting a low wall and sprinting directly into traffic to get to it.

Just as he made it to the first cab, he heard what sounded like gunfire, a block back in the station, but he was breathing too loud to be sure. He climbed into the cab and slammed the door. The driver glared back at him.

"Jesus, buddy, you—"

"Wife!" Ray shouted. "Roll, man! Take me anywhere but here!"

The driver floored it, and Ray looked back just as screaming people foamed out of the exits of Thirtieth Street Station.

▶ BADDEST OF THE BAD, REVEREND HORTON HEAT

He had the cab drop him off ten blocks from the Salvation Army on East Lansdowne, and from there he trudged through the snow making calls. First was Agnes.

"Gruben Media," she answered in her secretary voice.

"We got a situation. Turn the lights out."

Agnes hung up. Protocol was for her to call building security first; she knew half of them by name. The story was that she'd been frightened by a strange man testing doors in the hallway. Then she was supposed to hide under Ray's desk with the only gun she knew how to use: the sawed-off assembly built into his desk. It activated by pressing two buttons, and the desk fired only once, four double-barrels of twelve-gauge buckshot. It was an extreme measure. Security was to escort her from the building, where she would relay through a miracle labyrinth of cabs and SEPTA to a bed-and-breakfast in University City.

Next was Skuggy, who answered a fraction of a second through the first ring.

"Switchin'." He hung up. Seconds later Ray's phone rang—a Delaware area code.

"Yo."

"Yo, Dog. Thought you were at the station."

"I was," Ray said. "Hit a snag."

"Six dead kind o' fuckin' snag? Muthafucka—"

"Wasn't me," Ray said, cutting him off. "What'd you hear?"

"All over the news, man. Thirtieth Street is locked down. Single shooter, six dead, dozen injured, shooter fled on foot."

"Description?"

"Nada. So you there or not?"

"I was. Somehow I got tailed all the way out of Chinatown. It looked like it was gonna be a gunfight right there in the middle of everything, and then this bitch comes out of the blue and tries a shank 'n' glide."

"Where you now?"

"Almost to the Salvation Army. I'm going to do a costume change and. . . ."

"And?"

"Shit, man. When was the last time you heard from Hakeem?"

"No way." Skuggy sounded like the air in his lungs had frozen.

"Call you back. You roll out, take the phone you're on now."

Ray slowed to a casual stroll as he approached the Salvation Army. The snowy parking lot had four cars and a van. He gave all of them a wide berth and entered, his heart rate approaching normal for the first time since the station. He went straight to men's clothes. It took less than a minute to find a faded brown overcoat. He took it out and sniffed it and then took it to the register. The old black woman didn't try to make small talk, and he didn't try either.

Once he was outside, he took a left and headed for the nearest busy intersection. The four corners were a laundromat, a gas station, another gas station, and a donut shop. He went to the back of gas station number one and changed into the eleven-dollar coat, transferred the contents of the pockets, put the good coat in the bag, and went inside.

It was a run-down place, with a tiny Pakistani woman behind bulletproof glass. There was a coffee machine, so Ray poured some in a Styrofoam cup and went to the slot. She smiled pleasantly.

"Pack of Newport menthols too, in a box. Matches. Thanks."

She rang it up while he sipped the bad coffee, and then he went back outside and down the street. There was a halal grocery store and a vacant place with a bench in between them. He went and took a seat and smoked.

Someone was trying to kill him, and they wanted him bad. Bad enough to have a team waiting in the train station. That was interesting. Scraping tails there was a habit, and habits were risky, as he'd just seen. Knowing he would be there, banking on it, meant he was made in a significant way. Agnes was safe. She was the ultimate in low-priority targets in most ways. Skuggy was in the red zone, but he was also incredibly dangerous.

Abigail.

Ray took out his phone and called her office.

"Hydrogenesis," Anton answered.

"Hi, I need to speak to Doctor Abelard."

"Dr. Abelard is busy at the moment. May I ask—"

"Tell her it's her boyfriend, Ray."

There was a pause, then muffled cursing, and then Mozart as hold music.

"My boyfriend Ray!" Abigail answered. "Oh, I like the sound of that! I was just running a folding dynamics algorithm and thinking about bathing suits."

"They have little mermaids on 'em?"

"Mnn. I was thinking of sticking with the classics. Greta Garbo, big sun hat."

"Sweet. So I have—*had!*—a super-busy weekend lined up, but the cinematographer had to reschedule and now I'm free. I was wondering. . . ."

"Yes?"

"Would you like to spend the weekend with me? There are so many things I've discovered doing location scouting over the last few years. Magical things. I'd like to share some of them with you."

"Raymond, you want to take me away for a long weekend to magical places. Let me think about it."

"There will be snow involved. Caviar. I'm going to have to shop for a winter coat for you here in a moment if you say yes, and I don't want to hear anything about my selection. And—"

"Yes," she said. She sighed, and he could hear the smile in her voice, almost see the dreaminess in her eyes. "We can talk about Pasadena . . . your swimsuit options. . . ."

"Excellent. What time do you get off?"

"Pretty much make our own hours here. When's good?"

"I'll be passing right by your lab in about an hour and a half. I can pick you up, and we can stop by your place to pick up panties and your toothbrush and go from there."

"I wait with bated breath."

"Smooch." He hung up, waited a minute, and then called back. Anton answered again. He was a former bank robber and not a bad fighter, plus he probably had a gun.

"Hydrogenesis."

"Hey, it's Ray again. Anton, right?"

"This is Anton." Barely civil.

"Right on, man. I'm picking Abby up in a couple hours, but I wanted to grab some dude time with you if you're gonna be around."

"Dude time," Anton repeated in a flat voice.

"Yep. You and Abs are pals. Maybe you got a little advice for me, shit like that."

He could hear the static of deep space.

"I'll see you then." Anton hung up.

Ray dialed the Kimpton and booked three rooms, all suites on the top floor, and then he called Skuggy.

"Dog," Skuggy answered.

"What's the word?"

"Hakeem and Little Elijah and Bobo G still be circlin'. Bad news big-time. Your bitch Mary be meetin' with Carlo Hardshell. The Indian Carlo Hardshell. No way that good, Ray. I'm wearin' my vest, and I got all kinds of don't be knockin'. Street's got eyes. We see."

Carlo Hardshell was the head of the Mohegan Indian security apparatus. Almost seven feet tall, ponytail, cheesy buffalo-skin coat with tassels, human killer times twenty plus, and he collected antique dolls and vintage dentures and nineteenth-century wheelchairs. It made perfect sense. Mary was selling the blackmail back to them. They were the ones on the line for the sixty mil, after all. She'd found out too much and decided she wasn't being paid enough, and now she was going to bring fire down on all their houses and walk away with a hefty commission.

"So Tim Cantwell is getting played from the inside. You know what this means, right?"

"Means we might have identified the biggest player. Time to run our exit burn."

"Bingo."

"Except the train station. Someone took out the hit squad and got away. There's one last player at the table, Skug. We can't snap our trap closed until we got a name for every face."

"Probably too late to cut an' run anyway." He blew out a breath. "Maybe too late the whole time. You call Cody?"

"I'll leave him a message later. If I tell him anything now, he'll just worry for the whole flight. Best if he gets the news when he gets off the plane and checks his messages."

"Truth. What's the plan?"

"I have to set a meeting with Hardshell. Sell him those documents myself. But right now, I have to go get my chick. But before that, shit—I have to gamble the whole fuckin' thing."

"How's that?" Skuggy sounded grim. Ray did too.

"Gotta go get my fucking dog."

▶ GO TELL THE WOMEN, GRINDERMAN

Ray had cab number three drop him off a block south of his house. It was newly dark, and a cold wind was blowing. He crunched over the ice to the house behind his and looked both ways. The streets were empty as the next wave of winter storm descended on Philadelphia. He scanned the yard for anything remotely like a skater-kid killing machine. Nothing.

The best way into his house when it was in lights-out mode was through the back of the garage. He went through the gate of the house in front of him and up the walk. At the edge of the porch, he dropped low and cut sideways, just in front of the snowdrift that had formed in front of the frozen shrubbery. The side of the house was unlit, so once he was there he rose to his full height and ran flat out until he got to the corner of the back yard. There was a gnarled old pear tree there that he'd already climbed in the dark once or twice, so he jumped and his hands found the right branch. He levered himself up and then swung sideways onto the top of the fence. It was only two steps to the four corners of the fence. He rapidly made them, balancing with his hands out, but slipped on the second one and fell into his back yard, only barely catching the edge of his garage roof. He pulled himself up on top and paused, listening.

Nothing. Moving as low as possible, he scuttled sideways until he was over the ventilator. He'd rigged it to open, but there was a booby trap. Wired into the frame was a trip that would set off the house alarm. He clipped the trip line and yanked it open and then dropped silently into the darkness.

His house was extremely hard to break into. The motion sensor in the garage had already activated, so if he didn't punch in the code on the pad by the door in thirty seconds, the alarm would go off; if he didn't enter the code a second time, the timer on the bomb in the upstairs safe would activate. It wouldn't harm the house, but valuable records would be destroyed. He moved quickly to the pad and punched in the sixteen-digit code twice and then drew one of his guns.

He went to the '77 Coupe de Ville and took the spare key out of the wheel well, unlocked the driver's door, and then put the key in the ignition and gently closed the door again. Then he went to the tool cabinet and took out a twelve-gauge sawed-off. He was ready to go in.

Quiet. He listened with his mouth wide open, tilting his head slowly to either side. Nothing. He crouched and stole through the kitchen to the dining-room table and took out the rifle, slung it over his shoulder, and then snuck into the living room. Pepper wasn't on the couch. Ray cursed silently and went up the stairs.

He found her curled up in the center of his bed. Silently, he went to the closet and took out a duffel bag, put in three suits—pausing to hold one up and then return it in favor of another—and then added three ties and some folded undergarments. When he was done, he zipped the bag closed and picked up Pepper. She licked his chin as he risked a low peek out the window at the street, and then he carried her down the stairs into the living room. As he passed through the kitchen, he paused and then took a paper grocery bag out from under the sink, dumped in his sharpened bicycle spokes and the bowl of clementines, and then stole back into the garage.

Pepper was excited to be in the Cadillac. He put the squirming dog in the passenger seat and tossed the bags in back, laid the rifle over his knees, and opened the glove box to grab the garage-door remote. Then he started the engine. It turned over on the first try, and he let it warm for a moment. Pepper barked once, softly because she seemed to sense that they were sneaking around, and he made shushing sounds. The engine settled into a low, throaty purr, and he put one Beretta on the dash, glanced at Pepper, and hit the button on the remote. The garage door shuddered and broke the ice around it and opened rapidly. Ray put it in drive, pushed the brake pedal all the way down, and put his foot on the gas. The second he had clearance, he hit the remote again to reverse the door's direction and floored the gas as he took his foot off the brakes. The car surged forward.

ǁ

CHAPTER EIGHTEEN

The 1977 Cadillac Coupe de Ville was front-wheel drive and as long as any car ever made, designed for transporting a dozen business gangsters, two statues, assorted paintings, and a picnic table. It handled well on dry streets at low speeds, but the 440 engine was designed for high-speed collisions rather than performance, the seven feet of hood to give the driver a chance of surviving it. The vehicle roared out onto the ice and staggered, then it slewed to the right into the yard as a single wheel caught traction.

Ray turned into it and kept the gas pedal to the firewall. Various kinds of landscaping hedges exploded in snow and ice as he plowed down his street over his neighbors' yards. At the end of the block he expertly put the massive vehicle into a controlled donut, skipped off the last curb while spinning around, and all four tires found purchase on the salted black sleet on the street.

Pepper howled with glee. They raced a block, and then Ray did another long, controlled slide onto a busy street. One more block, and they slowed. He looked in the rearview. There was no sign of any pursuit, which would have been as insane as what he'd just done.

"We did it," he said, patting Pepper's head. "Sit down and be quiet. I'm driving here."

There was a mini-mall two blocks down, full of artsy little boutiques and a café, all closed for the night. He pulled into the parking lot and slowly rumbled through it, came to a stop on the side in front of the dumpster, and cut the engine. For a moment they sat in silence, Pepper panting and waiting for round two of the excitement, Ray waiting for his heart rate to return to normal. When it did, he opened the glove box, tossed the remote in, and took out a small flask, looked both ways, and hit it. Pepper tried to help in some way as Ray put the flask back and took out a pack of Newport 100s. He lit one and took a drag and then looked around the car.

"Neighbors are going to be so pissed, Pep," he said. "We'll have to blame it on Cody's new girlfriend somehow."

He put the gun on the dash back in the holster and then looked back to make sure the parking lot behind the car was free of people. He hefted the rifle, gave Pepper a stern look she ignored, and got out. He kept the rifle low and behind him as he went to the trunk, opened it, and set the rifle inside and closed it. That's when he noticed the bullet holes. Two of them, one to each side of the license plate, and a third, low on the right side of the bumper. Someone had been shooting at him.

Ray paused and smoked, just looking at the holes. They were small and neat, no spall. The sniper had been reasonably close, so either he or she was inept or an offensive communicator. He looked up at the night sky. The snow was coming down harder, which was good. Visibility was a factor, so there was that. He flicked the cigarette away, got back in, and started the engine. Pepper sniffed at the heater vent when he cranked it and then angled her face back and forth like she was blow-drying her hair. He took out his cell phone, ripped the battery out, and tossed it out the window, and then got a new one out of the duffel bag and called Cody. It went straight to voice mail.

"Yo, Code, it's me. So . . . ah, slight complication. When I pick you up tonight at the airport, I'm Gruben Media and you're . . . oh, Roger Hubbard, cinematographer here to look at the light or some shit. I'll have a, uh . . . oh, my female companion—not companion companion, but the other kind, like the dating—I'm bringing a date when I pick you up. Shit sorta hit the fan here, so. . . ." He hung up and called Skuggy.

"So you livin'. Goddamn fuckin—"

"Where the fuck is Mary Chapman?"

"She done with Hardshell. Fuckin' yeti headed back out to the rez. Chapman went straight to Tim Cantwell's office. They up in there drinkin' wine, probably thinkin' up fancy ways to get pee up in our graves an' steal our fillins. While you fuckin' wif dogs an' science pussy. You did call Cody, right? His momma hid up in a pancake house, an' he walkin' into the crazy parade wif no trombone. Boy gonna—"

"Skug, I'm not bringing you chicken, not with that mouth."

"Fuck you!"

"Someone shot my car when I was leaving my house."

Skuggy stopped his wind up and listened while Ray told him the story. By the time he was done, the snow was coming down hard enough to turn the wipers on. When he was finished, Skuggy chuckled.

"Yo own neighbors shot the Caddy, dog. Sick of your spooky ass, and now you ruin all them yards. Boom boom white lady rage. Fuck with they grass like touchin' they hair, dummy."

Ray laughed too.

"So now what, man with a plan? You got a dog and some guns. Lose a tooth and rub an onion on you head, you blend right in wif da Philly white pop now. Deesguise, baby."

"Gotta pick up Abby, drop off Pepper with Mrs. Capsule, check into the Kimpton for night one of a romantic weekend vacation, eat a room-service dinner, have you call at eight and interrupt it so I can explain why I have to pick up Cody, then get Cody at the airport and hope he got the message I left him, and then have drinks at the lounge on the roof at the Kimpton with my chick and see if anything shakes out of the shadows before . . ." Ray sighed. ". . . before

Abigail and I take a bath in that huge tub and I wash her hair while we drink champagne."

"Sheet." Skuggy coughed. "Just get a little puke up in m'froat. Taste like air conditioner water and . . ." He smacked his lips. ". . . beach diaper."

"Skug, dude. You shouldn't know what either of those things taste like."

"Pussy that you don't, Ray. So, you gots the dog. Now you go get the lady saint of the revelation and point your fierce at the world."

"That's the size of it, Skug. Want me to come get you first? You like the Kimpton."

"Nah." He sipped something, probably boozy. "Glad you got a woman, Ray."

"Agnes said the same thing. She told me a story about an acid bender and her subsequent reflections in an AA meeting."

"Hmm. Tell you what. One time—oh, long time ago now—I was fifteen. My uncles were runnin' horse out of this motel. I used to hang around, go get shit from the corner store. Momma gunned down in the kitchen year before, didn't have shit to do." He paused. Ray never talked about the years before they'd met, and neither did Skuggy. Ever. Ray lit up a second cigarette and listened, watching the snow fall on the dumpster in front of the car.

"There was this girl worked the corner. Chicky. Sometimes they called her Dulce, but I always rolled with Chicky. My Chicky. Puerto Rican, and she had jungle butt, little waist. Blue lipstick, she like that. I had this huge love on that woman, follow her around and I sing songs to her. . . ."

▶ LOVE AND HAPPINESS, AL GREEN

Ray prepared himself for something horrifying.

"My uncles got me a piece of that for my birthday. I so excited, gonna fuck on Chicky—like a dream inside a dream inside a dream, jus' can't be real. Big blowout night, tickets to Journey. I used ta love that band. They get me an' Chicky a room, and she come in an' she smell so good, Ray, like popcorn and grape candy. We got some blow and some ludes and some crystal, an' Chicky, she do a few lines and then she do a thing I ain't seen 'fore or since. She make a mix, lude an' blow, an' she shoot me up and get suckin', and right when I gonna pass out, she bring me back up on the crystal. I'ma blow, back on down on a poke o' that lude juice. Up an' down, up an' down, an' I think I'ma go crazy, baby. Hour after hour, like a crazy roller coaster in Coney. Damn. . . ."

Ray was quiet.

"I's so in love. I wake up a day later, an' my arm . . . my arm all slick, an' it don't work right. My uncles think that so damn funny. Damn. So I just kinda hang back, keep all quiet, and 'bout a month go by, I get me a sling. Make it from a pillowcase. Chicky, my Chicky . . . like she don't even know any kinda skinny little whistlin' boy wif no funny arm."

"Fuck those people," Ray said eventually, when he realized the story was over.

"Oh, I did, Raymond. I did."

Ray got the flask out and drank again, and then he sat there watching the wipers go back and forth.

"So you're saying be careful."

"I am," Skuggy said. "But you Deadbomb Bingo Ray. Maybe you keep that in mind, you up in a bathtub all Keanu Reevin." He snorted and hung up.

Ray put the car in drive and edged out into the storm.

Traffic was light and cautious. Pepper sat in the passenger seat, small in the center of it, and after a few blocks she put her front paws on the dash so she could look out. The swirling white must have been instantly boring, because she dropped back onto the seat and walked over to Ray's lap and curled up.

As he drove he monitored the rearview, but he couldn't see more than forty feet behind him. Gusts of snow periodically swirled through in minor tornadoes and dropped visibility even further. Anyone who could successfully tail him through that deserved a fair shot, he thought. Still, in case someone already knew where he was going, he skirted the edge of the parking lot three times before he pulled in with the headlights out.

Anton Brown was actually standing when Ray came in, his arms crossed, waiting for him. In an instant, Ray surmised from his expression and body language that he wasn't alarmed or being held hostage: no, Anton was spoiling for a fight. Ray raised a finger.

"Rain check on the chat. Abby!"

Anton reddened, and the door to the lab flew open. Abigail came out doing ballet, twirling as she advanced and falling into his arms.

"Raymond," she said with dramatic flair, "take me away!"

Ray dipped her and then twirled her once before bringing her in for a kiss. He winked at a fuming Anton and then kissed her hand.

"I drove the sled."

"Goody."

"Grab your stuff, and let's boogie. Your car'll be safe out front. We can buzz by your place and pick up your unmentionables, and then I have a surprise."

"Ahh. Let me get my purse."

Abigail went back into her office, humming. Ray took out his phone and ignored Anton entirely for the minute it took for Abigail to get her things. She came back out wearing her giant raincoat, and Ray couldn't help but smile. There was no doubt she had anticipated the weather, but somehow turning it into a fashion statement was contrary to her concept of perfection.

Ray waved at Anton, who smiled at Abigail.

"See you Monday, Anton."

"Doctor. Enjoy your . . . weekend."

If Abigail noticed the pause and the glowering expression, she breezed by it with great elegance. Ray opened the door for her, and they stepped out into the storm. He pointed out the Cadillac, and they hurried toward it. He opened her door for her and then rushed around to his side and got in. Pepper was already in her lap.

"Aw, Pepper gets to go for a ride," she said, scratching Pepper's cheeks.

"Dropping her off with Agnes. The two of them are thick as thieves."

"Good." She looked over at him. "This car! What is this?"

"My cool old Caddy. It's a better weekend ride than anything else I have. So, where to?"

"Down off Thirtieth by Penn. My place is a faculty apartment. Free Wi-Fi."

They buckled in and started out. Anton stood in the window watching them, his arms crossed again.

"So the surprise is huge," he said, glancing in the rearview. Black with swirling white. "We booked three suites at the Kimpton for the entire weekend for the folks from LA, but with the storm and the rest of their misadventures, none of them can make it, so I vote we begin there. Room service, an incredible lounge on the top floor with a panoramic view of the city in the snow, giant bathtub in the room. And then?"

"And then?" Abigail was delighted.

"And then we make it up as we go along. Ever been to Atlantic City?"

"Nope."

"Maybe we hit the coast, or go south, or take the train up to New York and go coat shopping in Manhattan."

"I love it. The plan is to enjoy each other's company, you're saying."

"Pure. I thought you might like that."

"I do."

Ray drove, one eye on the swirl behind them. Abigail's place and Agnes's bed-and-breakfast were reasonably close together, which was good. It was a straight shot, but he opted for the scenic route.

"And you get to meet my secretary," he said, making it jovial. "She's the sweetest old gal. Loves Pepper. Spending the weekend at this B-n-B she loves, wants Pep to play house with and go for walks. Staycation. She picked the concept up from this playboy son of hers."

"Staycation," Abigail said, relishing the word.

"Yeah. Kinda like what we're doing."

Abigail became transfixed by the swirl of oncoming snow. She seemed peaceful, and he knew her thoughts had returned to work, maybe Pasadena, and from the faint smile on her face he could tell they were good ones. Her vibe seemed to get to him. In spite of it all, he was enjoying himself.

The Hampton House was a giant four-story colonial on Chester, restored to *Architectural Digest* glory and filled with antiques. The gay couple who ran it were excellent hosts, and one of them was an exceptional breakfast cook. In the snow, with the blazing gold lamps and the touch of early holiday decorations, it looked exactly like the kind of place an eccentric old lady would spend the weekend with a stolen Pomeranian.

"Here we are," Ray said. "The home away from home of Agnes . . . Agnes."

"I can wait here if you like," Abigail offered. Ray shook his head.

"I'd never hear the end of it. You carry Pepper, and I'll be in charge of her luggage."

Abigail got out with Pepper in her arms and waited while Ray gathered up the bag of dog food and Pepper's favorite bowl from the back. Together, they went up the walk and the freshly shoveled stairs. The door opened as they approached, and Agnes held her arms out for Pepper, making chirps of delight.

"There's my little granddaughter," she said, taking the dog and kissing her head. Pepper wiggled and furiously licked her face. Agnes transferred her to the cradle of one arm and held her hand out to Abigail.

"You must be Doctor Abelard," she said pleasantly. "Ray has told me so much about you. Under all that confident bluster, he's quite fragile, you know." She winked. "A real hothouse flower. Can I interest you two lovebirds in a sherry? Carl just set up the evening cocktail buffet."

"We should be moving along," Ray said quickly. "You're all set for your weekend?"

"I am, dear. Thank you." She stroked Pepper's upturned face. "The boys missed Pepper here." She looked at Abigail. "We might watch *Annie Hall* tonight. That's a film by the director Woody Allen, the one who fornicates with his oriental daughter, so I may drink the entire bottle myself." She looked back at Pepper. "My little friend is all the babysitter I need."

"I'll check in later," Ray said.

"May I have a quick word with you, Raymond?" She looked between them.

"I'll just wait in the car," Abigail said, smiling. "Nice to meet you."

"You too, dear," Agnes said. "Please make sure Raymond takes his vitamins. And he's cranky if he doesn't get milk before bed."

"I'll take charge," Abigail replied. She nodded to Ray and gave him a stern look of authority and then went back down the stairs. Ray turned to Agnes.

"One minute and you're a drunk harping on the fornicator."

"Up yours," Agnes growled. "You tell Cody to call me on my cell. I assume the bloodbath at the train station was you?"

"Indirectly. Someone tried to kill me, got waxed by the competition. Shot my car when I went to get Pep."

"Ah, well." She snuggled Pepper. "I have that giant knife under my pillow and enough cash to get to Bermuda. We're cool."

He patted her bony shoulder. "You aren't really watching that movie, are you? 'Cause I have all kinds of shit going on and—"

"Don't worry, dear. I just wanted to test the water. We're going to watch reruns of *30 Rock*, the best television programming in the history of the invention. Now, Cody needs to call me, and I don't want any kind of conspiracy between you two boys. My nerves—"

"I'll call you tomorrow," he said. "Gotta run. Need to pee."

"You might have a bladder infection," she called after him. "From the friskadoro!"

"She's so sweet," Abigail said when he got back in. Ray started the engine.

"Sure is. She, ah, she has this way of poking fun at movies. She's old, so—"

"Left up here," Abigail said, letting him off the hook. "I told you my place is cardboard boxes and a futon, and I wasn't joking."

"You wanna just pop in while I make a few quick calls? Finish clearing the decks at the office and get a line on some beluga?"

"Sure. And what happened to your no-cell-phone rule?"

"Contract," he said. "Has a Colorado area code and everything."

When they pulled up in front of her apartment building, Abigail dashed in to get her travel bag. While she was gone, Ray scanned the area and then put one of his guns in the pouch on the back of the driver's seat and then got out to deal with the rifle. He opened the trunk and, after looking both ways, reached in and lifted the carpet flap, put the rifle under it, and closed the trunk. Abigail was there the instant he slammed it shut. He shot her a smile, and she held up her bag.

"Back seat with mine," he said. "It'd just roll around in the trunk. They made it for transporting pianos."

"I watered my plant," Abigail said as she buckled up. The streets were still close to empty as they headed downtown.

▶ BOP 'TIL YOU DROP, THE RAMONES

Ray had booked the rooms at the Kimpton for a few very good reasons. He had accounts there under various names associated with various businesses, none of them Gruben Media, so he would be hard to find in the eleven-floor maze. He also had the hotel memorized in a way that perhaps no one but the architect did. In that respect, the tactical advantage was his. The bathtubs in the penthouse suites were more like Jacuzzis. And Cody would be in the next room over, armed, as close as he could be without compromising his identity to any of the unknown players, while simultaneously keeping his cover with Abigail.

"Goodness me," Abigail said as they walked in. The penthouse suites were huge, with a sitting room full of antiques and original oils—more tasteful than valuable—and a small half bath just to the right of the door, in case the opulent master bath was occupied. Through frosted-glass sliding doors was the bedroom. The doors were open, so Ray followed Abigail through and smiled at her delight. The bed was oddly bigger than king size, the abnormal king jumbo reserved for high-end hotels and the gutty princes of Dubai. The floor-to-ceiling windows on the far wall were curtained. Abigail tossed her small bag on the bed, rushed to the windows, and threw the curtains open.

"Oh, Raymond, look."

He dropped his bag and went and stood by her, putting his arm around her. The storm was spectacular on the eleventh story, with swirling snow above and below. Lofting bigger flakes swirled briefly through the small envelope of stillness just outside the window. Abigail reached out and pressed her hand on the glass.

"You can almost feel the history of this window," she murmured.

"How's that?" He kissed the top of her head.

"It has witnessed so much change. It radiates it. If windows were minded things, Ray, what would this one tell me? A story of the transit of light and the shapes of temperature." She turned to him and gave him a curious look, as if she were trying to focus. He looked out the window, taken by her impression. His poker face held his frown in a vise.

The gray city below was a vast graveyard, the buildings tombstones of crumbling commerce, their interiors honeycombed with termites. The white snow, a perfect illusion, fell from the same sky that killed birds on summer nights. The geometric white flakes lofted down to the icy trash below, where the poor had been demoted to something lower and new and mean, generating a frenzied human heat that could in no way be differentiated from the zombie fiction of the day except in the profit projections of the ever-dropping bottom line.

"Hungry?" he asked.

"Starving!" Abigail ran her hand along his arm and stepped away from the window. Ray took one last look and then walked over to the minibar, which could be referred to as "mini" only in a very loose way. The glasses were real glass, and there was a wine selection. The room-service menus were front and center. He took them and joined Abigail on the edge of the bed. In the end, they looked at the one he opened, with Abigail holding her head next to his.

"Oysters," he suggested.

"Everything looks so good. Oysters and . . . mussels."

He looked at her. "And crab. And two lobsters."

"One lobster," she said and kissed him. "Unless you want to save one for a midnight snack."

"The bar has crackers," he murmured. "I could feed you lobster snacks in the bath."

"I can't imagine."

Ray called in the order while Abigail looked through the wine, presenting the bottles one at a time until he gave the thumbs-up to a chardonnay. She uncorked it and poured two glasses, handed him one, and took her boots off while he was on hold and then pulled his shoes off too. Then she lay back on the bed with her wine and stared at the ceiling, listening to him charm his way into a bowl of strawberries. When he was finally done, she sighed.

"Sounds like you have a plan with those strawberries, Ray," she said.

"I will be making that up as the evening progresses." He tried his wine, and then he got up and walked back to the window. "Guy might call tonight, so we might have to go to the airport."

"Work?"

"Yeah. I usually try to greet them and get them settled. Can't have Agnes out in this weather. If we have to go, I'm glad to have you as my wing lady."

"We're on. Agnes is so sweet."

"She is." Ray turned and looked at her, but Abigail didn't say anything more. Instead, she got up and went to the television.

"Has to be a radio station. Music?"

"Sure."

"I'll let you pick. You're the music buff."

He went over and picked up the remote. Abigail put their bags by the closet and hung up their jackets and then walked into the master bathroom.

"Did you see this bathtub?"

"I've seen it before. These are the same rooms we always get." He turned the TV on and looked at the guide. Abigail peeked out.

"You—never mind." She disappeared, and he heard the sink water turn on.

"I stayed in a hotel in Switzerland that had an elevated shower in the center of the bedroom," she called. Ray hit the channel for CNN.

"How'd that work out?"

"Strange. It was also round. Everything was round."

CNN was leading with Atlantic City. Massive fire at a charity event. More than a hundred injured, more than twenty unaccounted for, assumed to have been burned alive. The Orphan Foundation— long plagued with rumors of fraud and criminal conspiracy—was now embroiled in an underworld struggle that had escalated to horrific proportions. Images of old men in tuxedos sitting on the curb with oxygen masks, wild-haired and covered in soot, overdressed women with pearls and diamonds screaming hysterically, black smoke vomiting from the shattered windows in the background, dozens of ambulances and an armada of fire trucks.

Ray turned the TV off as Abigail emerged from the bathroom, wiping her hands on a towel.

"It was a work trip," she continued, "but we did go out to eat a few times. There was a wild mushroom restaurant. That's all they had."

"How was it?" Ray carried his wine over to the chair by the window. Abigail picked up her wine.

"Fantastic."

"There's a little place on the Washington coast that does the same thing during the mushroom harvest," he said casually.

"I've always wanted to see the Columbia River Gorge." She walked over and drew the drapes on the rest of the windows.

The reason Gordon wanted Atlantic City cleared—so almost two dozen incredibly rich people could be burned alive. Everyone still living was a smoke screen, he guessed. The real targets were smoking skeletons. Ray tried to think. Abigail sat down on the edge of the bed.

"Want to hear some neat stuff about Pasadena?"

"Sure." Creating a stillness in the underworld was useful when you were looking for out-of-town traffic. Gordon or the people he represented had been tracing a money trail.

"Next week at the Pasadena Civic Auditorium, they're hosting 'An Evening with Neil deGrasse Tyson.' We could attend the event, but the after party should be amazing. Most of the people I'd be working with will be there."

"Cool." Dropping local criminal traffic would alarm the federal monitors. The local players would fall under a microscope, allowing all kinds of activity that might otherwise be instantly flagged.

"The Pasadena Museum of California Art is what it is, but I understand there's a fantastic fish taco place right down the street. Dr. Cole, she's at the Institute, she eats there twice a week."

"I love fish tacos." Gordon created a vacuum to light a charity event on fire.

"And the Pasadena Playhouse—oh, Ray, it looks adorable. It was established in 1917. Adobe, with exceptional palm trees. You want to help me pick out a swimming suit?"

"I sure do." He smiled. CNN was already talking about allegations of corruption, and that meant that the story was already in a spin cycle at extreme altitude. Immolation was, in fact, a time-honored combat tactic among heavyweights and bantams both, but to do it publicly and on that kind of scale, with those targets. . . .

"Good. You know, there's also the Space Flight Operations Facility. They have tours, but I'm sure I can get us a private one. That sounds neat, to me anyway. But you have to pick some stuff too. We can't just do what I want to do."

"I will." He smiled and sipped his wine. "Maybe I'll call one of my contacts in the area and ask for recommendations, restaurant-wise." So Gordon must have been monitoring him for some time. Cooling Atlantic City was no small thing, and Manny Trujillo and his crew were key players right on the line in several places.

"What a view," Abigail said, touching the glass again.

"Something, isn't it?" He looked out too. Gordon knew what Mary Chapman's blackmail was about the entire time. He also knew that Ray could cash in some chips to create quite a crack in the nightworld for his operation to move in and out, without attracting the one kind of attention that would matter. No one cared if the Feds put you on a suspect list, especially not in Atlantic City. But criminals noticed everything, and they only made lists of dead people after a massive distortion like burning a charity event full of rich people. Gordon's operation had escaped the notice of the only people who mattered—the other criminals.

Abigail came and sat down in his lap and put her arms around his neck.

"I'm so glad about this California trip, Ray. I love the snow, but I think it will make the sunlight all the sweeter."

"You're absolutely right." If Ray was killed and the word got out, that crack would close within hours. Gordon's people wouldn't like that. "We have to rent a car for a day and hit this little place I know in Santa Monica. The best stuffed grape leaves on Earth."

The skater-kid killing machine in Thirtieth Street Station was Gordon's.

▶ MOTHER SKY. CAN

The airport could have been any kind of mess on a weeknight in a snowstorm, and Ray had seen them all: Panic with screaming children. Panic with screaming college kids. Panic with screaming drunk people was the most common, followed by blanket depression. It was rarely the empty, echoing abandoned sanitarium they walked into. Flights were coming in but not going out and cabs were running, so the place was drained of bodies. Good for limo drivers; bad, bad, bad for someone being stalked by a new set of killers.

"Do you know what this man looks like?" Abigail took his arm. "Maybe we should have made a sign."

"The memo gave me a typical Hollywood description," Ray said. He looked up at the nearest arrivals display. "Plane landed fifteen minutes ago, so he should be . . . ah, there he is." Abigail looked in the same direction. A small group of people were approaching a baggage carousel.

"Which one?"

"The giant black guy who looks like he ate the pilot and landed the plane himself." He nodded.

Cody's father—one of the many and varied lovers of Agnes Capsule—had been an extraordinarily huge black man she'd known for a single night of debauchery. Ray had tried to track him down a few years ago, but the trail stopped at a grave with no headstone outside of Houston, circa a long time ago. Agnes had raised Cody alone, though various men had pitched in along the way. Ray had met Cody when he was fifteen and still growing, a hungry, pissed-off young giant who smoked weed, loved Tupac, and had a volatile mixture of crime and Chaucer in his veins. They needed each other. After Cody had tried to kill him twice—once with a spear and a second time with a moving van—he'd become Ray's protégé.

They shook hands like strangers, so either Cody had gotten his message or the presence of Abigail had him in cover mode. Ray smiled up into his wide, beaming face.

"You must be Cody," Ray said. "No one else here fits your description."

"And you must be Ray," Cody rumbled, oozing charisma. He was wearing a black turtleneck, a knee-length orange rubber construction jacket, black jeans, and huge boots, so in many ways he looked the part of an exotic Hollywood dignitary. "They didn't tell me you'd be so . . . short."

"Do you have cameras coming in?"

"Traveling light," Cody replied. He looked at Abigail. "This cannot be Agnes Capsule."

"Abigail." They shook hands, and Cody couldn't help giving her a curiously piercing look.

"I've reserved a room for you at the Kimpton," Ray said. "It's one of the locations in the scouting file. Marble floors and brass fixtures, old Philadelphia charm. And it's close to many of the other things you'll need to see."

Cody hefted a single bag off the carousel, and they started walking.

"Fantastic. I could use a smoke. Would you two mind if I popped out for a quick one before the drive into the city?"

Ray and Abigail looked at each other.

"You both smoke," Abigail said. "Why don't I visit the women's room and join you both here after? And would anyone like coffee?"

"I'm good," Ray said pleasantly.

"I would absolutely love some," Cody said. "Lots of sugar." He bowed minutely and took Ray's arm as Abigail let go. "Ray and I will endeavor to keep cigarettes out of the hands of children by smoking them all. Sir?"

Ray glanced at Abigail as Cody pulled him toward the revolving doors and the snow and made a "yikes" face. Abigail stifled a laugh.

"Let's keep her in our line of sight," Ray said as they stepped out. "And when did you start smoking, Code? And what's up with the whole 'short' bullshit, you lobotomite? That's my fucking girlfriend."

They hugged and then turned and watched Abigail enter the women's restroom. Cody held his hand out and made a gimme motion.

"Smokes. I know you have Skuggy's menthols. I can smell them on you."

Ray fished the pack out and shook one loose. Cody took it, and Ray lipped one out for himself. They lit up, staying close to the glass so they were out of the wind.

"She's nice," Cody said. "I can feel it. You bring her 'cause of the shit-hitting-the-fan deal you left in the message?"

"Big time. Someone tried to kill me in Thirtieth Street Station. They were stopped by someone else, so six dead and we're looking for a skater kid or small Asian man, didn't get a good look. They shot my car when I went back to get Pepper. No way anyone followed me through this storm. But then again it didn't seem like anyone could trail me out of Chinatown to the station either, so I'm jumpy as fuck."

"Guns?"

"You sit in back when we get to the Caddy. Beretta's in the seat-back pouch. Rifle's in the trunk, so we'll get it into your bag and bring it into the Kimpton."

"Agnes?"

"Bed-and-breakfast with Pepper. She actually seems happy to be there. Gets on with the gay dudes. They're all playing canasta. Sort of like three months ago with the Jamaicans, except no Jamaicans."

"Skug?"

"Holed up in his pad. He's running the surveillance on Mary Chapman, and he doesn't want to leave. That crazy bitch met with Hardshell, of all people, so it looks like we have to do the same."

"That isn't good."

"No shit."

"So who the fuck am I supposed to be?"

"Cinematographer." Ray turned away from watching for Abigail, and Cody gave him an innocent look. "Code, do not, and I can't stress this enough, do not go escapee from the Island of Misfit Toys on this. If you start yammering about fractals in Bollywood or the underlying civil liberties for cetaceans found in the subtext of Norwegian cinema, she will swear-to-god bust us."

"Spoilsport," Cody rumbled, turning his attention back to the window. "So. Christmas."

Ray sighed. "I talked to your mom about it when I dropped off Pepper. She's not happy, man. Not happy. I'm not taking sides here, but try to put yourself in her shoes. She loves you, and here you are all fixated on this woman, and you're being secretive, Code. At least with her you are, and she can tell. This whole communication problem between you stems from your inability to accurately summarize your mother to strangers."

"You *are* taking sides, Ray! That's what taking sides sounds like, right there! Accurately summarize my mother! Listen to yourself! What am I supposed to say? 'Oh, baby, here's my itsy bitsy white mommy. She took enough hallucinogens to kill everyone in a square mile and she wants to whack Woody Allen, but no worries, she won't carry a gun, no, ma'am, and she looooves dogs.' Horseshit. It's too—"

"Code, a family therapist costs more than me just to suggest that you suck it up. You guys want to stay at my house, fine. But no fucking under my roof. How you like that?"

They stared at each other again and then turned back to the window.

"I can't believe I'm hearing this," Cody said eventually. "From you, the man with a thousand watches and a thousand hands."

"Believe it."

"Fine. We'll stay at the Kimpton."

"You great big bitchy dumbass. You wanna hurt both of our feelings? I was going to get you a new model train set for Christmas, but now I'm just going to get you a checkup at the dentist and new school pants."

"Fuck you."

Ray punched him on the arm. Cody turned on him and poked him in the center of his chest with his index finger. Ray got him into a wristlock, lightning fast. Cody bared his teeth and growled.

"Coffee for one," Abigail said, emerging through the revolving doors. Ray and Cody sprang apart, and Cody smiled warmly.

"Thank you so much, Abigail," he said, taking it. "Shall we? Ray was just giving me more details about the Kimpton. I frankly can't wait to have a drink at the bar and begin my tour there. Round out the evening with a nine-hour nap."

They started walking. Abigail took the arm Ray offered. Cody breathed deep and turned his face up to the sky. Snow swirled around them, and he was clearly happy about it.

"You miss the snow, Cody?" Abigail asked, smiling at the big man's evident pleasure.

"So much," Cody replied. "I was on a shoot in Norway a few years ago. Haven't seen it since. I'm just glad my plane made it in."

"Philadelphia isn't all that good at letting planes out in this weather," Ray explained, "but incoming flights are full of potential targets. Everyone from the Mayor to the mafia wants as much fresh meat as they can get."

"Raymond!" Abigail scolded. Cody laughed.

"I've been here before. He's unfortunately correct, but you can't beat the place when you need to film a horror movie for under thirty million and you need it to look big. Apocalypse budgets are rock bottom here."

They got to the Cadillac, and Ray unlocked the passenger door.

"If it's okay with you two, I'll sit in back," Cody said. "Best if I sit sideways, whole back of this toboggan to myself."

"If you insist," Abigail said easily. "It's a good thing Ray drove this today. What did you call it? Your sled?"

"I did." He kissed her and closed the door when she was in and then turned to Cody.

"Let's put your bag in the trunk," Ray suggested. They walked to the back and Cody briefly inspected the small bullet holes. He gave Ray a confused look, as if to say this should be questioned and pondered at great length. Ray shrugged with his eyebrows and opened the trunk. Cody looked both ways while Ray swept the carpet aside, and together they looked at the rifle.

"See if you can fit it in your bag," Ray suggested softly. Cody unzipped his bag and put the rifle in. It barely fit.

"How many rounds?"

"Ten. No spares."

"I'll get more tomorrow."

"Good." He reached under the lip of the trunk lid and pulled out a spoke. Cody took it and it vanished up his sleeve. Ray slammed the trunk and handed him the room key for the suite next to his.

"It's good to be back, Ray," Cody said quietly. "Think they'll recognize me at the Kimpton?"

"My guess is yes, even though your hair is normal. Go to the bar when we get there, and come up in the next elevator. Twenty-second lead."

"Check."

The ride to the Kimpton was uneventful. The storm had lessened, but traffic was still light enough to make them hard to tail. Ray still took random advantage of every sudden gust to change direction, claiming the big car was struggling for traction. Cody napped, appearing tired but actually avoiding conversation with the incredibly intelligent Abigail. So it was quiet.

Since the car was drained of guns, Ray used valet parking. Cody stretched after he got his bag out of the trunk and waited with Abigail while Ray got his ticket.

"I'm going to check out the bar and get that drink," Cody said. "Food's good?"

"You bet," Ray replied. "Feel free to call me or Agnes at any time."

They shook hands, and Cody went in and took an immediate left into Casey's. Ray held his arm out for Abigail and she took it, and together they strolled in to the elevators. As they stepped in, Ray glanced sideways and just caught sight of Cody exiting the bar to follow. He smiled at Abigail and pressed eleven.

"He's nice," Abigail said.

"I really like him," Ray agreed honestly. "We might see more of him over the weekend. He'll be visiting some of the same spots we are."

Back in the room, they took their coats and shoes off and Ray poured them drinks. The leftover lobster and strawberries from dinner were in the mini-fridge. Abigail rubbed her hands together and tossed her thumb at the bathroom, wiggled her eyebrows. Ray nodded, and she went in and ran the bath. He went to the window and looked out.

Cody would be set up in moments, with the rifle pointed at the wall, ready to fire ten rounds through it at chest height in one-foot intervals. He sipped and abruptly caught sight of his reflection— worried, when his poker face wasn't in play. He tried to relax.

"So tomorrow, you have anything in mind yet? Or do we stay in bed all day and . . . stay in bed all day?" Abigail asked.

"There's a beautiful place I'd like to take you to in the morning," Ray said, turning. "Out toward the bird sanctuary. Fantastic little place for brunch, if you're up for it."

"Good." She sat down on the edge of the bed, and Ray joined her.

"Maybe we should invite Cody along for brunch," she suggested. Ray shook his head.

"We'd just talk shop. No, me and you, the open road, maybe ice-skating, maybe a little making out at this amusement park, if the Ferris wheel is running and it isn't too windy."

"Ohh." She made her eyes round.

"And you, little miss, need a fuzzy hat of some kind."

"The bathtub fills on turbo."

"Race to naked." He stood up and tore his shirt off, buttons and all.

"Cheater!" Abigail crowed, struggling with her pants.

Ray stripped as he went, tossing clothes to either side. Abigail hopped after him and then sat on the floor, rolled up and back and shucked her pants and underwear in one fluid move, all part of a sudden dance.

"Raymond!" she called. He paused in the bathroom doorway and looked back. She pulled her shirt and sweater off and looked down at her side. "What . . ." She put her pale hands on her side and peered down at something. "Tell me this is a mole."

He took two steps in her direction and stopped. Abigail came at him slowly, still looking down at her side.

"Better look," she breathed.

"You just can't stand the thought of losing," he said. She grinned and bolted around him.

"No empirical evidence to that point," she cried. He heard a splash. "To establish that, we have to do more than project my estimated reaction to such an unlikely scenario. Hypothesizing just won't do."

Ray poured a glass of scotch at the deluxe minibar and went into the bathroom. Abigail was in the bubbly water facing him, her face already wet, eyes shining. He set his glass down within easy reach of her, and she instantly picked it up.

"You cheat to get in the bubble bath and then you steal my drink," he said, easing into the hot water. "How, pray tell, does that affect your chances of getting into heaven, Doctor?"

"Depends," she said, sipping and smiling mischievously, "on the outcome."

"So the outcome factors into the judgment? Since when?"

"Since always," she said, swishing toward him. She slowly spun around and settled into his arms.

"I know what you're thinking," he said eventually.

"I usually have a great deal going on in my mind, Ray."

"You do—your pursuit of the perfect string of perfect moments, the blessed mind that will stand out like a gem made of blue starlight on an endless beach of black sand." He whispered in her ear: "But right now, Doctor, I can read your thoughts."

She closed her eyes. "Do tell."

"You're wondering if the conditioner at the Kimpton is the good stuff."

She took a deep breath through her nose.

"And you're wondering what it will take to get a foot massage out of me."

She smiled and made a little noise.

"And now that I've suggested it, you're wondering if I'll be any good at it."

"You're gifted at touching me, Raymond. I have every faith in you."

"C'mon, then," he urged. "Feet first, then your hair."

Abigail spun around in the water and slid to the far side and then presented her foot. Ray took it and began massaging it. She sipped the scotch and closed her eyes.

"I was thinking about our trip to California," she said softly. "It seems like an especially good sign, picking up Cody tonight."

"Think so?"

"A cinematographer from LA? We're going to have such a beautiful trip. Sun, the pool at the hotel. Even this hotel is a good sign. Total godsend—just fell in your lap."

Cody had flown in from Boston, where they were enduring blizzard conditions moments after his connecting flight made it out.

They were staying at the Kimpton because someone was trying to kill him—possibly two different groups of people at this point, in fact. And it was entirely possible that someone had been close enough to him since it all started to know about Abigail and take her hostage, maybe torture her to get him to do whatever they wanted, to tell them anything.

"Abby, this vision of the future you have. When the physicists of a hundred years from now find all of the souls ever born and bring them back—what happens then?"

"You mean the afterlife?"

"Sure, I guess. You never gave me the big picture."

"Difficult to speculate, like I was saying the other day. The upward limit of information, of 'soul' in this context, that you can fit into a single proton might be infinite."

"Meaning?"

"Meaning a trillion trillions of souls might fit on the head of a pin."

"Your number pi again."

"Pasadena. It all fits together. We're cut from the same cloth, though, Raymond. I can feel it. We'll find each other, no matter what the afterlife in a single proton looks like. I'm more sure of it than I've ever been about anything."

▶ SAD ABOUT GIRLS. ELVIS COSTELLO

After they got out of the bath, they made love until Abigail had a seizure. Her eyes fluttered and she convulsed, and Ray worried that he might have hurt her somehow. But when she finally looked into his eyes, it was like looking into the eyes of an alien thing—beyond the world of grass and rain and rocks, far into something that for a moment transformed his own eyes—and, locked like that, they held each other until her shuddering subsided and her eyelids closed.

Ray stared at her face for a long time. Abigail's breathing gradually returned to normal. He realized that he was experiencing something like fear, a fear that she might speak and that it would be in a voice he had never heard before. When he knew she was finally asleep, he untangled himself from her embrace and rose. He was covered in sweat, and all his old scars stood white against his hard, sun-blasted frame. He looked at his body until he realized his mouth was too dry to swallow and then went to the minibar and took out both the vodkas, draining them one at a time. Then he went to the window and stood naked, looking out at the storm-swept city. After a moment, he put both hands out, pressed them on the freezing glass, and closed his eyes.

Something had just happened to him that had never happened before. He opened his eyes and looked to the side. Then he looked up through the window at the black sky, alive with fluttering white as the snow entered the small halo of light spilling out around him. He didn't really think so much as feel the moment, the echo of it. He stared up for a long, long time. Then he took another small bottle from the minibar and picked up his phone and carried them both into the sitting room and closed the sliding door. Cody answered on the first ring.

"Trouble?"

"Nah." Ray sat and opened the little bottle. "Nah."

"So the doctor's asleep? What the hell were you guys doing in there?"

"Why?"

"Ray, I'm sitting here with the rifle pointed at the wall. I made a tripod out of a freestanding lamp and the courtesy ironing board. But that, ah. . . . She's noisy, yo. The walls were shaking."

"I can't talk. But I need you to call Skug and say hi. He missed you."

"Jesus."

"Yeah. And tell him to set up a meeting for me with Hardshell. Tomorrow. Skug is to tell him that Deadbomb Bingo Ray has sixty million reasons to listen for five minutes. You get your ride out of storage first thing in the morning and tail me with additional guns."

"When and where?"

Ray told him.

II

CHAPTER NINETEEN

In the morning, Ray woke up to the faint sound of Abigail singing to herself in the shower. The sun was bright around the edges of the curtains, and he could smell coffee from the little service in the sitting room. He sat up and listened. Too soft to make out the words, or even the melody. He'd stayed at the Kimpton more than a hundred times, but he'd never before woken up in this way. He glanced at the clock. A little after seven on a Saturday morning, and she was singing.

He got up and walked naked to the window, pulled the curtains, and immediately shielded his eyes. Gradually, he lowered his hand. The sun was out, and below him the city was white, cut with a grid of black roads. His eyes rose, and he squinted into the pulsing blue horizon—motionless, calculating the odds, seeing a thousand futures, mapping the avenues of change.

"Beautiful," Abigail murmured behind him. He turned.

"I've been watching you," she continued. "I don't think I've ever seen anyone stand so still inside of a thought." She smiled. "I understand something about statues now. The better ones don't strive to capture the beauty of the body so much as the soul of transiting emotion. You were thinking about numbers."

Ray smiled and nodded. "You have a lovely singing voice. Good morning, Abigail."

She smiled and stepped closer, touching the belt of her robe. He held up his hand.

"Do not remove that robe, Doctor. The first part of the dream begins. But you will soon be naked, never fear."

While she was dressing, he carried his phone into the sitting room and called Cody.

"Yo, Ray," he answered. "She in earshot?"

"Gruben Media. I'm calling to confirm a reservation. I made it late last night. Spur of the moment, I know."

"My boy Todd got my ride, and it's parked across the street. Got all the ammo we need for the zombie apocalypse and an NRA free pork-and-donut sampler combined. Did I just say that? Coffee. Your meeting with Hardshell is at nine. I'll follow you and set up with the rifle a hundred yards out."

"Fantastic," Ray said.

"Good. When you guys heading out?"

"Soon."

"Text me two minutes before and I'll go first, make sure your walk is clear."

"Thank you." Ray hung up. "Abby! You're going to love this."

"Are you going to get dressed?" She appeared in the doorway.

"I am." He got up and stretched. "First this place—you won't even believe it—and then brunch. We'll be good and hungry." He walked past and playfully swatted her butt on his way into the bathroom.

▶ SAIUN. YOSHIDA BROTHERS

"Behold, the Katenkoi," Ray said expansively. "It's a spa run by the Mohegan Indian tribe. They've made some serious casino bank and done some really interesting stuff with it. Scouted it about a month ago."

"I've never actually been to a spa," Abigail said, studying the building. It was a sprawling structure made of bone-colored birch and glass, seamed with ribbons of coppery metal, and surrounded by forest. "Exactly what do we do?"

"In this case, we check in and shower. I've reserved a private heated pool." He sighed. "It might not be your kind of thing, actually. We have to sit in the steaming water, surrounded by snow, ice sculptures, the winter gardens, that kind of thing. Once you get really hot, you're supposed to roll in the pristine snow and ponder the statuary, then reimmerse yourself, repeat. It's cleansing and spiritually invigorating and blah blah blah."

"It's a temple," Abigail murmured. She turned to him and cocked her head, looking through him as she sometimes did.

"Our pool, I'm told, is a glacial shade of blue," he continued. "Color 304. So maybe we can rename it while we're here."

She gasped. "I don't have a swimsuit!"

"Me neither. I told you naked was involved." He looked back at the lodge. "Naked is the rule."

They got out and walked in. Cody had pulled in and parked as they did, but he hung back in the parking lot as Ray and Abigail approached the front desk. The lobby was spare and elegant and almost Oriental, except for the long, ornately painted canoe hanging from the ceiling and the traditional recurve bows on the walls. The attendant was a small Indian woman in a black business suit. She didn't smile as they approached.

"Welcome to the Katenkoi." She bowed.

"Gruben Media, party of two."

"Men's dressing rooms to the left." She gestured. "Women to the right. You may disrobe and shower and store your possessions in any of the lockers. Robes and towels are available from the attendant. Then please proceed from there as directed to your private pool, the Dawn Glacier. If you require anything at any time, simply ring the bell or notify one of the attendants."

Ray turned to Abigail. "Meet you outside in ten."

Abigail nodded and went into the women's dressing room. Ray looked back at the attendant, and they stared at each other with dead eyes. She gestured for him to proceed and then took a step back, lowering her head.

Ray went through the arched wooden doors into the men's changing area. As he did, he removed the loose razor from his jacket pocket and put it in his mouth, gently adjusted it with his tongue. He could carry on a conversation, run, even yell with it hidden along the side of his mouth, and Cody could too. They had both learned the hard way that only singing was not possible. The lockers were more like small closets, and there was a long bench hewn from a single log down the center. A lone attendant in a black suit stood by the door, and an old man with a towel around his waist sat in the center of the wooden bench, staring straight forward at nothing at all. As Ray approached, the old man glanced up at him. The attendant vanished without a word.

"Mr. Ray," the old man said in a raspy voice. "Disrobe." He pointed at one of the big lockers. "Your clothing and all of your items will be locked in here. Don't try to open it until your talk is concluded. When Mr. Hardshell is safely away from the premises, you will be discreetly notified. At that time, you may dress and leave. Do you understand?"

"Yeah." Ray sat down and took his shoes off. "Pretty tight. Hardshell have all of his meetings like this? You guys afraid of bugs?"

"No," the old man replied. "This exceptional caution is just for you, Mr. Ray."

Ray opened the closet door and slowly took his gun out, showing it to the old man as he put it on the top shelf. Then he removed a sharpened spoke from each sleeve and sat them next to it. He took all of his clothes off then and carefully hung them up and closed the door, and then he faced the old man, naked.

"Arms out, please," the old man directed. Ray complied.

"Slowly turn." Ray did. Once he'd done a full 360, he lowered his arms.

"Go on to the showers," the old man continued. "Make no sudden movements. Do not approach Mr. Hardshell unless you are instructed to, and then maintain a minimum distance of ten feet."

"You got it," Ray said easily. "Anyone touches my stuff—even breathes on it, even looks at it—and *you're* the one who dies. You better be sitting right where you are when I get back."

The old man nodded.

Ray walked down the short marble hallway to the showering area. The light was dim and diffused, the floor a glossy black. Steam curled from various pedestals and vents, and the walls were lined with large brass showerheads, spaced five feet apart. The room was empty except for Hardshell, who stood under a blast of steaming water on the far side of the room. His long hair was down, his face upturned, his giant, scarred body motionless.

Ray walked over and immediately violated the ten-foot rule by standing under the next showerhead over. Hardshell raised his hand to the two armed guards who appeared out of the steamy gloom behind them. Ray reached into his mouth and pulled out the razor and thunked it into the wood between them. Hardshell turned and looked down at him, giving him an expressionless stare.

"Deadbomb Bingo Ray," Hardshell said.

His voice was deep to the point of being comparable to the opening chord of a black metal song about elephants, punctuated by sharp, inhuman crackles of diction that exploded from his huge, dark mouth like exploding beer bottles. He turned his face back into the water. Ray turned his showerhead on.

"Sniper outside," Ray said casually. "I can probably murder my way out into his kill zone, starting with you, but I brought my girlfriend, so let's keep this clean."

"Sixty million reasons to talk to you," Hardshell intoned. He didn't seem perturbed in any way. More sleepy. "You're talking about Tim Cantwell. The deal we have going with him. We were approached by a woman calling herself Mary Chapman ten days ago. She claims to have an evidence trail implicating the Cantwell Fund in fraud, and she also claims she can present it to us for a finder's fee."

"What's her price?"

"One million dollars and a pass. The money, of course, we will give her. The pass, of course, we will not."

Ray let the water run through his hair. There was a bottle of soap on the shelf. He took it and sniffed. Lavender.

"Two and I give you the proof she's talking about, plus I give you Tim in person and kill his entire personnel roster, get your money back, and remove the woman calling herself Mary Chapman."

Hardshell turned his water off and walked over to the nearest cedar bench. Ray followed, and they both wrapped towels around their waists and sat. The Mohegan looked into the darkness, still without expression. Eventually, he started talking, in a slow, patient way, like he was talking to himself, as if his enormous rib cage was bent and painful and old.

"The madness with the tulips. That's when we first knew about you."

Ray said nothing.

"Five years ago now. May." He gestured with one hand. "Movement in the birds. The spring was so slow to come that year. My nephew, he won the lottery and wrecked his car. Roads in Connecticut. There was a man we did business with, a little Arab, Persian—I get them confused. His name was Ahmed. Slave of God."

Ray's poker face was granite.

"Slave of God moved things for the Wolf People. Sometimes in a truck or a bus. This time it was in a limousine. He was to transport the most expensive kind of woman. An escort, they call these intelligent whores. Blond. With the blue eyes. Slave of God was doing just this for the People that May. That May, when we hear about this Deadbomb Bingo Ray." He chuckled at his rhyme. A long moment passed. Hardshell didn't look at him. His eyes were staring through the darkness at the razor stuck in the wall.

"This woman, she had seen something. Something terrible and peculiar. And someone wanted to talk to her—many people—to learn what she had learned, and to make sure this secret stayed secret. We knew this. Slave of God leaves this city with her to drive her to New York, where she can make her case—maybe trade for her life, maybe not. But he does not arrive with her. No, this little man arrives with a single tulip bulb instead. The woman, she is gone, never to be seen again. The secret she was not trusted to keep was dark, so dark. The secret of a man who has many such secrets. He is a student of economics, and his favorite metaphor is the Dutch tulip. The fictional worth of all things in the marketplace."

Hardshell paused again, this time to rub his face with one fleshy, arthritic hand.

"So she was taken by someone who knew of him, who knew his secret, maybe all of his secrets. Someone who was able to find out so much, to read the cards, to deliver a message and with it an intimate kind of fear. And we took note. It was a man who is said to be death himself, a man who is never to be crossed, a man with a thousand watches and a thousand hands, with a black giant and an ancient clockwork bokor with the hand of the monkey.

"Then the United situation, with the fighting dogs and the parrots, the Night of the Burning Parrots. . . ." He chuckled again and shook his head. "Whispers. Whispers of this name again. Deadbomb Bingo Ray." Hardshell paused for a long moment before he continued. He finally looked at Ray, his eyes empty of anything remotely primate.

"With the two million, you will leave Philadelphia."

"Why?"

"Atlantic City," he rumbled. "You touched what happened there. Now this. The Feds are the least of your problems, Mr. Ray. The lawyer you did this favor for, when you cleared the path for his client, well . . . it is there that your troubles will come from. You will do this for us and then you will go on hiatus, until any trail leading back to you—and potentially to us as a result—becomes a trail lost in time. You already suspect this, Mr. Ray. I am merely confirming it. The underworld of crime has layers. Creatures larger than us were fighting in Atlantic City. They will come for you once the burned skeletons have been buried."

Ray rose. "I'll be in touch."

"Tim Cantwell." Hardshell rose as well and slowly headed for the dressing room. "He will be alive when he's delivered. Alive and unharmed before our questioning begins and the punishment for his crime commences."

Ray plucked a robe off a hook and picked up an extra towel, went past a row of slippers without stopping, and stepped outside into the blinding white. It was still bright and cold, and clouds were moving in with the promise of more snow. He surveyed the winter garden.

The three acres were unsheltered, with cleared wooden walkways winding through enormous clay pots, stone daises with burning braziers, frozen fountains, and unusual cubist ice sculptures. The private pools were enclosed in living bamboo and cedar. He followed the discreet signs to the Dawn Glacier pool and opened the gate. Abigail was inside, kneeling over the calm, steaming surface and running her hand through the water. She was wearing a large robe like his and thick slippers, with a towel wrapped around her head and another in her free hand. She looked up at the sound of the latch.

"This place is amazing," she said quietly. Ray took his robe off and hung it on a hook and then stepped into the water and descended the submerged stairs until only his head was sticking out.

"The bottom of the pool is incredibly hot," he reported.

Abigail disrobed and walked in and then glided over to him. Her hair was still wet from the showers.

"So we float and swim and look at the snow and the clouds, until our cores are so hot that rolling in the snow feels good," she said slowly. She arched onto her back and stared at the sky. "I find you acceptably romantic once again, Raymond."

"Hmm."

"It's moments like this"—Abigail backstroked and looked up through the steam with wide eyes—"this kind of beauty in memory, in action, that blesses. This instant and those like it, Raymond, entangled with passions. . . . In the great reckoning to come, when all the minds in all the past are laid bare, it will be to the final garden that the souls of our greatest pioneers go, and our champions of humanity, our thinkers who created cathedrals in their minds."

Ray watched her swim, as beautiful and elegant as a mermaid. When he was a little boy, his mother had once told him that he'd eaten his twin in the womb—absorbed and consumed him—which is why he'd been born with a second set of teeth. He wondered briefly about the soul of that creature.

"When you talk like this, Abby, about your vision of the future of science, it moves me to consider things in a new light."

"I'm glad," she said softly. "I'm glad for you, Raymond. You make me feel and understand how lonely I was before I met you. It's like we come from the same place, yet neither of us knows where that is. Kindred spirits on a journey with no beginning and no end. Have you read much about quantum entanglement?"

"I have not." He leaned back and floated, looking up as she was.

"Einstein called it 'spooky action at a distance.' In quantum physics, an unobserved photon exists in all possible states simultaneously; but when observed and measured, the same photon exhibits only one state. Observation has this effect on it."

"Interesting. And this relates to memory how?"

"The quanta in the water molecules in our minds. Our soul particle building blocks. If you remove them from each other, they stay what's called 'entangled' and interact over great distances at more than ten thousand times the speed of light, maybe even instantaneously."

Ray thought about it. "So two particles remain intimately connected."

"Through space and time, yes."

He considered. If this was true, then the physicists of Abigail's tomorrow had already cracked open his mind and knew his past, his present, and his future. It was almost depressing, or would have been if anyone had made the mistake of telling him the sum total of what they'd found and spoiling it all.

"Good for them," he said eventually.

"Who, darling?"

"Your panel of judges, or whatever you like to call them. They have a wonderful appreciation of privacy."

Abigail sighed and approached him. He was erect as she settled into his arms. Her eyes had taken on the same shade of blue as the deepest part of the pool.

"Knowledge is the wing wherewith we fly to heaven," she whispered into his mouth. "It's a quote I think about." She settled onto him and closed her eyes. "I think it means more than I'd previously considered."

He thought about last night as they began to move.

"Abby, the company I work for . . . I told them about Pasadena."

She opened her eyes.

"This place, where we are right now, it's one of the reasons I'm in such high demand. Here is this cursed city, with all of its filth and despair and sadness, in this place where all the dreams have tricked away and left a shell full of the mad and the desperate. I can still find places just like this."

"I can't wait to leave," she admitted. "My grant has run its course. What are you saying?"

"They want me to broaden my horizon to include the rest of the world. It's almost like I don't have a choice. We can leave whenever."

Her embrace became crushing as she pressed as much of herself into him as possible. At that moment, it was the most physical contact he had ever had with another since birth.

"Your house," she breathed.

"I'll rent it out. Even that Cody would love it, and he has to be here for months and months, maybe years. Maybe I'll sell it."

"I'm a scientist with a suitcase," she said, maybe just realizing it. She drew back and looked into his eyes. "I'm a woman with a suitcase. And even the suitcase has wheels."

"I'll keep Agnes on to run the home office. Or she can finally retire and follow her director around."

Abigail closed her eyes again. "I just have Anton. And my houseplant."

It was Ray's turn to close his eyes. They thrashed and floated, and after a time they left the pool and frolicked naked in the snow until they were both red, their breath coming in thick white plumes. And then it was back into the now-scalding water and then into the snow again. After their third immersion, there was a gentle rap on the gate. They disengaged and floated apart.

"Enter," Ray called.

The gate opened, and a small Mohegan woman dressed in white entered with tea and ice water and glasses on a tray. She gave Ray a private nod indicating that Hardshell was clear of the lodge, and then she departed with a bow. Abigail floated over and poured herself a glass of water and drank thirstily.

"Brunch?" he suggested.

"Starving," she replied. "What a glorious morning. I can't believe it, but I might need a nap after that."

"We have the suite all weekend. Brunch followed by nap time for you. Maybe I'll pop out and check on Agnes and pick up a few things to go with dinner. And then . . . another little surprise."

▶ STONES. NEIL DIAMOND

After brunch, they returned to the Kimpton, followed by Cody, who did an excellent job of signaling that no one was following but him.

Cody's preferred ride was a 2007 Land Rover, white with tinted windows. Ray thought it was too flashy, so at some point Cody put a Garth Brooks bumper sticker on it, shooting for bland, noncriminal dumbass in advertising. It worked much like the Dave Matthews sticker on Ray's Batmobile.

Abigail went to the bed and sat down, sleepy and content. Ray pulled off her boots, took her coat, and then dragged her to the center of the big bed and wrapped her up.

"I'll be back in an hour," he whispered.

"I'll be right here," she murmured. She stretched, and her curling toes peeked out. "What are you going to go get?"

"Couple quick things. One little stop to make."

He left quietly and went next door and knocked. There was a click, and then Cody appeared and motioned him inside.

"I'm going out for about an hour," Ray said. "Keep an eye on Abigail for me."

"Done." Cody flopped back on the bed. His suite was almost identical, except he'd transferred in three rifles with tripods. All were pointed at Ray's room. An Airweight was on the bed next to him, and there was a sawed-off on top of the minibar. "How was the meet?"

"Fine." Ray helped himself to a drink.

"Hardshell want the standard package?"

"I offered it. Clean up our mutual mess. The size of his end of this fiasco is way bigger, so he's coughing up."

"Good. That place all creepy, or what?"

"Nah. It was nice, actually. We went swimming."

Cody was watching the television with the sound off. It didn't seem like he wanted to hear the details, so Ray finished his drink.

"Need anything?" Ray asked. "Smokes, that kind of thing?"

"Enough with the cigarettes, Ray. Get out."

On the drive to Anton Brown's, Ray stopped to pick up a six-pack of beer and a pizza. It was still nice out, so he smoked in front of the place while he waited for his order to be ready. Then he carried it all out and put it in the trunk. He put a surprise in the pizza box and then drove leisurely, thinking. There was a small mall off Liberty Plaza with a women's clothing store. On the way back, it would be easy enough to pop in and pick up a coat and matching hat for Abigail.

Anton's car was parked out front when he pulled up. He'd spent hours following that car. It was nice to know that, one way or another, he'd never feel compelled to trail the hedge-fund scumbag turned bank robber turned accountant again. All the nights of watching Anton circle in confusion, torn between Chinese takeout and a cheesesteak, his slow cruising through Kensington while trolling for underage junkies, watching through the windows as he went up and down the aisles of Drugmart, in search of just the right acne cream. It was over.

▶ MIDNIGHT SPECIAL. LEAD BELLY AND WOODY GUTHRIE

Ray knocked on Anton's door, the six-pack of beer under his arm and the pizza in his other hand. He heard the approach of feet and then a muffled curse as Anton peeked out at him, followed by the sound of the worthless chain and the ineffective locks, all three of them. Anton opened the door a few inches and presented his incredulous best.

"Mr. Ray? What the . . . what the hell are you doing—" Then he saw the pizza.

"I wanted to ask you something about Abby."

Anton's eyes narrowed. "Doctor Abelard?"

"Got beer too." Ray shifted, and Anton's eyes flicked to the six-pack and back. Grudgingly, he opened the door.

"Place is a mess," he said, gesturing. "Wasn't expecting company." Anton walked a few steps in and then turned back. "How'd you know where I live?"

"Abby told me."

He nodded, but Ray could sense the shift from powerful irritation to paranoia. While Anton considered his next move, Ray stepped in and gently kicked the door closed with his heel. Anton's eyes widened a little.

"Nice place," Ray said. It was just as he remembered, spare and on the dirty side. The coffee table was cluttered with beer bottles and the takeout Anton had been eating for lunch. Chinese.

"Yeah. Well." Anton shrugged and crossed his beefy arms. "So, like, what?"

Ray handed him the pizza. Anton paused before he took it, but he did. Ray set the beer down on the edge of the coffee table and took one out, twisted off the cap, and handed it to him. Anton took it. Then Ray opened one for himself and they stood there, two men with beers. Ray gestured with his.

"So, how long you know Abby?"

"Why?"

"C'mon, man," Ray said smoothly. "Let's be friends here."

Anton looked surly, but he went to the bare dining-room table and set the pizza down. Ray sat in the only chair and waited until Anton sat back down on the couch in front of the cold Chinese food.

"I don't like talking about work," Anton said flatly.

"Me neither," Ray said easily. "But I have this thing, dude. Abby. I'm totally falling for her, but . . . what do you know about me?"

"Some kind of media dip—guy." Anton leaned back, hostility taking the emotional foreground again. "Fuckin' talks about you all the time. Can't be good for her work."

"Good to know," Ray said, nodding. "I can appreciate that. I really can. She tell you anything else about what I do?"

"No." Suspicion again. "Why?"

"I'm"—Ray looked away from him and gestured expansively with his beer bottle—"a researcher too. Nothing like Abby's work with the quantum elements of memory and the potential resurrection of it in the future. But I do sort of work with the soul, Anton. I research people. I read them like other people read traffic signs." He looked back at Anton. "I do it all day long."

"So you're like, an investigator?" Fear entered his eyes.

"Sometimes, Anton."

"Holy shit." Anton's pulse went into his temples in a visible way. "Holy shit." He gave Ray an astonished look. "So Doctor Abelard is under investigation?"

"No, Anton," Ray said. He shifted a little for easy access to his guns. "You are."

Anton went blank. Something just turned off in his mind, and Ray could see the bottom fall out. It was the look in an animal's eyes when it was being eaten, when it knew there was no escape. Ray snapped his fingers, and Anton's eyes flicked to his hand out of reflex. Ray made a kissing sound next, to draw Anton's eyes to his face.

"I know you crewed with Tim Cantwell. I know you went sort of crazy there at the end, when the federal heat came down. And I know that in the long crazy after it, you started robbing banks."

Anton registered that. His mouth opened a little, and a tic erupted under one eye.

"All those banks, Anton. Jesus. And then you just stopped. Boom!" Ray snapped his fingers again. "And then you start working as an accountant? An accountant, Anton? Who in the world is supposed to believe that?"

Ray waited. Anton eventually looked at his beer, and after he'd stared at it for a minute, he took a shuddering breath and looked up at Ray with tears in his eyes.

"Aw, man," he said in a hoarse voice. "Aw, man, you don't know. You don't know."

"Tell me."

"God." Anton's eyes went distant. He started talking in slow, measured tones, as though he'd never told the story before, even to himself. It had an eerie, out-of-place-revelation quality to it—a strange, sad sermon told in a grocery store. Ray listened without moving.

"We were shuffling money from one hedge fund to another, night and day. The nugget was an even mil, but we had to shift it constantly, in a triple rotation that ran in so many directions only Tim could keep track of it. Maybe that's the way it had to work. Maybe he didn't even know himself sometimes. . . . All the coke, so crazy, so fucking nuts, and the charts and the fake records. . . . We stole millions, man. Millions. Pension funds, everything. Everyone we touched went down. And . . . and . . . and I could see it all for what it really was—one enormous, colossal illusion, like mirrors that went on forever. And everyone was doing the same thing. Fannie Mae and Freddie Mac were running scams just like it into the billions, but no way anyone could stop that, so the Feds started to look around for . . . us. Us. People just like us. Doing what everyone was doing. Stealing with all the right papers."

He stopped talking and stared at the nightmare of those days. His face was a mess of conflicting greed and guilt, remorse and triumph, a morphing schizophrenic mask that hurt to look at. Eventually, he continued.

"When I made it out, I . . . I didn't have a life. I was dead. All I had was this place. This couch and this fucking coffee table. All that money went through my hands, and all I had was . . . nothing."

He went silent as he considered the transition, when he went from semi-legal to stone-cold scumbag. Ray watched Anton's pussy rationalization form, the lie about what he really was, and he almost smiled.

"That first bank, I just drove past it and I thought 'That's my money in there.' Just like that. So I watched it for an hour, and then I went in and handed the teller a note. Little Asian lady. Note said I had her family, that I'd let them go in an hour, that she needed to empty her till for me. And she did, just like that. Didn't even blink."

Anton took another deep breath. The memory brought some kind of life back into him. Ray watched, unblinking.

"Then I went bigger next time. Robbed the entire bank, and I was hooked. It seemed so clean after Tim's . . . after Tim. Clean, fast.

Quick! I was in and out. But . . . but . . . that time wasn't so smooth, 'cause I almost got busted. But I had it then. I'd been in and out. And I know banks. I have an associate's in accounting, so I know. I know."

He sat back like he'd been punched. Without thinking, he drained his beer.

"But someone else knew too. Fuck!" He finally looked at Ray. "I got ripped off! Fuck! Fuck! Fuck!" He got up and started pacing. "First it starts small. I had ten grand in the closet. I come home, and I know someone's been in here. I go and look, and the money's been moved. Oh my God, I counted it ten times, all fucking night long. One twenty-dollar bill was gone."

He was lost then, deep in the memory of the change in the quality of his sanity.

"I don't know. I don't know. I don't know, I thought maybe the tellers had stolen one of the bills, or maybe I was sleepwalking, like I used one of the bills for toilet paper in a nightmare. But then a week later it was all gone! All of it!"

He stood up and picked up the pace.

"I hid it in different places, all over the house, so I thought I was losing it. I moved it so many times, I think I thought I'd lost it. Week goes by, maybe two, and then I hit the Savings and Loan. Sixty grand, just like that. Ohhh." He looked up and the glory was back for an instant. "It felt so good! I was safe! I put the money under my bed. Can't get it from under me when I'm sleeping."

He spun and wheeled, lecturing now.

"I found this dog in the park. Mosey, I called her. Little Pomeranian. I gave her beer. Yappy piece of shit was the profiling tool I needed, 'cause no one stops a guy out walking his girlfriend's dog. Nah, fuck that guy. He's whipped. He's cool. So I make my biggest run. Stole five cars and set them all up. Went in and took that bank down like a motherfucker, two hundred large. Cops are combing a five-mile radius, copters over the freeways, and I'm sitting in a fucking Burger King a mile away. Different car, different guy."

He stopped as the final gears shifted through the wheels to the pavement.

"I get home and . . . I get home, and the money is gone. It's not in the trunk of the car. Someone . . . some motherfucker was following me the whole time." He choked a little. "It was right there, right out front. I open the trunk, and there's no money. And I thought I was losing my mind. I looked up and—the world was made out of plastic. None of the trees were real. The street wasn't real. The grass was fake."

He looked at his hands.

"I wasn't real. It was all like the kind of thing you see in the window of a toy store. I was in the TV. I was a mannequin in a commercial. In a plastic world." His voice lost half its volume. "And then I came in, and Mosey was gone. Her food was gone. This beer cap she had. Water bowl. And the sixty grand was gone, an' all my maps. I had these nautical maps, and they were gone. And I knew it right then. I don't even live here. I don't have a dog. I . . . I . . . I was all the way gone. No roots in the world. Like a spore that doesn't even come from anywhere, and there's no place to land."

He crashed down onto the couch. Ray had not moved the entire time.

"I got on my computer and Craigslisted accounting jobs. Doctor Abelard's post had shown up two minutes earlier. I was the first person who called. She was still sitting at her desk." He looked at Ray. "I went and met her, and she hired me, so I tried to become a real person. I'm trying to become a real person, Ray."

They stared at each other. Slowly, Ray raised his beer and took one sip, then another, then five, until it was empty. Anton watched him set the bottle down and take another one out of the six-pack, twist off the lid, and drop the lid onto the floor.

"That's quite a story, you crazy piece of shit," Ray said evenly. He took the three folded pages of Mary Chapman's blackmail out of his jacket pocket and held it up. "What would you tell me if I told you that, quite amazingly, I have the name of the man who stole your money and your dog and your"—he gestured with the paper—"everything. What would you be willing to do?"

Fire erupted in Anton's eyes, and he started shaking.

"Anything," he managed. Ray unfolded the papers and handed them to him. Anton took them with a trembling hand.

"Your old friend Tim is running some kind of burn, and I need to know what it is."

"Tim?" Anton lowered the papers. Ray shook his head.

"Tim wants you back. He has no idea what you've been up to. Read that, and tell me what it is."

Anton looked at the first sheet. Recognition crossed his face, almost immediately.

"These are EPA file numbers. The first sets . . . I know what this is. This is Tim!" He flipped to the second sheet and then back. "Condemned land, maybe asbestos, environmental toxins—can't tell from this. What we would do is get it rezoned, bury all that old data for just long enough to set up a shell on its value, incorporate it into a hedge fund as an asset, and then spin the money and have the EPA return its status to zero value. Inside job, all speculation." He turned to the last page. "Accounts. In and out, but someone is hanging for . . . sixty million! Score!" He looked up, and his smile faded a little. "I know the access codes to this account. I'm a signatory." The smile went all the way black, and his eyes widened in horror. "Is someone blackmailing Tim?" He rose. "Holy shit! Are you a fucking Fed? I have nothing to do with—"

"Sit down," Ray said. It was all suddenly crystal clear. Amazing. Anton froze and then unfroze and sat.

"Who are you? Who are you, really?"

"I'm the guy who's going to get you out of this. Someone is setting you up, Anton. When Tim goes down in a hail of bullets and fire, the only person left alive who can touch that money is you. And you will, after your feet are cut off and someone sews your tongue to the roof of your mouth. All she'll need is the one finger for you to type. She might not even let you keep your thumbs."

Anton went blank again.

"What are the access codes to that account, Anton? Now. Now and I tell you who trashed your world. You'd never see a penny of that bent money anyway, and that isn't even the way you roll anymore. You were perfect for this."

Anton scrabbled through the garbage on the coffee table and came up with a ballpoint pen. He turned the papers over and wrote on the back as Ray watched. A huge string of numbers. When he was done, he sat back. Ray picked up the papers and looked at what he'd written and then at Anton.

"You sure this is right?"

"I'm sure, man," Anton said confidently. "One hundred percent."

Ray folded the papers and put them back in his pocket. Anton licked his lips. They stared at each other.

"So, who is it?" Anton asked. "I gave you the code. Who's been after me this last year?"

"The woman setting you up must have found out that you were the final card up Tim's sleeve. That's why he used this account, because you're out of the loop for the moment. None of his current people know about it. Just him, two or three jailbirds, and you. He gets popped, you do the time. The lady who found this out and is selling Tim Cantwell to the meat grinder—then she's going to yank these numbers out of your head with pliers—she goes by the name Mary Chapman."

"So she . . . she isn't the one who stole my cash? My maps? My fucking goddamned dog?"

"No, Anton. That was me. Deadbomb Bingo Ray. I did all that shit to you after I burned Tim and your whole crew, and I fucked up your mind and stole your gal too. Because I was bored. But mostly because I just don't like you."

▶ JOLENE. ME FIRST AND THE GIMME GIMMES

Anton flipped the coffee table at him in a surprisingly slick move, and Ray rolled back as Anton surged forward with the speed and strength of a guy who had snapped for all time one second ago. Ray threw Anton over the top of him and rolled to his feet.

Anton bounced off the wall like he was already in a rubber room, and Ray had just enough time to punch him in the throat. Anton slid it off and tried to bite his hand, so Ray kept with his forward momentum and dropped, in a hard downward punch to Anton's crotch. Then he rose and landed a leg-powered uppercut to Anton's face, which was pointed down at him, and flattened his nose. Anton's legs went limp, and he dropped. His eyes didn't even flutter.

He didn't rise. Ray wiped blood off his mouth and then just stood there. The place was trashed, but there was a beer in the wreckage at his feet. He picked it up and popped the cap off, and foam shot out. He let it gush and then took a sip, and then he wandered over to the bedroom door and looked in. The bed was unmade, and there were clothes all over the floor. He carried the beer in and peeked under the bed and then slowly went to the closet and opened it. More clothes and shoes.

He walked back into the living room. Anton was still out, but he was breathing. Ray looked in the bathroom but didn't go in. There were two other bedrooms, both empty the last time he'd looked. Still panting a little, he opened the door on the first one. The air smelled musty and still, like Anton had never been in there. Ray closed it and walked into the dining room. Nothing new. He ran his finger over the table and inspected it for dust. The pizza box was still sitting there, unopened. He went to the second spare bedroom and opened the door and stepped back. A wave of cold went through his chest, and in one heartbeat the game changed. He walked slowly into the temple.

There were pictures of Abigail plastered all over the walls, hundreds of them, and what looked like a shrine of some kind made out of a stool, with candles all over it and a scattering of strange little curios stuck in the melted wax. He slowly walked over to it. An antique spoon with a fine koi-fin handle. A cracked camera lens. Three white Ping-Pong balls, each with a perfect red dot, pointed like eyes at the door. Ray slowly backed away and turned.

Anton was standing in the doorway, swaying, his face smeared with blood, his eyes rolling and unfocused. Ray drew his gun and fired in one fluid motion, and Anton fell backward in a spray of blood and brain, most of the left side of his head all over the dining room.

"Didn't see that comin'," Ray said. He still had the beer, so he drained it and tossed it aside. Then he holstered the gun and started taking Abigail's pictures down, all of them. It took twenty minutes, but when he was done, there was nothing left but the shrine. He dragged Anton's body in and laid it out in front of it. Then he stood back and looked at it for what it was: an altar devoted to his girlfriend, with a man he had slowly driven insane lying dead in front of it.

Last, he went out to the dining-room table, to the pizza box. He opened it and smiled. The dynamite wrapped in barbed wire with the thermal trigger was on top of the large pepperoni, dead center. He took it out and inspected it, and then he went into Anton's bedroom closet and took the laces out of a pair of high-top sneakers. It took a minute to pry the back off the trigger. Then he rigged the end of the shoelace around it and threaded the shoelace through the old-fashioned keyhole. When he was done, he pocketed the thermostat. It wasn't a comfort bomb anymore. He tied it to the inside of the door of the altar room and gently closed the door.

The next person who opened the door would see Anton for a fraction of a second, and then the apartment would move sideways in every direction in a torus of fire and molten shrapnel. The woman known as Mary Chapman's featherdusting days would be over.

Anton's computer was on the bed. Ray opened it and clicked on Anton's e-mail. He read for a few minutes and didn't find anything interesting. There were several e-mails from Abigail, all friendly and professional. She was an excellent boss, he was pleased to learn. The last one was from yesterday, sent from her apartment when she ran in to get her bag, telling him that she was leaving her computer at home and would have only her phone and wishing him a good weekend. He clicked on it and responded.

Dear Abigail,
Sorry for the short notice. I quit. Biz in Florida, so go go go! Good luck in Cali.
—AB

He hit SEND.

Back in the Cadillac, he took the phone out from under the seat and dialed Cody.

"Yo, dog," the big man reported. "No news. Sounds like your gal is sleeping."

Ray looked at the stack of pictures on the passenger seat. The one on top was of Abigail leaning over her keyboard in her lab, her eyes looking through the monitor at eternity.

"Just talked to Anton Brown. We had a few beers."

"That's it? A few beers? I thought you hated that dude."

"Code, I got . . . I got a code."

"Ah, good man. What kind?"

"Anton had the key. Tell you about it later. I'm headed back now, but. . . ." Ray sighed and glanced at the photos again.

"But?"

"Still gotta pick up that coat. Maybe a matching hat."

II

CHAPTER TWENTY

▶ IT'S NOT UNUSUAL, TOM JONES

Picking out a fashionable woman's coat in the neighborhood around the Kimpton was easy enough. Ray dropped the car with the valet and then walked the icy sidewalks to a little street lined with boutiques. He strolled with his hands in his pockets, mannequin shopping. He paused to inspect a red-and-gold three-quarter length and check the reflections in the window. Pedestrians with rosy cheeks, many of them just getting off work. He paused again in front of an emerald-green velvet coat with gold stitching. Nice, but a tad too big. Eventually he came to a row of seven black coats with white collars, just the right size, and peered through the window. Hats of every description.

An attractive blond woman in her thirties was stocking a garment rack. She looked up and smiled when he entered, and then her smile broadened when Ray smiled back.

"Can I help you?" she asked, pausing in her work.

"The women's coats in the window," he replied, turning. "The long one in the center caught my eye. Just the right size. I'll need a matching hat and gloves."

"Certainly!" She went to a rack and took out the coat in question and held it up for him. He nodded. "Hats and gloves. Does she have a particular look? What color is her hair?"

"She's a physicist," Ray replied. "Blond. Not into makeup."

"Plain?" she asked. "As in wholesome?"

"No."

The woman looked uncertain.

"Wholesome is a word for cow's milk, or a Dutch landscape painting in a liposuction clinic lobby. Warm breakfast grain." He cocked his head. "She's . . . unique." He considered and then snapped his fingers. "Clean."

"Ah." She picked out a soft white hat-and-glove combination and presented them. "They match the coat, of course, but. . . ."

Ray beamed. "Ring me up."

On the walk back, he watched all the reflective surfaces for a hint of a ripple in the people behind him, but there was nothing. Zero could only mean that everyone knew where he was, in the Kimpton, the only place he knew as well as the train station, but with better security.

Stanley the doorman was just coming on his shift when Ray walked up.

"My man!" he said. "How you like this weather?"

"Time for a change, my friend." Ray paused. "The equator runs through the center of the world and here we are, so far away from it the sky has frozen. Does that make us adventurers or dipshits?"

"Ain't no Belize, baby."

Upstairs, Ray knocked softly on Cody's door. It opened almost immediately, and he went in. Cody had put the guns away for housekeeping at some point and then taken them back out and rearranged them. Now all three tripods were pointed at the first ten feet of Ray's room. Cody noticed him note the changes and tossed a thumb at the row of guns.

"Figured I'd focus on the entry," he said. "Anyone makes it past that has you to say hi to, so. . . ."

"Good thinking. So, weird shit." He put the box containing Abigail's new coat on a chair and sat.

"Lay it on me." Cody poured them wine, a borolo.

"Hardshell might know more than he let on, but at this point I think the shooter in the train station wanted me alive to keep a window open in Atlantic City. When I set up the all-quiet in AC with Trujillo, I stepped in something bigger than I thought. Whole shitload of crooked politicians and blue-blooded aristocrats burned alive, et cetera. I think it might have already been traced back to me. Someone wants to know who had me do that. And someone else wants me alive but quiet."

"The creepy skater kid slash little Asian killing machine is the fixer for group number two?"

"Right. The shooter is group B—Gordon's, the lawyer. It's possible that he killed all the others to keep me from capturing one of them. Might have been my first move if . . . I could see it in the hitter's eyes when she looked over my shoulder. Different bad news. I was surrounded, and there were too many variables. Had to blow. But trying to find out who hired the dead people in the train station is impossible at this point."

"Like Russian dolls," Cody said. "Setup inside a setup inside a setup. Inside a setup."

"Yeah." Ray sipped his wine. "That spa was awesome this morning, though. You gotta go there when all this settles down."

"Good idea. Take my gal over Christmas. What else did Hardshell say?"

"Not much." Ray smiled. "Remember the Dutch tulip?"

Cody laughed and nodded.

"Guess that freaked him out. It's like those guys never heard of the Internet. He called Skuggy a witchman with a monkey hand."

"You do the razor-in-the-mouth deal?"

"Yep."

Cody stared into the middle distance. "Fuckin' Depeche Mode, man."

"That was a hard day," Ray said sympathetically, remembering Cody's failure and the horrible thing he'd done to his tongue when he tried to sing in the same situation. "Anyway, upshot is we can expect bad news later, so we might have to fuck up this hotel."

Cody carried his wine over to the window and looked out. "I always liked the view." He was silent for a moment, remembering. "First big job you ever gave me? The Swiss guys? Ran it right out of room 904." He shook his head. "I was sixteen. Can you believe that? Agnes was in Baltimore, shacked up with that guy Kevin, sending me food stamps and boxes of walnuts. Poor, sweet little bird was in love. And in comes Deadbomb Bingo Ray, the white demon who ran the Clancy Street guys into plastic bags. You and Skuggy ruled that patch of hell until you were done burning those idiots, and then you hired me, after I tried to kill you that second time. Got me my first computer, my first suit, and my first really good white hooker." He smacked his lips. "Clarissa."

"And then we stung those Swiss guys on those blueprints to an imaginary meth superlab in the former Clancy Street patch and sat back in room 904 and watched the street eat them alive. That was a sweet burn from the ground up."

"Yeah." Cody finished his wine and poured another. "I spent my first big score on books and more pussy."

"And the motorcycle you wrecked in a single day."

Cody shrugged. Ray looked at the clock and rose.

"What's the plan for tonight?" Cody asked.

"We play it all the way out," Ray replied. "Rooftop lounge opens at eight. I take Abby up, and we have a few drinks, dinner. Look at the city lights. You watch and wait. And when our hitter shows, you do too. You join our table, and I go to the bar. Wide open for a hit or some talking. It's a hit, you cover Abs and kill everyone I miss. It's a talk, well. . . ."

"All this is cover for your new gal, Ray," Cody said. "I dig that this is happening to you, but man. She will die if we don't send her packing. And I'm not talking about sending her home, either. Someone already has your number, which means they have her number too. We withdraw our protection for one hour, and she's a hostage in surgery, best-case scenario."

"I have a plan."

Ray walked over to Cody's munitions pack and peered in, rummaged around, and came up with a grenade. He held it up and winked and then dropped it into his overcoat pocket.

▶ BITTERSWEET FAITH, BITTER:SWEET

"There you are!" Abigail called from the bed as he entered.

"I brought you something," Ray called back. "Close your eyes!"

"Closing! Closed!"

Ray set her new coat aside and hung up his overcoat. He took the grenade out and put it on the top shelf of the entryway closet and then added one of his guns. After unclipping the second gun, holster and all, from his back, he took it out, checked the clip, and put it in the breast pocket of his suit coat. Then he put the holster up with the other gun and closed the closet door.

"Still closed?"

"Getting sleepy again."

He took her coat and the hat and the gloves out of the bag and carried it all into the bedroom.

"Open."

Abigail was still in bed. Her hair was a wild mess, and her blue eyes were huge and bright. She looked at the coat in momentary confusion and then laughed her clean, bright winter bell of a laugh.

"My winter coat!" She scrambled forward on all fours. "At long last! After two years I'm finally getting a coat, right before I move to California!"

"Try it on," he suggested. She got up and put it on. During her nap, she'd lost her pants and her shirt and had been reduced to panties and one sock. The long black coat fit her perfectly. She flipped up the white collar and vogued her best, bit her thumb and twirled, cocking her butt out, smiling and tossing her hair. He was briefly paralyzed at how easy it was for her to transform in an instant from a sleepy woman with messy hair and a single sock to something fresh to a Paris runway. It was part of her dance with perfection, he knew, but she was doing it . . . perfectly.

"You take my breath away."

Abigail batted her eyelashes. "It is a simple thing, this breath of yours, tricked from your chest. I would catch it in my lungs and breathe it back into your mouth for one small thing."

Ray grabbed her, brushed his cheek along her upturned face, and purred in her ear and then whispered into her mouth. "Ask."

"Come with me," she breathed. "Come with me into this tiny eternity." She dropped the coat and stepped back. Shyly, she removed her sock.

The next hour was a swirl of impressions Ray would never forget: Abigail's eyes pulsing from distant, to unimaginably distant, to watching his mind, to looking inward, to focused on nothing at all; the curve of her back; the shape of her molars; clouds passing over the sunlight streaming through the window. Frames—fast and scattered throughout—of three white balls spinning on Anton's altar, the bullet holes in the trunk of his Cadillac, black birds swimming after flashing minnows, fire and smoke and flashes of blue from the morning pool, the bending of a forest. And then finally her seizure, hot and convulsive.

Afterward, Abigail stared at the ceiling, shaking and mute, unblinking, mouth open, her body slick with sweat. Somehow empty, he rose and walked slowly to the window. It was getting dark, and the sunset was a rolling splendor of burning orange and vanishing blue. Low, heavy clouds appeared in the distance, like the dust of an advancing army of metal and coal. Splayed contrails were flattened by the weight of the hidden structure of the heavens.

He put his hand out and touched the cold window and looked down. Somehow he could see the outline of SEPTA below the darkening white, see the desperation in the pace of the figures, and his mouth tasted like blood. He walked back to the bed and sat, staring at the blank television until complete darkness fell.

▶ DANCE ME TO THE END OF LOVE, MADELEINE PEYROUX

Ray shaved and dressed in the best suit he'd brought along for the ride, a Brioni Colosseo. While Abigail showered and fussed with her hair and changed into an elegant dress, he carefully stowed his guns and spokes. The grenade was hard to fit anywhere, so he put it back in his overcoat. If Abigail discovered it, he could always claim it was a prop from Gruben he was using for stills.

"So this rooftop lounge is one of your location finds?" Abigail called.

"Yep. Only open on Friday and Saturday nights. I took a few photos the last time, but I'll probably take more tonight."

"They don't mind?"

"You kidding?" He walked up and watched from the bathroom door as she moisturized. "If anything I shoot attracts a real photographer—for an ad campaign or a commercial, or something bigger like the project Cody is working on—it's huge exposure, all kinds of revenue. Total jackpot."

"Interesting," she said. She smiled and went past him, picked up her new coat and put it on, and then examined her profile in the mirror. "I might not need this, but I had to look."

"By all means wear it," he suggested. "Bring the hat and gloves too. There's actually outdoor seating."

"Twelve stories up? In this weather?" It pleased her.

"It's partially enclosed. Big propane heat lamps, but still kinda nippy. I reserved us a table inside and out."

"You can do that?"

"I can." He put on his coat and held out his elbow. Abigail donned her hat and draped her long gloves over one arm, looped the other through his, and squeezed. Her transformation was nothing short of astonishing once again, from nerdy science woman to knockout with a minimum of effort. They stopped in the entryway and vainly looked at themselves in the mirror across the hallway, smiling simultaneously.

"We make an interesting pair, Raymond." His darker skin and piercing gaze at once contrasted and complemented her fair skin and wide blue eyes.

"I'm not sure we look like real people," he said admiringly.

"This might be the worst disguise ever," she agreed. Her smile changed a little, and the distance from earlier crept into her expression again. He tugged her arm.

The hallway was empty. As they passed Cody's door, Ray heard a light rasp on the inside, signaling that Cody knew they were on the move. They strolled arm in arm to the elevator, and Ray pressed the UP button. Behind them, Cody's door silently opened and his head appeared. If the elevator door opened on the wrong person, he would step out and begin shooting. Ray watched his blurry reflection in the polished metal door.

The doors opened on an empty car, and they stepped in. Cody vanished back into his room to grab his jacket. Without thinking, Ray pulled his arm free and put his hand on Abigail's butt; and without thinking, she leaned her hip into his side.

"It's been a long time since I groped anyone in the elevator," he said, looking straight ahead.

"Why is that, Ray?" Her voice was part purr.

"In all honesty, I date whores."

"Hmm. I'm glad. You saved up all your genuine passion for me." She looked at him and licked her lips.

"I guess I did," he agreed.

"A normal man would have the decency to blush right now, Raymond." She looked forward again, satisfied. He did too.

The Debarre Lounge had been designed by a Basque maniac named Bireli Langrene, and it was not locally popular. The elevator doors opened on a slightly disheveled black attendant, who smiled and revealed the Philadelphia standard in teeth—a mélange of gold and brown and missing. The bar was to the left, torn from a hallucination of the Roaring Twenties, with brass fixtures and mirrors with silver tracery, towers of colored glass bottles, and strange mechanical things that may have been for espresso or Spanish squeeze donuts but were probably just for show. The tables were arrayed in a pattern that faced the bar, in a radiating amphitheater fashion. Confusingly, there was a small stage for the jazz band that would never play opposite it. The floor-to-ceiling windows were a panorama of neighboring rooftop antennas, blinking warning lights, and the bottom of clouds lit fish-belly white from the city below. They were the first people to arrive. Abigail gasped.

"Someone captured the essence of the city," she whispered in awe.

"Astonishing, isn't it?" Ray led her past the attendant toward the bar. "Langrene is a visionary genius of rare distinction. I follow his work closely."

"Amazing."

The bartender smiled as they approached. "Reservations?" he asked in all seriousness.

"Always," Ray replied. "Though I'll put them on hold for the moment."

The bartender cocked his head quizzically.

"Gruben Media. Two, please."

"Ah, right! The photographer." He picked up two menus. "I was told to give you the run of the place, which, as you can see . . ." he gestured apologetically. "House music starts at midnight, and then the place goes insane."

"So we hear," Ray replied. "I guess a table by the stage over there, close to the window. Then we might move outside for a few."

"Excellent." He went around the bar and led the way. "What kind of stuff are you working on, don't mind my asking?"

"Just general, really. Location scouting, that kind of thing. I have a cinematographer in town right now, might pop in at some point tonight or tomorrow."

"Super." He gestured at a two-top. "Good?"

Ray nodded and took Abigail's coat and then pulled out her chair. He draped both of their coats over the back of his chair.

"Drinks?"

"I guess I'll have a Macallan, neat."

"I might try one of those too," Abigail said. The bartender nodded and then departed. Abigail fixed Ray with a look of open admiration. "So tell me. Tell me your vision of this place."

"I picture this as the background of a particularly destructive action scene in a made-for-TV movie," he replied. "Deep cable. Winner of the Oxygen Award for Best Nobody. Maybe kung fu mixed with an awful clash of flamenco and a child violin prodigy. Or a Chinese cigarette commercial, something suitably mushroom-driven, with live camels and praying-mantis masks."

"There's something so . . ." she sought for the right word. ". . . fractured. Have you ever been to Hong Kong?"

"Sure."

"A colleague of mine told me about a Mexican-food restaurant she went to there. It was the strangest thing, she said. They'd never sampled the cuisine, of course, or even had a Mexican visitor, so the food was made entirely of what the cooks imagined it would taste like based on photographs."

"Was it good?"

"I don't recall her impressions." So, no. Their drinks arrived.

"You two dining with us tonight?"

"We are," Ray replied. He looked at Abigail. "Appetizer?"

"Oysters," Abigail replied.

"It's the season," the bartender said. "Inside word is the crab cakes are out of this world tonight."

"Dozen oysters and the crab cakes," Ray said. There was a commotion by the door, and he turned. A small man dressed in a black suit exited the elevator, gliding with the grace of a dancer or a matador. Ray recognized the man's frame instantly. It was the shooter from the train station. Just as the elevator doors were almost closed, a giant black hand shot out and they opened again. Cody emerged, talking in an animated way on his cell, laughing quietly at something the imaginary person on the other end hadn't said. He and Ray met eyes for an instant. Ray's eyes flicked for the shortest possible time in the direction of the shooter and then back to Cody and then narrowed. He tilted his head in a minute nod. Cody raised his hand to them as the shooter took a seat at the bar.

"Coming up," the bartender said.

"Cody's here," Ray said to Abigail. She turned.

"Well, I'll be. Should we invite him over for a drink? We should."

"If you don't mind a little business." Ray waved and Cody waved back and headed in their direction.

"I wonder what he'll think of this place?" she whispered. Cody put his phone away as he arrived and leaned down.

"This place is brilliant, Ray," he said, answering her question. "The angles, the lines of sight. Crazy cool."

"Pull up a chair," Ray said, smiling.

"Please join us," Abigail said warmly. "I'd love to hear your impressions."

"Reflective," Cody said. He pulled up a chair. The bartender made to approach, but Cody stopped him by pointing at Ray's drink and holding up three fingers. "There is a juxtaposition, a contrary lunacy that itself is a burlesque of lunacy itself. Delicious."

"I couldn't have put it better," Abigail said. "I sometimes get the impression that Raymond sees the city in a unique way."

Cody smiled and turned his attention to Ray, enjoying having him in the spotlight. His giant bulk was positioned to cut off the shooter's line of sight, but there were so many shiny surfaces, it didn't matter. The shooter ordered a drink, and the bartender said something and smiled.

"This is a city that could change in a single generation if the poor had decent jobs," Ray said guardedly. "But it would take an entire generation at this point. No one can deny, however, that this crushing desperation breeds its own singular magic."

Cody and Abigail exchanged a look.

"I could never function in paradise," Ray continued. He put his hand over Abigail's. "At least in the way I do now."

"I guess I couldn't either," Cody said thoughtfully. "Advertising only works because we sell good dreams to people who live inside never-ending nightmares."

"Well," Abigail began and then stopped. Their drinks arrived with impossible timing, and Cody held his up and toasted them.

"To all that is good in the world," he said, sensing the right direction like an eel in muddy water, "no matter where we find it."

"I'll drink to that," Abigail said, raising the remains of her first drink. They clinked their glasses and drank. Ray wiped his lips and watched as the shooter went through two sets of glass doors out onto the enclosed balcony and lit a cigarette under one of the heat lamps. He then glanced Ray's way.

"If you two will excuse me for just one moment," he said. "That gentleman smoking outside just reminded me that I need a smoke. Be back in a flash."

"So, tell me about California," Abigail said to Cody. "Ray and I were just talking about palm trees."

Ray put on his coat and walked to the glass doors. The shooter watched as he came through them with his hands in his pockets, and then he turned his back and looked out into the night. Ray slowly walked over and stood next to him. The enclosed balcony had no ceiling and was open to the snow, which didn't fall so much as gust in from time to time and then gust back out into the dark. The wind wasn't as bad as it could have been, and the heat lamps were set to roar. They stood like that for a moment until Ray turned to him.

"Got another one of those?"

Without turning, the shooter produced a pack of cigarettes and a small, crack torch–style lighter. Lucky Strikes, no filters. Ray shook one out and lit it and then handed the pack back. They smoked.

"I have a grenade in my pocket. Guns. I think you know that I don't even need them. It was pretty slick, the train station. I get the feeling you might want to talk to me. So talk. But be super-cautious. If I feel even a little bit bummed out, well—over the side you go."

The little man considered for a moment. Then he finally turned, and they met each other's eyes. Ray saw no fear at all, not even a high degree of interest—just hard little eyes in a bland little face. Maybe traces of jet lag; maybe not.

"In about three minutes, two hitters will enter," the little man said, just loud enough to be heard. Ray had no reaction. "Both of them work, I assume, for one of the parties who currently want you dead."

Ray nodded. "They usually do."

"I don't."

"Good for you." They both looked forward, just two guys chatting about nothing at all. Far below, the snow was winning the race with the snowplows, and the black circulatory system of the city was reduced to ribbons of gray.

"I guess you have less than two minutes to tell me what you want," Ray continued. "The next people who get off the elevator are going to die, and I might get so carried away that even the bartender catches some. But you won't make it."

"I understand. Indirectly, we work for the same party. I am a direct contractor like you, through the lawyer Gordon." He turned back to Ray. "Atlantic City, you see. I am to make sure you don't answer the wrong kinds of questions, though how I proceed is at my own discretion."

"That's a good rule," Ray said. "I like discretionary room myself."

"So," the little man continued, "let me share my read on the situation with you. That scientist in there is your girlfriend. You killed her accountant earlier. The gentleman with her is the accomplished criminal and killer Cody Hooper, your protégé. In less than one minute, we will be joined on the balcony by two extremely competent assassins, who will either attempt to kill you in retribution and then question your associates or attempt to subdue you and kill your associates as they exit."

"Messy."

"And then there is . . . us. I am your equal, Mr. Ray. I propose an entirely different sequence of events."

"I like where you're going with this. It has to have style, of course."

"Naturally."

Ray gestured at the night sky. "A certain panache. You know I have my reputation to consider."

"I as well."

"Good. Let's hear it."

The shooter leaned over and whispered. Ray saw Cody begin to rise and held up his hand, motioned for him to sit, and then flashed the thumbs-up. Then Ray and the shooter pulled apart.

"That will work nicely," Ray said. The shooter nodded.

"I'll get the drinks." He made to turn away and then turned back. "Sippai—my name."

Ray nodded. He smoked and watched in the reflection of the glass as the shooter went back inside and ordered two scotches, neat. Beyond him, as the bartender poured, a man and a woman stepped out of the elevator arm in arm, deep in conversation. They smiled and spoke with the greeter, who gestured at the bar. Sippai ignored them and paid for the scotch as they walked over and took two stools. The bartender nodded to the couple and poured them two shots of vodka from the top shelf. The man paid, and they toasted each other and drank. Sippai was ignoring his two drinks, texting someone. The man asked the bartender something, and he pointed at the balcony. The man and woman nodded, and the man took a pack of cigarettes out of the breast pocket of his suit jacket. Arm in arm again, they headed in Ray's direction.

The sequence of events began. Sippai summoned the bartender and pointed at Cody and Abigail, ordering them a bottle of champagne. The bartender nodded and vanished into the back to retrieve it. The two assassins exited through the glass doors out onto the balcony, and Ray turned and looked and then turned back to his view of the city. He watched in the reflection of the heavy window glass in front of him as Sippai picked up the two drinks in one hand and came their way, awkwardly pushing through the doors.

Both the man and the woman had their hands in their pockets, their eyes on Ray as Sippai came out. Ray turned toward them, and everyone froze.

"Riley Cline!" Sippai yelled. "You crazy bastard! What the hell are you doing in Philly?"

The couple turned. Sippai stumbled and rammed a finger right into the woman's eye. Ray kicked her in the back of the knee, and she dropped. In the same instant, Sippai dropped as well and neatly swept the man's legs out from under him, while in the same motion Ray grabbed the top of his body and rolled to the right, toward the nearest wall of the tall enclosure. Sippai sculled forward and rose, grabbing the man's knees with one arm. Together—with Ray holding the man below the armpits and Sippai his knees—they tossed the man over the top in one smooth, coordinated second, like they'd practiced it a thousand times.

The woman regained her composure just as Ray grabbed her. Sippai kicked a chair into the backs of her knees, and the three of them sat just as the bartender emerged from the back and headed for Cody and Abigail, both of whom were laughing at Cody's ten-second distraction. The entire production was a well-oiled Charlie Chaplin clip. Sippai hadn't spilled a drop of either drink. He'd played his part one-handed.

"Hi," Ray said.

"I got the good stuff," Sippai said, sliding Ray a scotch.

Ray took a sip and nodded his appreciation. The woman glared at them with her good eye. Sippai took his cigarettes out and lit one and then offered the pack to Ray, who politely declined.

"So, was the plan to kill me, or question me?" Ray didn't expect her to answer. Sippai evidently didn't either, and withdrew a petite pair of needle-nose pliers from his suit coat.

"I cannot say." German accent. She didn't seem especially angry.

"'Course not. Tell you what. I'm going to let you go, because I want you to deliver a message for me. Can you do that?"

She nodded.

"Good. Give me your hand."

She held out her hand. Ray took out the tape and the grenade. He popped the pin and then closed her hand around the grenade and swept the tape around her hand twice. Then he passed the tape to Sippai, who taped her other hand to the back of her belt.

"That's the message. Get out."

The woman rose and pushed her way through the glass doors with her shoulder. They watched as she approached the elevators and the attendant pressed the button for her. She said something that made him smile and nod, and the doors opened. She stepped in, and the doors closed. Ray rose.

"Be seein' ya."

"Enjoy the rest of your evening, Mr. Ray."

Ray went back in to find Cody and Abigail laughing again. He took off his jacket and sat down, and Abigail took his hand.

"Cold out there?" Cody asked.

"Yep. Ran into a consultant for another media company, if you can believe that. Music-industry goon scouting locations for a video."

"Small world sometimes," Abigail said. "Did you compare notes?"

"Totally did," Ray replied. Cody expertly concealed his interest. "Friends today, enemies tomorrow, though. Name of the game."

"Well, I'll leave you two," Cody said. "I have a few phone calls to make and another location to look at. Ray, sorry to pull you away, but maybe later we can grab a quick chat? I want to run through my itinerary for tomorrow. Take ten minutes, tops."

Ray looked at Abigail, who didn't seem to mind the idea.

"No prob. Looks like more snow out there, so we were just going to grab dinner and maybe go down to the bar later."

"Good." Cody rose. "I'm going to grill the bartender about local history and see if he knows what those contraptions behind the bar do. Abigail, it was a pleasure."

They watched him go to the bar and take a stool, order a drink, and take out his phone again.

"Interesting man," Abigail mused. "Do all the Hollywood types lie that much?"

"Fiction is part of their industry," Ray confirmed. "Keeps them sharp. They're nothing compared to music executives."

"So." She turned her intelligent gaze on him.

"So."

"Pasadena. I checked my e-mail on my phone earlier. They want me, sooner the better. And my accounting assistant just quit. That has to be a sign. I'm free."

"Wow." Ray sat back. "Wow."

"I know. Wow."

He pretended to think. She watched him do it. Eventually, he drained his waiting drink and gave her a keen appraisal.

"Snow and more snow is in the forecast. My people want me to see the world. Your grant is done, and your one employee is out of the picture. I say we blow town. Like, tomorrow. Turn our long weekend into something else."

It was Abigail's turn to sit back. He watched it compute.

"Tomorrow. . . ." She rolled it around.

"I'll call Agnes and have her reserve a month at someplace with a pool. Total write-off for me, so it's like a free vacation. You set up shop, create your new contact list and schedule meetings, get your bearings and all that before you start at the new place. Get a jump on it. I'll tidy up my office all day tomorrow, and we can fly out tomorrow night."

"My lab equipment is on loan from the university," she mused. "They don't need me to supervise the pickup, really. Grad students do all that. My apartment. It's just seven boxes and a futon. I . . . I . . ." She looked up. "I think I want to. Now is better—far better. I can get to know the place before I bury my head in science for a change. Are you sure you can write this off?"

"If we move fast, yes. Yes, I can. And I mean fast."

"Incredible," Abigail said. She reached out and took his hand. "This is easily the most romantic thing that's ever happened to me."

"Me too." Ray squeezed her hand. "Tonight I have to zip by the office and pick up some files. Hit my place real quick in the morning while you tidy up yours." He sighed. "This is the best part of not getting tied down in life, I guess. Come and go as we like."

"It's almost like . . . almost like we aren't even real people," she agreed. He smiled at that, and then for a fleeting instant they both looked confused. Abigail's face settled into distant examination. Ray switched immediately to croupier, surprised he'd let his guard down. She continued: "I feel like you're changing me, somehow. Like I'm blooming."

"How. . . ." He trailed off. He felt it too. He didn't want to admit it, but he did.

"It's okay," she whispered. She could see through his mask, all the way to the shifting surface of the revelation.

"I wonder," he began, almost to himself, "I wonder if all this has . . . Abby, do you think it's possible, this blooming, if we're acting like a catalyst on each other? My life has . . . exploded. It started when we met in that café."

"Love, as an agent of transformation?"

He nodded. Her smile was full of Einstein's mystery.

"I'm sure of it."

He didn't remember dinner. Afterward, they made love for a blurry time, until the ribs in his back hurt and her eyes rolled back in her head, and then her body shook like she was connected to a giant, unseen machine. Her mouth foamed this time.

Afterward, he went to the window and pressed his hand on the glass and stood there, the lights of the city below burning like campfires, until Abigail finally stirred.

"Raymond," she called in a hoarse whisper. He turned and looked into her burning eyes, mute.

"I love you," she said.

"I love you," he echoed in return.

Abigail stared through the ceiling until her eyes closed. Ray put on his clothes and left.

II

CHAPTER
TWENTY-ONE

▶ MAN OF MYSTERY. JOHN JORGENSON

The drive to the office of Tim Cantwell should have felt like a domino progression or a long piano introduction that built itself for seamless insertion into the muscular innards of a sweet and clever pop ditty. Instead, he saw a trail of omens, signs that his time in the weeping city was drawing to a close. The dolmens of his past were bright spots in the black-and-white wasteland, and in the blowing snow it was hard to tell the huddled forms of the living from rushing ghosts. The dark side of the moon shone like antilamp from the SEPTA cavities, and it was almost as if all the street signs had fingers on them, or hands; they projected the rumor of pointing, all in the vague direction of "away."

Ray turned on the radio.

▶ DANCING IN THE MOONLIGHT. KING HARVEST

Every street led to a place he had visited with fire and painted with blood. The wind would howl through the wires above the feeding grounds and graveyard parks when he was gone, he knew. If the city was a boat, a giant ocean liner, then he had been a creature of rust and bending and a new magnetic misdirection for the busted compass, to be sure. But his efforts had fallen short compared to the general desire to deface that ruled the moody ethos of the place. He thought about London, in an effort to distract himself.

Eugene Gordon, Esq., had been sincere when he'd offered it as a way out; it was in his eyes. But they had whale on the plate in LA too—probably far more—and they also had tacos, palm trees, frenzy, and Abigail. He shook his head as he turned onto Baltimore, a street he had haunted hard enough to know as only a phantom could. He passed the place where he'd stabbed the man tailing them. Of course, there was no sign that someone had died there, except in his memory. A block farther was Clark Park, where he and Abigail had had their snow picnic. A year ago, he had walked through the park with the rep for a stock scam—a prescription junkie named Clarence Puckett, who was in the final tight circle of a death spiral after his twin sister died in London. Puckett was playing the system for some kind of escape, hitting it hard to make the big score and get out, or maybe get killed for trying; he didn't care. Ray had taken three active contacts off him and then snapped his neck, leaving his body sitting in the rain on the very bench he and Abigail had eaten on. He'd chosen it for the view, in some way considerate of what Puckett would watch as his brain ran out of oxygen and his eyes went waxy.

Tim's office was in a little fourplex past the anarchist café. Ray parked just around the corner and got the bombs out of the trunk, put them in his inner coat pocket, and lit a cigarette. It was almost midnight—the opening hour of the burglar's window—but he didn't see any point in waiting. All the lights were out and the parking lot was empty. He smoked across the street until he was sure and then crossed with his head down.

Getting in was easy. The dead bolt opened like a baby bird's mouth, and the security system was the kind they used to train burglars, top-shelf Radio Shack, no doubt installed by Tim himself because he was too paranoid to have anyone else do it. Ray stood inside the door and listened, one hand on his gun. The light slanting in from the street was good enough to work with.

The office was almost exactly what he'd been expecting. It was small, with a reception area, Tim's office, a conference room, and an adjoining bathroom. The furniture didn't fit the place. It was all hideously expensive, for one thing, but it was also from Tim's old office, which had been far bigger. It gave the off-putting impression of being the office of an oldest child who'd borrowed his powerful father's impressive leftovers. A suit that was one size too big. It must have been factoring into Tim's psyche on some level.

Ray clucked distastefully and walked to the thermostat. Sixty-four degrees. He went around and opened all the windows and waited as the wind dropped the temp, one degree per minute. When it hit fifty-five, he closed everything back up and took out the bombs, set them to blow at sixty-one degrees, and strategically hid them. He put the first one in the conference room, on the floor behind the lone plastic plant. The second he taped under Tim's desk, carefully dangling it by two inches so the thermostat wouldn't be thrown off by contact with the metal. The third one went in the reception area, on top of the partitioning wall separating it from the short hallway leading to the other two rooms. All three would reach the same temperature around the same time—though in many ways it didn't matter, since when the first of them did, the resulting explosion would rip the thermostats on the other two through the detonation line almost instantly.

Back across the street, he lit one final cigarette and looked at the office plex once again. It was the last time he would ever see the building. He froze the image of it in his mind like a postcard. Then he turned away and walked back to his car. There wasn't any point in going back to the house he used to live in, so he drove back to the Kimpton.

▶ WHEN I'M SMALL, PHANTOGRAM

‖

CHAPTER TWENTY-TWO

"I'll see you at the airport," Ray said. The morning had been quiet, pensive. While Abigail showered, Ray shaved, dressed, and then made coffee and drank it in front of the window.

Abigail stared into him, sensing on some level that this day would be more difficult for him. She gently touched his face but said nothing. He reached out and did the same, and they stood like that. He waited for her to say something, anything, but she didn't. Maybe she was afraid that there was a spell between them, something so fragile that a single word could break it; maybe she didn't want this moment to end, as if her silence could assure them that they could stand there until the end of time. He embraced her and felt her heart fast against his chest. She took a shuddering breath, and he kissed the top of her head, the crown of her forehead, inhaling her hair, feeling the warmth of her body rise up along the skin of his neck. He closed his eyes and reluctantly pulled away. Abigail looked down, and Ray turned and picked up his bag. The click of the door closing when he stepped into the hallway sounded like the snapping of a hollow avian bone.

Cody opened the door before he could knock, his face set. Ray entered and walked past him as the giant locked the door. Three young black men were lined up, as if for inspection. There was a forced bravery set in their faces that spoke from the early lines around their hard eyes. All three had lived a life of crime and often surreal violence, surviving the Darwinian nightmare jungle they'd been born into by embracing death as more than a lifestyle or a philosophy, but as something like a religion. They knew who he was, and they could feel how close the universe had become. Each was standing in an upright and invisible coffin, and they knew it. Ray slowly walked past them, pointing each out in turn. He'd never met them, but he knew who they were too.

"Hakeem." Ray looked him up and down. Hakeem was in his mid-twenties, the oldest of the three, dressed in khaki pants and a long-sleeved blue dress shirt. He looked like he worked at an office-supply store. Ray knew Hakeem had been making people disappear since he was twelve, starting with three of his cousins. Skuggy had taken him in, and he lived in one of his houses. Hakeem liked cars.

"Yes, sir, Mr. Ray." It had been a long time since Hakeem had called anyone "sir," and it came out like a Spanish word he read off a menu. Ray moved on.

"Little Elijah." Ray squinted at the next young man. Elijah was indeed little, an even five feet tall with his shoes on. Three-time cop killer. He was wearing Patagonia everything.

"Yes, sir, Mr. Ray." A singsong chirp. Ray kept going.

"Bobo G." Bartholomew Gable worked part-time at the pet shop where Skuggy bought rats for his snakes. Jeans, sneakers, heavy work coat over a thermal shirt. The worker disguise. Gable had been running with Hakeem for almost two years on the side to put himself through school. He had power of a kind spilling out of his pores, bubbling up from an inner artesian fount of serious wrong, wrong, wrong. In ten years he'd be royalty—enthroned at the head of a red carpet of unlikely horrors and crowned with a headdress of fingers—or he'd be dead.

"Mr. Ray, sir." Gable nodded, but he met Ray's eyes and his piercing gaze didn't waver. He was scared, but not like the other two: he was scared that Ray would know what he was.

"Okay, kids," Ray began. "You three are following my lady friend today. She's in the next room over. Blond hair, blue eyes, black coat." He didn't look away from Gable's face. "She's going home.

She's going to her office. Maybe her bank. Then she's going to the airport. You three will follow her. Now, I want to be clear—there's a good chance someone will try to take her. Not kill her, just take her. You are to kill that person or persons without her ever knowing about it. I don't care who they are, so you don't need to pick up the body. Just keep the ball in motion at all times. Clear?"

All three nodded.

"Now, you know who I am. You know what will happen if you fail. It would be far, far, far better to die trying to protect this woman."

Three nods again.

Ray turned to Cody and motioned for him to follow. They went into the bedroom, and Ray closed the sliding door.

"We're good," Cody said quietly. "Those boys are armed to the teeth, all three of them are wearing vests, cars are proofed."

"You shadow the operation. Hang back and let Hakeem call the shots, but stay in the loop. Shit hits the fan and Abigail gets picked up, those three kids die, I want you to follow whoever has her to where they go to ground and then call me."

"Got it. You, ah, you think we got blood in the forecast for these three?"

"You talk to Gable?"

Cody frowned. "Bobo G? At least one of them is gonna pull through, I agree it's him. We should keep an eye on that kid when this is done."

"Everything set up to make the bank transfer?"

"Yep. One call and the funds bounce out of the old Cantwell Fund account and right into your Geneva number. This Anton guy had impeccable writing."

"No shit." Ray stuck his hand out. Cody looked at it, confused for a second, and then they shook. They didn't usually shake unless they were playing a part. "Luck on you, Code."

"Back atcha," Cody softly replied. The big man's eyes were large as he studied his mentor's face, looking for signs. He sighed. "You know, Ray. You know, my life, it would have never been . . . I mean, I'm alive because of you. Everything I'll ever be is because—"

"Code, man."

"Abigail will make that flight," Cody said, suddenly grim.

Ray realized in that instant that his poker face had become permanent sometime in the night, or perhaps even right then, at that very instant. No one would ever read his thoughts again, even if he wanted them to, no matter how well they knew him.

He clapped Cody on the shoulder. Hakeem and his crew were quiet as he walked out.

▶ PLAY IT ALL THE WAY, LISA MANN

Skuggy was waiting on the corner of Sixth and Market, dressed in a vintage blue suit and a tan overcoat, with a short-brim black hat. He looked like a fifties-era banker, except his bad arm was in a red silken sling and the long fingernails jutting from the end of his wizened hand were brown and sharp and glistening with a fresh coat of clear polish. He was staring east with his eyelids reduced to slits in the glare. Ray beeped once, and the old man got in.

"Something fuckin' with the pigeons." Skuggy fastened his seat belt. "Maybe the Alka-Seltzer man be around again."

"I thought you killed that guy." Skuggy's Alka-Seltzer villain had killed thousands of pigeons over the years by blowing up their stomachs with chips of the stuff.

"Philly, baby. Million more where that muthafucka came from."

Skuggy ate pigeon and considered them an eternal food source. He claimed to have learned the culinary judo in Portugal, of all places, though it could have been from a cooking show.

"Coffee?"

"Nah." Skuggy brightened a little. "Talk to Hakeem just now. Guess they all ready."

"Good. That kid Bobo G. . . ."

"Bartholomew Gable." Skuggy let it hang. "Him an atypical monster."

"How so? I could see it in his eyes, but I'm curious."

"Gable be what the Freestyle Butthole Illuminati call a serial killer. 'Course, that describe half the ghetto that boy crawl up out of, but he a special case jus' the same."

"In what way?"

"Well"—Skuggy paused and lit a cigarette—"him got serious peculiarities. See, he's a boy got crushed flat 'bout a billion times. Cruel world and blah blah boo hoo, but there be the raw kinda rodeo tweak him just so. Cain't never tell the truth 'bout nothin', tells the stone-cold in lies. Complicated head. Spooky thing? You really wanna know?"

"Bring it."

"Near as anyone knows, Bobo G—Bartholomew Gable—he ain't never committed a single crime. Now, you can feel what he is. But there never, ever be proof. None."

"Ah."

They rode in silence after that.

"This gonna be an interestin' couple hours," Skuggy said eventually. He didn't seem particularly energized by the notion. "Wish I's gonna be there to see Tim Cantwell's face when this goes down."

"I got a phone today."

"So you do!" He brightened at the idea. "You snap me a picture."

They pulled up in front of the steak house down the street from Gordon, Pritchett & Hughes and parked. Skuggy offered Ray a smoke, and he took it and lit it with a match. It was almost time. One by one, he took his guns and sharpened spokes out and put them under the seat.

"Tim's people will be in place by now with the heater running."

"I know what you gonna say, Ray. My boy Rollie at the anarchist café havin' coffee and waitin' on a boom, you want him to snap you a picture, 'cause we all about pictures today."

"Good. Everyone will be taking pictures. He won't stand out."

"Deal."

"See you in an hour, old man."

"I be ready."

Ray left him smoking in the car. The glare was intense, so he put on his Ray-Bans and buttoned his coat. Slowly, he walked into everyone's trap.

▶ AIN'T NO GRAVE CAN HOLD MY BODY DOWN, DIAMANDA GALAS

Hardshell and two of his witches were in a Lincoln with tinted windows on the corner. He walked past them without stopping. By now, Tim Cantwell and two Feds were in the first-floor lobby of the Pearl Building, waiting for Ray to emerge from the elevator after visiting Eugene Gordon and picking up the blackmail documents. He wouldn't see them when he went in, obviously, but they were somewhere. Mary Chapman was parked one block up. He walked to her car and got in.

"Ray," she said tensely. She was dressed to the nines like she was going out on the town. Her luggage was in the back seat. Ray gave her the once-over.

"Here's how it's going down," he said. "Your lawyer pal is at a resort right now. I have his keys. I go in, get your file, return the keys before he notices, and we're all done."

"So you just walk in and walk out?"

"I've had people following Gordon all week around the clock. This was easy. The main thing now is you. I give you that file, and you go back to Chicago, right?"

"Right." She smiled a little.

"And when he calls you for the next payment?"

"I decline," she said, smiling a little more at the developing fiction.

"And then?"

She shrugged. "Tell him to fuck off."

Ray shook his head. "Whatever. Back in ten minutes. You're not here, I'll be the one blackmailing you. Clear?"

"I will be right here." The leer in her smile turned up.

Ray got out before he could decide not to and walked to the Pearl Building and went up the wide stairs. The enormous lobby was empty. He went to the elevators and pressed the button, waited with his hands in his pockets until the doors opened, and then rode it up to the fifth floor.

The reception area of Gordon, Pritchett & Hughes was quiet. The secretary was nowhere to be seen, but the door to Gordon's office was open and voices were coming out. Ray walked slowly to the doorway and stopped.

Gordon was at his desk. Across from him was the Asian hit man Sippai, dressed in a black suit, coffee in one hand and folded newspaper in the other. They looked pleased to see him.

"Deadbomb Bingo Ray," Gordon said, obviously relishing the name. "Here to talk about London?"

"I was just telling Attorney Gordon about this tiny park I discovered," Sippai said. "More than a hundred years old, and it has no name anyone is aware of. May have been there for three centuries now."

"Real estate is an opportunistic mess over there," Gordon said. "The early billionaires are gentrifying the millionaire set out of entire neighborhoods. Imagine, block after block of empty apartments, lavishly appointed ones at that, stilled by economics. Miniature ghost towns with the lights on and the tables set."

"I love it," Sippai said casually. "Sleep in a different million-pound-plus apartment every night, drive whatever I want. Can't imagine giving it up for more than a week at a time."

"Interesting." Ray went to the bar and poured himself a small glass of scotch.

"Timothy Cantwell and two federal agents are in the men's restroom on the first floor," Gordon said. "I'm sure you know that already. When you're finished with your drink, we can go talk to them."

"Thanks." Ray sipped. "I just need you to tell them that I didn't break in and that I don't have any documents on me."

"Of course." Gordon put his feet up and leaned back.

"Need me to watch your guns for a few?" Sippai offered.

"Nah, left 'em in the car. But thanks."

"What's your plan with Chapman?" Gordon asked. Ray sat down in the chair next to Sippai.

"I'm turning Cantwell over and giving his mark his money back. Chapman, though . . . I still need to find out if she works for someone else, if she's making a run at a graduation ceremony, that kind of thing. Pretty much every variable around Cantwell is an hour away from closing time. I just need a couple final answers, and then I close the book."

"Tidy," Gordon admired.

"Cheers." Sippai raised his coffee.

Ray finished his drink. "Ready when you are." He rose and straightened his tie. Gordon did the same and then took an envelope out of his desk. Ray looked at it and raised an eyebrow. Gordon smiled and tucked it away in the breast pocket of his suit coat.

"Little present for the Feds. I would have thought they would have learned to never enter this building."

They walked to the elevator and waited silently and then got in when the doors opened. Ray hit L.

"Sippai told me about the hotel," Gordon said. "The body landed right on a cab. It took the police three hours to look up. They never did make it up to the lounge."

"Knew they wouldn't," Ray said. "So many windows to check first. And how in the world would anyone get over the top of the windscreen on the balcony of that bar without help? Bartender would have noticed."

"Your grenade message was received, but that won't be the end of it."

"Noted."

The doors opened. Two men were standing with Tim Cantwell in the center of the lobby. All three were wearing suits. Ray and Gordon started toward them, and Tim's triumphant smile began to fade.

"That's him!" Tim's face contorted in sudden rage. He was a pale man, with a small paunch he had sucked in, short sandy hair, and a slightly sunken chest. He pointed a skinny, trembling arm at Ray. "Arrest that man!"

Ray held his hands up. He and Gordon stopped in front of them. The Feds showed their badges. Brown and Irving.

"You again," Ray said sadly. "I can't believe they let you just walk around like this."

"These men would like—"

Gordon interrupted him and produced the envelope.

"There's been a misunderstanding," Gordon said patiently. "This is a restraining order we were preparing to file. Mr. Cantwell is a convict who's been harassing my client for some time now. It's doubtful he's dangerous, but can I ask, have either of you searched him for a weapon?"

"Hang on," Agent Brown began. "Mr. Cantwell has been cooperating with our office in the investigation of—"

"We're well aware of his crimes," Gordon said. "Do you have a warrant? Is my client under arrest? Exactly what is going on here?"

The Feds looked at each other.

"Cuff him!" Tim screamed. "I can't believe I'm hearing this! What the hell kind of—"

Agent Brown stopped him with a sharp gesture and fixed Ray with a bored stare.

"Sir, do you have any documents in your possession right now that could be used against Mr. Cantwell?"

"Search me, and let's all go home," Ray said. He held his arms out. Agent Brown nodded and patted him down while Gordon handed the envelope to Agent Irving. Tim Cantwell crossed his arms, fuming and thinking fast. Abruptly, he turned to leave.

"Mr. Cantwell," Agent Irving called out, stopping him.

"You're being played," Tim said coldly, wheeling back. "Played right in front of me. Unbelievable."

"He's clean," Agent Brown said, stepping back. Tim hissed. Agent Irving handed Gordon the papers back. Gordon turned to Ray.

"Sorry for the interruption in your day. I'll have this filed sooner rather than later."

Ray nodded. "Right on. Agents. Mr. Gordon. Psycho." He tipped an imaginary hat and headed for the door. Behind him, Tim started yelling for them to stop him. He stepped outside and lit a cigarette and then took out his phone. Mary Chapman was still parked in the same place. He dialed the number for Hardshell and let it ring once and then hung up. Then he called the number for Cody and let that ring once too.

The Feds and Tim Cantwell came out. Tim stopped outside the doors, and the Feds kept walking, shaking their heads. Tim waited for them to move out of earshot, sneering, until he spoke.

"I know who you are," he said coldly. "I know where you live. Where you work. I know everything about you. I own you."

"Cantwell." Ray took a long drag, shaking his head. "I have one minute to fill you in." He looked at the phone and found the camera function, activated it, and looked up. "The Mohegans have this security chief named Hardshell. Medicine man, but not the healing kind. I have his money as of about ten seconds ago. Anton Brown is dead, you're about to be tortured to death in an unimaginable way, everyone who works for you is probably on fire, and Mary Chapman set you up." He raised the phone and snapped a picture, looked at it, and laughed, shaking his head. "Damn, dude. I didn't know people could make that face."

Tim Cantwell took a step back, face ashen, his mouth slack with horror. His eyes looked ready to pop out of his suddenly sweaty head as he turned to see Hardshell lumbering up the stairs, flanked on either side by a slight, hatchet-faced woman in black.

"Glad I'm not you," Ray said quietly.

"No, no. . . ." Tim tried to run back into the Pearl Building, but the doors were locked. Gordon waved from the other side of the glass and then turned and disappeared. Tim wheeled back as Hardshell reached the top of the stairs. The giant Mohegan reached out and took him by the arm and stared down into his trembling face.

"These two ladies with me will keep you alive for an extra week if you try to run," Hardshell rumbled. Tim wobbled, and his legs almost gave way. Hardshell held him in place and glanced at Ray, who smiled.

"Your money will bounce back to you before midnight," Ray said.

"Now," Hardshell said.

"Not until I walk with Mary Chapman." He glanced down at the street. "One of your boys is holding her."

Hardshell made a gesture, and the man by the driver's-side window on Mary's car nodded. He glanced back, and Ray nodded.

"Please," Tim gushed. "He's lying! I have your money! We have a deal! This is all a huge mistake! My God, can't you see—"

Hardshell broke his arm, and Tim fainted instantly. The woman closest stepped in, and the entire group made their way down to the Lincoln, now idling in front. They got Tim in the back, and Hardshell looked at Ray one last time.

"What we talked about in the sauna," the giant said. His eyes flicked back to Ray, and they were almost sad. "I know what you are now."

Ray's eyes narrowed.

Hardshell got in the car, and they left.

The man tending to Mary Chapman peeled away as Ray got in. Mary turned to him and smiled uncertainly. He was supposed to be leaving with the Feds in handcuffs. She was supposed to be sitting next to Tim, counting her money, and then be on her way to Anton Brown's to rip him off. She was doing her best to hide her confusion, but she knew it wasn't working. Ray patted his chest.

"I got the document," he said. "Feds were there with my old pal Tim Cantwell and a giant fuckin' Indian. Weirdest thing I've ever seen, Mary."

"I . . . I . . . Feds. A man named Cantwell and an Indian. But you do have my file?"

"Drive." He picked up her purse, took out her gun, and pointed it at her. "You know where I live, right? Let's go have a drink and talk this through."

"There's a bar right—"

"Drive, or I shoot you in the foot."

She drove.

Mary stared straight forward, both hands on the wheel. Ray smoked, his free hand holding the gun in his lap. Finally, she spoke.

"When." It didn't come out as a question.

"Unbelievable. You mean you don't know? Sitting there, you still don't know? And here I was wondering if you were a hard-news player or a chip with legs and a wet spot."

"Unbelievable," she repeated.

She stayed quiet for the rest of the drive, but her dignity was back. When they pulled up in his driveway, he glanced sideways to read her, but there was nothing there. She hadn't been the sniper. She turned to him and gave him a liquid smile. Whatever kind of complex lie she'd been forming on the drive must have been a good one.

"Tour of the bedroom?" She looked away and took in the torn-up landscaping. "Love what you've done with your yard."

"No more with the snark," he said. "Only warning. You say the right things, I'll give you a head start before I sell your last known location to the most enraged bidder. One more witty remark, and you go straight to the taco wagon."

"Okay. I'm just nervous, is all."

He gestured with the gun. "Out."

None of the neighbors came out as they walked up the icy sidewalk to the door. Ray punched in the code, not caring if she noticed what it was, and the act shook her a tiny bit. When the security pad blinked green, he entered a second code and unlocked the door. They went in.

"Straight out of *Décor*," she admired.

"January 2015. Bought the entire thing. I liked the way it looked."

They sized each other up. Ray turned away and walked through the house, all the way to the kitchen, while she watched, clutching her purse to her stomach. He took down his most modest bottle of red—the 2005 Domaine Dominique Mugneret Vosne-Romanée—and two glasses. The wine was often overpriced, always oversweet, and he'd read somewhere that the grapes were machine-harvested, so mice wound up in the mix. It suited the moment. She remained still while he opened it with his back to her. When he was done, he poured two glasses and gestured for her to join him at the dining-room table. She did, and he slid one of the glasses over.

"So, Mary," he began. "I think I've already made it clear that I'm not fond of you. That poor latte kid? I did kill him. But you ultimately fucked him worse, leading him around by his dick and his heart until he was broke—I'm just guessing here. But then you got him blown away in a rental car in Chinatown. In Philadelphia. That kind of shit shouldn't happen to anyone."

Mary Chapman sipped her wine without tasting it.

"Tim Cantwell is under the pliers by now, but he's going out hard-core Indian mafia traditional. Those fucking psychos will keep him alive for days. One guy? Fucked 'em really good. They had him on an IV for three weeks, fluids and an antibiotic drip, so he could appreciate being eaten alive by beetles. That's almost Egyptian, isn't it? Don't tell them I said so."

"I don't think I'll be telling them anything now," she said slowly. She toyed with her glass. "There's a reason you didn't take me to Kensington and toss my body out. You need me alive. Why don't we skip the theatrics and get to it?"

"'Kay." Ray swirled his wine and sniffed and then drained half the glass. "Tasty. So yeah, you and the commuted death sentence. I do need you alive, for the next little bit. The Indians. I'd rather have them after you than me."

"How much do you know about their deal with Tim Cantwell?"

"Lots of money."

"My documents?"

"The lawyer burned them. Turns out you didn't pay him near enough to get mixed up in your shit. Guy is a little pissed at you too, come to think of it."

"You're sure."

"Three pages of math. Torched them right there in front of me."

"Christ." She thought, and he watched as she put it together. Anton Brown was her only hope for walking away with a dime. There was still a chance. She drained her glass. "Christ. Okay. Here's the deal. Tim Cantwell hires me to pull you in. Says he has a way to shift the blame on a burn you ran on him and spring some of his people from federal lockup. Fine. About a week in, it all starts to look like I'll never make it out alive." She stopped talking, and her eyes became distant. Ray waited. Either it was a stellar performance, or she really was remembering being scared that first time; the two often overlapped in great liars.

"You found out about the money."

"He just let too many little things slip. Guy is a hedge-fund manager. Brilliant planner too, but he's a piss-poor criminal. Of course, I found out about the money. And as soon as I did, I followed it right back to the source. Huge fucking mistake. Giant Mohegan named Hardshell was waiting at the end of the trail. Nightmare of a man. My god, right then is when it started." She looked at her wine glass. Ray poured the rest of his into her glass, and she gulped it down.

"Keep going," he prompted.

"I knew Tim was going to use you as a back door. If it all went to shit, he was going to put them on your trail. See, that's the other thing I was scared about." She looked up. "You. Deadbomb Bingo Ray. The more I found out, the worse Cantwell's plan seemed. You . . . ah, your reputation. You're a rumor—like the boogeyman or Bad Man Jodie. Mythic bad news, from coast to coast, way down under everything. No one even knows why you live in this ass crater of a city, but the word around every single campfire is to steer clear unless you have long green or a death wish."

He smiled and went into the kitchen, brought back the wine, and poured for both of them.

"So you're between a rock and a hard place," he said.

"More like between a broken microwave someone plugged in and a fifty-gallon barrel of poison. So I lied. I lied to everyone. I lied my ass off. I told Cantwell I was swinging you by the dick and had you on a dog collar. I told the Indians I'd found a way to get their money. I . . . I told my man this was my last job in the underworld, that I was going legit. Get us to Costa Rica. Maybe change my name again and dye my hair, get us a little ranch in Texas. Do blow and drink tequila and work on some cherry skin cancer." She sobbed a little. He drank and watched.

"Here's what you're going to do," he said eventually, "woman-who-calls-herself Mary Chapman." She looked up. "You are going to go get in your car and drive straight to the freeway. Then you're going to pick a direction and take it. No stops. Straight from here to way gone lost forever. I have a line of communication with the Mohegans, of course. What I'm going to do with it is none of your business, but make no mistake—they aren't going to be looking for me. Clear?"

"I don't understand." She sniffed.

"I'm using you as bait. Everything points at you if you split town. Their bloodhounds will come after you, and that will give me plenty of time to slide out of this."

"How do I know they're not waiting right outside?" There was real hope in her eyes.

"My reputation, Mary. Who would be crazy enough to wait out there right now, in broad daylight?" He took her gun out of his jacket and put it on the table. Mary looked at it and licked her lips. He slid it across and then leaned back. Trembling, she reached out and picked it up.

"You . . . you're giving me my gun back?"

"Gutsy, I know." He crossed his arms. "You need me for the same reason, kid. They catch you, you tell them I got the codes off the lawyer, that I'm the one who ripped them off in the end."

She pointed the gun at his head.

"Or I kill you," she said softly. "Right now. That's a good plan too."

"Think it through, dumbass. You send them after me if you get caught, how many of them do you think I'll kill before they take me down? Maybe every last one of them? It all boils down to what you heard, lady. Who do you think is worse—me or them? You looked into Hardshell's eyes, and now you're looking right into mine. Who are you willing to bet on?"

Gradually, she lowered the gun and rose, backing away like she was backing up from a wild animal. Halfway across the living room, she turned and bolted. The instant the door slammed behind her, Skuggy stepped out of the pantry and lowered his revolver and then stowed it in his sling. He walked to where Mary had been sitting, and Ray poured more wine in her glass. Skuggy drank and smacked his lips, raising his eyebrows.

"Dis the super fancy stuff?"

"Yeah." He refilled his glass and poured more in Skuggy's. "We'll give her a two-minute lead."

▶ HYPNOTIZE. THE NOTORIOUS B.I.G.

Ray drove.

Skuggy fiddled with the heater before he settled back, stroking his withered hand. They passed landmarks without talking about them, in the way that men who have known each other for years and done much in each other's company sometimes do. Skuggy didn't seem distracted; more a touch wistful. His ancient, glassy eyes played over the passing city, his expression hard to read except around the edges of his mouth, which were turned down in the distant cousin of a sad smile.

Mary Chapman's car was parked in front of Anton's, and she was just getting out. Ray pulled into a parking spot half a block down and cut the engine. They watched her hurry to the door and knock and then take something out of her purse, slyly look both ways, and then let herself in. A moment passed.

The roof above Anton's apartment lifted off in a burping ripple of fire. The front door blew across the street, and the windows disintegrated in jets of white light and rolling inferno. Car alarms went off in a ten-block radius, and the big Cadillac swayed in the shock wave. A second later, black smoke poured from the holes. Ray started the engine.

"Kinda anticlimactic," Skuggy observed. A flaming shoe landed on the street in front of them. He motioned at the burning wreckage with his good hand in a twisting motion. "Little copper for some green is all I'm sayin'. Old pennies is fine."

Ray headed for the airport. Skuggy took his cigarettes out and lit one and passed it. Ray smoked while he lit one for himself. When he was done, he opened the glove box and took out the flask.

"Gone miss this, Ray."

Ray didn't say anything. Skuggy twisted the cap off with his teeth and took a pull.

"Airport . . . now, we had some good ol' times up in there. I think back, maybe the best was that one time, Thanksgivin'. We was following someone, forget who, had him a ride hid up in long-term. Night come an' I ain't bitchin', but I'z thinkin' damn, shitty we ain't got no ham. Least a ham sandwich, maybe beans. An' holey boy damn!"

"I remember like it was yesterday," Ray said, smiling inwardly.

"Calf brain taco picnic! With them crazy peppers you put up in home vinegar! But Ray, you know you got the touch, boy, cause my third taco, that be the one with the bullet in it. Peeshaw. . . ."

"It was an accident."

"So you claim! All these years with that same fuckin' lie. Now you tell me, tell me one more time—you cookin' scramble, and you don't notice no slug in da pan? C'mon, baby. Gimme da truth. You write it onna napkin you needs to."

"The truth, Skug, is that I was amazed and delighted to discover that bullet in the brain. I've made that dish a thousand times, and I've never seen one. And it wasn't really a bullet, man. It was the tip of the pneumatic hammer they use at the end of the chute. But I knew it would freak you out—and man, Skug, you almost changed religions."

Skuggy laughed and slapped his knee. "I sho did. I sho did."

"I guess it's always surprised me, the way you take to Mexican food."

"Mebbe I jus' dig your cookin'. Mebbe I's fakin'." Skuggy's smile eventually faded, and he took another sip and passed the flask to Ray. "So. This woman."

"Abigail?"

"Yeah." Skuggy rubbed his chin with his good hand. "She waitin' at the airport. But I ask you a question, Raymond. You know this ol' town be like a big-ass rat nest, right?"

"Can't argue with you there."

"Right. Now, you know—'sides fleas and whatnot, bedbugs— you know what kinda creature come around the rat nest? What that rat momma be hidin' from?"

"Possums?"

"Snakes, baby. Snake, now, him creep along an' sneak up in there and have him a big breakfast, then he curl up and take a nap, move on in. Ain't a rat nest no more then, Raymond. Then it be a lair."

"A . . . lair." Ray repeated it in a whisper.

"You know it, baby. In all the old writin' in all the old books, that snake laze 'round long enough, gets himself his wings. . . ." The last part came out with a tune in it.

Ray thought for more than a mile. "Like . . . pupating."

"Metamorphosizin'," Skuggy clarified softly, still half singing. "Think on it. See, this world, there be patterns everywhere—all day and all night, some years long an' some not so much, some loopin' inta forever. But I see 'em, an' you know I do, Raymond. You and this woman, you wake up somethin' in each other. You both drawn to this place, but the reason, it ain't the same. You, baby? You a tickin' time bomb all these years. And just like in bingo, you lucky number come up. You changed, boy. Stirred. But Raymond." He turned in his seat, and Ray could feel his attention. They slowed, and Ray turned too.

"Yeah?"

Skuggy's eyes were wide and yellow. "Raymond, ain't neither one of you the dragon. The woman, she walkin' the long blue walk. You mebbe somethin' else, sprouted slow like the drought acorn, long last ready ta walk his winding way through creation. So you kin, but"—his wide eyes narrowed—"y'all got different daddies, so to speak."

Neither of them said anything until they pulled into the loading area. Ray cut the engine, took out the keys, and handed them to Skuggy.

"Keep it real," Ray said.

Skuggy squinted at the keys. "I will."

▶ A CHANGE IS GONNA COME, LEELA JAMES

The Cadillac pulled away as he walked through the nearest double doors. The airport was relatively full. He checked the gates to confirm where Abigail was and then walked in that direction. Cody had watched her pass through security and was gone by then. With twenty minutes to spare, Ray entered the check-in line and eventually went through the metal detectors.

Abigail was waiting in the boarding area with her carry-on. She kept an anxious eye on the incoming foot traffic, watching for him. She'd brought flowers, and her eyes were worried. He took a seat fifty feet away and called her phone and watched her answer it on the first ring.

"Raymond!" she said brightly, and he smiled at her smile. "I'm at the gate. They're about to make the final boarding call, sweetheart."

"I'm going to have to catch the next flight," he said apologetically. He watched as her smile faded and she lowered the flowers.

"Oh, no." It came out softy and breathy. She looked at the ground, waiting for him to explain. There was a tiny lag between the movement of her lips and the sound of her voice, as some part of her traveled to space and back.

"I love you, Abby."

"Oh." She looked up and smiled a little, and even from that far away he could see her eyes look through the walls in front of her. "I love you too, Raymond. I love you so."

"Get on that plane, baby. Have a safe flight."

"Okay."

He watched her lower the phone and rise. She gave her ticket to the gate attendant, an older black woman, and walked a few paces before turning back and placing the flowers in the trash can by the gate. Then Abigail was gone. The attendant looked down the causeway and then at the trash can and shook her head.

A few minutes later, Ray walked to the windows and watched the plane taxi to the runway. The sun was setting. The white plane sped up and raced into the sky and quickly became a silhouette, a fast black form in the fading sky, and then it vanished.

"Beautiful."

Ray turned. Sippai stood next to him, admiring the view. He turned back and watched more.

"It is. In every way."

"You ready?" Sippai rubbed his hands together. "Six hours to London on the company jet. We have reservations at this place. . . . Man, they have blowfish."

"Perfect."

The plane to London was a blinding nova of white that lingered in the rich black before it abruptly vanished in the direction of midnight.

■

THANK
YOUS

Thanks to Jon O'Neal, Stephanie Beard, and all the other people at Turner; my Philadelphia pals Susan Watson, Adam Pietras and Masami Inagaki; Cowboy Mark Gottlieb in New York; and Sylvia Mann.

CPSIA information can be obtained
at www.ICGtesting.com
Printed in the USA
BVOW08*1535241217
503611BV00005B/10/P